*A cu[...]*
*terribl[...]*
*to waste.*

# PROGRAMMED
# CELL DEATH

Jonathan Hendricks

Clockwork Pines

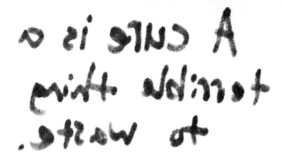

Cover photography: Fineas Anton and Andre Benz

Published by Clockwork Pines

ISBN-13: 978-1-951143-01-5 (Paperback v. 1.0)
ISBN-13: 978-1-951143-00-8 (E-book)

Clockwork Pines
1027 85th Avenue
Amery, Wisconsin 54001
USA

www.clockworkpines.com

*To my wife Sara,*

*the fastest reader I know.*

Transmortification Process 3.0


PROJECT LEAD: █████████████████████

    Patient A /
    Experimental Subject: █████████████
    D.O.B.: 10-31-82. 23:29.
    Weight: 2671 g / 5 lbs 14 oz APGAR: 07
    Mother: ████████████████████
    Father: ██████████████████

    Patient B /
    Control Subject: ██████████████
    D.O.B.: 10-31-82. 23:16.
    Weight: 3855 g / 8 lbs 8 oz APGAR: 10
    Mother: ████████████████████
    Father: ██████████████████

    22:13: Trial explained. Mothers opposed.
    22:45: Parents of A shown ███████████
    23:00: Father of B accepts ███████████
    23:53: All forms signed.
    23:57: DNA samples obtained.

MINNEAPOLIS POLICE DEPARTMENT
  Case Number: 20-1101-0127G
  Subject: Garcia, Arturo J.
  Confession


"It's not like I planned any of this. Not
even close. I hit him on the head and shoved
him off a roof. That's about it."

# PART I.

# ONCOGENESIS

*Onset*

CLIFFSIDE WELLNESS CENTER
  Patient: Baker, Adam
  Initial Session

   A B: Where do I start? I'm up to my ears
in this whole cancer project thing. Total
pain in the ass. They've got me running
interference with the media and the ethics
people so the eggheads can try to get some
work done. Doesn't leave much time for the
campaign.
   Dr. M: You must be under a lot of stress.
   A B: No kidding. And by the way, let me
tell you up front that this whole therapy
thing is pretty much unacceptable in my
family. Seeing a shrink--no offense--taking
happy pills… I've been conditioned against
all of it. Not that I don't believe it
works. Call it a religious objection. But
let's not kid ourselves--it's not like I'm
about to go take the Sacrament of Confession
any time soon, right? So here I am.
   Dr. M: So here we are.
   A B: Right. It started back in October,
right before we announced the project. My
flight to Chicago went off without a hitch
as always, and I picked up my rental and

4

headed for Lakeview. I got stuck in traffic.
I remember the sun on my dashboard...

Adam Baker, a dark-haired white man in a black suit, was running late for a meeting on the eve of a major research conference at the Lakeview Cancer Institute. Drumming on the steering wheel of his shiny black rental car, he drilled financial and oncological terms in a desperate attempt to keep his thoughts off of Maria. *Carcinogenesis. Termination of funds.*

Traffic was bumper-to-bumper on the freeway into Chicago. He signaled right and worked his way to the nearest exit, raising a polite hand to the driver of the pickup truck he was cutting off. The ramp led him up to a street that ran parallel to the freeway. Traffic up here was just as bad. The light at the end of the block turned yellow. The cars in front of him sped up. Adam took his foot off the gas and let the car roll to a stop. First in line at the red.

Straight ahead, glass-shelled skyscrapers cast down the afternoon sun at odd angles. The car's dashboard was hot. Adam put the windows down. On the right a strip of dead grass and bare trees lined a run-down transitional zone between the suburbs and downtown. On his left Adam could see down into the clogged freeway.

He caught himself imagining his fingers in Maria's hair. *Ethics committees. Shareholder accountability.*

The silver grille of the pickup filled the rear-view. He pushed the mirror out of alignment to avoid the laser eyes of the woman driving the truck. Pedestrians in the crosswalk pointed at something far away, on the other side of the freeway.

Her skin was so soft. His heart was pounding. *Cell division. Random genetic mutations. Metastasis.*

There was something, past the freeway, beyond the train yard... There, near the river, under a stand of drought-withered pines. Thick brown fur rippled over layers of fat and muscle, glowing golden in sheets of reflected sunlight. It was looking at him. He shook his head, looked again. Despite the distance, the bear was looking right at him.

Muscle memory sent his fingers to the center console, reaching for the cigarette box he knew wasn't there. His shoulders fell, lips moving automatically in unfulfilled anticipation. The bear was on the move. It made short work of a rusted chain-link fence, then bounded across the train yard, somehow knocking whole boxcars out of its way. A line of perspiration formed on Adam's forehead. He pulled at his tie. *Long-term liabilities. Apoptosis. Programmed cell death.*

Adam rolled up the windows and told his phone to call 911, stepped on the gas when the light turned green, then jammed on the brakes just as fast, because there was nowhere to go. Empty vehicles blocked the intersection, doors left open. People crowded the sidewalk, aiming their phones at the bear.

"911, whats your emergency?" asked a tiny voice. Adam noticed the phone in his hand.

"Yes, I'd like to report a bear."

It descended the concrete bank on the opposite side of the freeway, then leapt through ten lanes of traffic. An eruption of horns drowned out the crunch of metal on metal. Adam saw a flash of teeth.

"Excuse me?" said the voice in the phone.

The bear appeared at the top of the nearest bank of the freeway, then climbed onto the railing. Green and yellow vines snaked up the slope and wrapped around the rail. The bear dropped onto the sidewalk. A fire hydrant shot up into the air on a blast of water, and a young jack pine grew there spontaneously. The crowd backed away, but kept filming.

"Umm, I'd like to report a bear. It just crossed I-94 near Goose Island. Traffic is stopped."

"Is this some kind of prank? This line is for emergencies only."

Adam blinked and sighed. "No, this is not a prank. There's a real bear here, and it's uncomfortably close to my car, and I'm probably going to have to sit here and watch it eat some of these morons who won't stop shoving their phones in its face."

"I wonder how it got there."

"You—you wonder how it got there? How about sending the DNR and an ambulance? Waste any more time and you might as well call the coroner."

"Sir, calm down, please. I'm dispatching the authorities now. Please stay on the line."

"Hold on, something's happening."

A large form moved past Adam's window. It was the angry woman from the pickup truck. She was short and round, and she walked with purpose. She had curly red hair and a twelve-gauge side-by-side.

"Holy shit, she has a gun," Adam whispered.

"What? Who has a gun?" said the tiny voice.

Adam ended the call.

Ignoring everything else, the bear approached the front of Adam's car and reared up on its hind legs, front paws up in the air, massive claws shining in the sun. It balanced there for a moment, then slammed down hard on the hood of the rental. The whole car tilted forward. Adam shrank into his seat.

The short, round woman from the truck now struck a powerful stance at the front-left corner of the car, leveling her shotgun. The bear looked from the woman to Adam, and seemed to make up its mind. It climbed onto the car's hood, which caved under the weight of the thing. It stared directly into Adam's eyes.

A spectator suddenly found her conscience: "Stop! Don't kill it!" she shouted. Her cry for amnesty drew the bear's focus. It looked back over its shoulder, contemplating the woman, with her shining golden hair and heaving chest—and her boyfriend, who was cowering behind her, frozen and pale. The bear snapped out a short, sharp growl in their direction, then shook its massive head like a dog. Some of the people in the crowd stepped backward and found themselves up against the railing. Others produced handguns.

Claws screeched on glass as the bear walked its front paws up to the top of Adam's windshield. There was a loud low pop, like a frozen lake in the spring thaw. A long diagonal line appeared. Fractals radiated through the glass. The windshield popped out of its frame and fell into the car. To get a clear shot, the woman with the gun sidestepped to a position next to the driver-side door, next to Adam as he cowered under laminated glass. Before she could fire, the bear thrust its face into the car, snapping for Adam's head, but it was blocked by the spider-webbed safety glass.

The peanut gallery on the sidewalk experienced a change of heart. Animal-rights-based objections withdrawn, spectators begged for deliverance from the horrible scene. The armed among them took aim. Double-barrel shotgun to her shoulder, the orange-haired woman pulled both triggers. There was a deafening boom, followed by absolute silence, and a pair of butterflies emerged from the shotgun's twin barrels. They pinwheeled through the air and landed side by side on the tip of the bear's nose. The bear sneezed into the car, spraying honey on the broken windshield. The woman cracked the shotgun's breech and loaded two fresh rounds. The bear turned to face the gun and belted out a roar, its hot rancid breath spilling forth. The mob on the sidewalk opened fire, and soon the air above the street was swarming with bees, which turned on the crowd. Confused and angrier than ever, the bear raised its snout and began to cough out wispy tendrils of color. The colors floated up toward the sky, and the bear's hind legs began to fade. The bear coughed confetti into the air, and more of its body disappeared, as if the bear was throwing itself up from the inside. A cloud of multicolored smoke issued from its gaping nostrils. A moment later, it was gone.

The orange-haired woman opened Adam's car door. He crawled out and stood up.

"I thought you were going to kill me," he said, "the way you were glaring at me before."

"Oh, that? No, I'm just late for an important meeting."

"Me too."

"You might want to put on a different suit." She brushed flecks of glass from his lapel.

"Right. I will. Umm, thanks for saving me."

"Don't mention it. I, umm, I don't know what to say. I have no idea what just happened."

"Me neither. I'm Adam Baker."

"Cathy Peterson. Pleased to meet you." They shook hands. Her strong grip reassured him. "This kind of thing happen to you often?" she asked.

"All the time."

# The Fight

CEDAR CREEK POLICE DEPARTMENT
Case #19-1017-0032G
Subject: Garcia, Arturo Javier
St. Luke's Family Hospital
Surveillance transcript

"I'm afraid he's still sleeping, Officer."

"I understand that, but I need to see what we're dealing with here. I suppose you gals have him all cleaned up… Jesus."

"He needed thirty-seven sutures. He may want to elect for scar-reduction procedures, if he can scrape together the money, that is--on top of everything else."

"Broken bones?"

"Nine in total. The nose of course, plus three fingers, a metacarpal, three ribs, and the right clavicle. And the poor fellow doesn't have insurance."

"That's a damn shame. Has he said anything? AJ, can you hear me?"

"I wouldn't expect too much just yet, Steven. All we've gotten out of him so far was some babbling in the night. Nothing coherent. He was crying for his mother."

"Poor kid. You know him?"

```
   "Everybody knows him. He carries my
groceries. Such a nice young man."
   "We've had him down at the station once or
twice. Never anything serious. Never
anything like this."
   "Did you catch whoever did this to him?"
   "Well, yes. But I'm not fully at liberty
to discuss the particulars, as they say. Do
me a favor, will you Margie? Give us a call
when he wakes up, and I'll come right back.
Need to get his side of the story."
```

AJ and Carl were at Old Bill's drinking beer and tequila and arguing about zombies. Carl thought they only ate brains. AJ was incredulous. "Zombies eat everything," he said. "They tear you apart and eat your whole body clean down to the bones. They don't rampage either. They stumble."

Carl swore fast zombies were scarier. He made a whooshing motion with his hand and knocked his own beer off the bar, straight into AJ's lap. AJ looked up from his soaking wet crotch just in time to see Tommy Erickson and the Steinholtz twins walk in. The cowboys. The leader was skinny, but the other two were huge, and they all wore cowboy boots, and shiny belt buckles, and they had handkerchiefs tied around their necks. The cowboys had never made it out of Cedar Creek. Everything was still high school to them.

Tommy locked eyes with AJ, then tipped his hat to Bill Mischler, the owner of the establishment. AJ couldn't stop himself from laughing out loud.

"Well look here, boys," Tommy said. "We got a live one over here. Hey, Billy—this Mexican kid giving you trouble?"

AJ was born and raised in Minnesota.

"No, Tommy. He's fine. Now don't start anything in my bar tonight, hear me?"

Carl suggested that maybe the cowboys ought to mosey on down the road to another bar. He could make himself look tough, sometimes.

Tommy took it in stride. "Shut up, Carl," he said. "You shut your mouth right now." Then he zeroed in on the wet spot on AJ's jeans. "Look, boys—Pedro here pissed his pants! He pissed his fucking pants. What's the matter, little boy? You crying about your dear departed sister again?"

That was it. AJ stood up too fast, knocking over his stool in the process. "Fuck you, Tommy," he said. Silence filled the room. The jukebox's CD-changer whirred. The song AJ had picked half an hour before came on with guitars screaming. It was hair metal from the '80s.

Tommy's friends stood barring the door, looking like a pair of wood ticks with their arms crossed over their chests. Tommy clucked like a chicken, strutting with his chin stuck out and his shoulders back. He flapped his arms, then pretended like he was going to draw pistols. He twitched his fingers, about to draw and fire. The whole scene made AJ want to laugh even more. Old Bill must have been relieved to see they didn't actually have revolvers strapped to their hips. But on second thought, they probably were packing something. Seemed like everybody but AJ had a carry permit.

Tommy leaned in close. "You listen here, AJ Garcia, and you listen good." He spit on AJ's face as he talked. "Nobody laughs at me. Nobody. Certainly not no goddamn illegal. You keep your mouth shut and consider yourself lucky your sweet sister Maria ain't here no more. Or else I'd make you watch."

Bill was ready to call the cops. Said he wouldn't have this kind of shit going on in his bar. Said he wanted them out. Told them they could come back tomorrow. He stood there holding his phone, ready to dial.

Tommy turned his head towards the old man, who shrunk back and started shaking right there on the spot. Then Tommy sucker punched AJ square in the gut. AJ doubled over in pain, then managed to stomp on Tommy's foot. Tommy yelped like a child.

Old Bill yelled, "No guns!"

The metal band wailed on their guitars.

The Steinholtz brothers came striding forward. Edgar Steinholtz, the slightly bigger one, pulled AJ off the floor, saying, "You're gonna die, you little shit." The other one, Willie, grabbed Carl by the arm. While the goons took AJ and Carl out the back door, Tommy stood up and dusted himself off. He looked Bill Mischler square in the eye, pointed his finger, and said: "Don't you dare call the cops, old man."

Tommy swung hard. AJ was too drunk to react in time, and Tommy hit him square in the face, splitting his cheek open. He fell on his back on the pavement. He rolled to one side and saw the Steinholtz twins standing over Carl.

"You think you're better than me?" Tommy said, and he kicked AJ in the stomach. "Who the fuck do you think you are?" AJ stuck out his tongue. Tommy knelt down to punch him again. AJ rolled over and got up on all fours. The blacktop was cold. His face bled onto his hands. Tommy kicked him in the side and he went rolling. He got to his feet and turned to face his assailant.

Tommy said, "You need to get the fuck out of town, AJ. Everybody in Cedar Creek hates your stinking guts."

AJ started shaking all over and laughing like crazy. He charged at Tommy, who took a swing, but AJ ducked low and slammed his shoulder into Tommy's stomach, tackling him to the ground. Tommy's henchmen hustled over and yanked AJ up by the armpits. Tommy stood up and hit AJ in the face, ribs, and stomach, again and again.

# *The Conference*

LAKEVIEW CANCER INSTITUTE
  Dr. Mikayla Springer
  Personal audiolog
  10-26-19

October has traditionally been a strong month for Black Americans advancing the state of humanity. In October 1953, Dr. Charles Greene became America's first Black board-certified neurosurgeon. In October 1964, Dr. Martin Luther King Jr. won the Nobel Peace Prize. In October 1967, the Supreme Court reconvened with its first Black justice, Thurgood Marshall. In October 1993, Toni Morrison won the Nobel Prize in Literature. In 1995, again in October, the Million Man March stormed the National Mall. And one year from now, in October 2020, I will introduce the world to the cure for cancer.

The theoretical groundwork has already been laid. The missing pieces will fall quickly into place--I'm sure of that. I've brought some of the greatest minds in medicine here, to Lakeview, and I'm providing them with technology so powerful that it seems to have come from the future.

My hero through all of this has always been a man called Abraham Springer. He was an amazing man, capable of such feats of strength, and bravery... He was a model of perseverance. He never gave up on me, and he never let me give up on myself. He was my mentor. My guiding light. And so much more. Abraham Springer was my father.

And today, this morning, he passed away.

...I saw you just this morning, Daddy. You asked me if I had your train tickets. You haven't taken the train for years, Daddy. And now, you're gone. Dead. I can say it. Pancreatic cancer. Dead.

If only I could have done it sooner, Daddy. You always said that saving people didn't always mean keeping them alive. That's what you taught me. But is it true? I was going to keep you alive, Daddy. The whole thing, the Project, it was for you. I just needed more time. I just...

No. Stop it. Pull yourself together, Mikayla Springer. The pity party's over. You are a surgeon, and a scientist, and the director of a world-class facility. It's time to show them what you're made of. This is your life's work, Mikayla. Don't mess it up.

Adam Baker never overslept. At 5:00 on the morning of the conference, the hotel room's clock radio blared static and he sat up in bed. He shifted to a cross-legged position and focused on the white noise from the untuned radio as he performed a series of breathing exercises and seated stretches. His mind was clear. No hangover. He rolled his neck forward, then side to side. He brought his shoulders up, then pushed them down. No cigarettes today: that was the goal. Well, maybe just one, before the conference, to settle his nerves. He extended his hands, palms up. Arm circles. Then he got out of bed. Standing on the carpet in his shorts, he bent his elbows and turned his palms outward as though he were projecting a forcefield. Trunk twists, then side bends. He tried not to think about the bear.

He turned off the clock radio and picked up his phone. He smiled at the camera and the phone unlocked. He asked Minerva to read the morning headlines. Minerva was Adam's digital assistant. She lived in his phone, tablet, and laptop. She began to summarize articles related to medicine. Adam laid down and performed his core conditioning routine—plank, push-ups, bird dogs, crunches, bridge—as Minerva briefed him on emerging research on T-cell activation through ion channels.

He showered, put on a black suit and tie, picked up his black leather briefcase, and avoided eye contact on his way out of the hotel. As he climbed into a taxi, he happened to notice a random Chicagoan smoking a cigarette, and that was all he could think about for the next twenty minutes. Not the dense traffic, not the modern urban atmosphere, not the way the morning sunlight shot up from the horizon to glance off the tops of the skyscrapers. He saw these things, passively, but he couldn't think about them, or anything else, until he was standing on the sidewalk, three blocks away from Lakeview, finally holding an unlit cigarette between his fingertips.

He placed it in the palm of his left hand and studied it. Crisp tobacco in delicate ivory paper, the filter end brown like cork. He gave it a little push with his right index finger and watched it roll back and forth in his palm. This is the day, he thought. The big one. The last hurrah. Hell, Elena still thought he'd been quit since the last time. He lifted his palm toward his face and savored the aroma, as if he were holding a handful of coffee beans or a piece of fine chocolate. It wasn't going to be easy—this first one was going to have to last a few hours, then he would sneak out of the conference somehow and suck down a second, maybe a third. Smoking would be prohibited on the

Lakeview campus, of course. But tonight, after dinner, after the rest of the team got too tired or too drunk and went home, he'd be free. He'd smoke more than he ever had in his life. Two whole packs. Maybe three. And that would be the end of it.

He thought of his daughter Mary, a quizzical look on her little face, and her sister Lucy, always smiling. He could feel the softness of their hair, smell their shampoo. Every night after dinner they'd play in the tub, put on their jammies, then they'd get about ten minutes of Daddy time. Twenty if they were lucky. Just normal stuff: wrestling, tickling, maybe a book. Mary would say something amazing, like she was the smartest person alive, then Lucy would ask something silly, like what was the full moon full of? Full of shit, Adam thought. Just like your dad.

The cigarette was gone. He couldn't even remember lighting it. He opened his briefcase and took out a pack of floral-scented wipes. He carefully wiped the tips of his smoking fingers, the index and middle fingers of the left hand, frequently rotating the scented wipe so as to use the whole thing evenly, removing any trace of residue from his persona. A quick spritz of body spray on black lapels—not too much—and he was ready. Nobody would ever guess he was a smoker—nobody who mattered, anyway. Couldn't have that, in his line of work. He popped a stick of spearmint gum in his mouth and walked around the corner.

The front gate of Lakeview Cancer Institute came into view. Adam pulled out his phone and said, "Minerva, we're here."

"I know," she said. "Here's your pass." Minerva had constant access to Adam's physical location via his phone's GPS, so she had preemptively loaded Lakeview's custom app, which displayed Adam's credentials. He held up his phone for the guard as he walked through the front gate.

The Schleiden-Schwann Memorial Gardens began just inside, and covered every exterior inch of the campus. Seven o'clock in the morning and already the gardens were filling up with patients. Some could walk under the autumn colors, but most rolled in wheelchairs, their attendants and life-sustaining machinery in tow.

Adam tried not to look into the trees. In the trees were birds and squirrels, and their nests. Thousands of crawling and flying insects. Hypnotic silver spider webs, hidden in the crimson leaves like malignant cells in a drop of blood, visible only upon magnified examination. There was no pollen in the frigid fall air, thank God, but despite the cold, Adam began to perspire.

There was a map of the campus on the phone app, but Adam didn't need it. He had played a consulting role in Lakeview's planning, and he'd been back numerous times since construction was finished. The campus consisted of three main buildings and a number of smaller facilities. To Adam's right was the College of Medicine. It was a long, low building, four stories of red brick and neoclassical extravagance. Satyr and cherubim frolicked with lion and ox in high relief above elaborate Corinthian columns. The left or northern wing contained classrooms and lecture halls, and the south wing was a dormitory for medical students, visiting doctors, and even some of the patients. (Only those who could afford the upgrade, of course. Cancer care was devastatingly expensive.)

Looking north over the treetops, Adam saw the simple yet elegant white hospital that was the heart of LCI. And beyond that, looming in the distance: the Montgomery building, a hypermodern mirror-plated skyscraper. Home of Montgomery Medicine, the corporate parent of the Lakeview Cancer Institute.

Movement in the branches pulled Adam's attention down from the sky. He turned left and hurried to the administration building, his eyes glued to the pavement in front of his feet.

At reception, Adam introduced himself to a young Japanese woman, a doctor named Arisu Suzuki. "Call me Alice," she said, and she explained that she was a pediatric oncologist, currently working at a hospital in Los Angeles. Adam offered to help with Alice's bags. She accepted. They walked down a short hallway to a vast sunlit atrium. Hundreds of people were hard at work setting up booths representing dozens of corporations, research labs, hospitals, universities, professional organizations, and patient advocacy groups. The booths were a major part of any conference, and Adam was pleased to see that his organizational efforts were paying off. Within a few hours, thousands of guests would be subjected to a whirlwind of information overload. The inaugural Lakeview Lifeline Conference was shaping up to be a success.

"There's my group," Alice said. "I have to drop off my things."

She headed for a line of tables operated by none other than Montgomery Medicine.

"Looks like we're working for the same people," Adam said.

"Oh? And what do you do for Montgomery?"

"I used to be a drug rep, but I graduated. Now I just sort of get things done."

"Sounds important."

After navigating a gauntlet of small talk with the latest crop of industry underlings, they found an elderly gentleman reading a book at his table in the far corner of the gallery, where fewer conference-goers were likely to notice him. He was a small old man, his bald head barely higher than the stacks of books he had for sale. He offered none of the corporate-sponsored pens or thumb drives which attracted guests towards the other booths, nor did he have so much as a hand-written sign declaring his affiliation or purpose.

"Aleksei Brandt, at your service," the man said, without lifting his eyes from whatever he was reading.

"Dr. Brandt," Adam said.

"Mr. Baker."

Adam turned to Alice. "This is Dr. Brandt, the famous geneticist. Dr. Brandt, meet Dr. Alice Suzuki. She's researching the side effects of new drugs on children."

Dr. Brandt finally raised his eyes, a pair of oversized orbs behind thick glasses. "Lovely," he said. "A pleasure."

"Nice to meet you, too. I'm sorry, Doctor, but I'm not familiar with your work."

"Telomeres and microRNA."

"Fascinating. Tell me more."

Dr. Brandt was normally reticent in the extreme, having tired long ago of trying to explain things to people who were mentally incapable of grasping the complexities of the human genome. This included the majority of general practitioners. But when presented with a young victim such as Dr. Suzuki, whose overall politeness and deference to the aged overpowered the impulse to escape, he tended to ramble. Presently he invited Alice (and reluctantly, Adam) to take a seat at his table. He spoke at length on the nature of microRNA. Adam already knew most of that stuff: microRNAs were little chunks of genetic material, floating around loose inside cells, and for a long time after their discovery, nobody thought they could do anything. But it turned out that they actually switched genes on and off. Cancerous cells could make their own custom microRNAs that could turn off tumor suppressor genes, which normally kept cells from turning cancerous in the first place. Or something like that. Adam couldn't focus. He was thinking about cigarettes again.

"And then we have the telomeres. They are the protective caps on the ends of the chromosomes, and they play a vital role in cellular mitosis." Alice appeared to be listening intently, if not genuinely enjoying the experience. Adam honestly couldn't tell if she was faking it. He had heard this all before. Each time a cell divided, it lost some bits off the ends of its telomeres. He could see the shoelace metaphor coming from a mile away.

"Some compare the telomeres to the plastic tips on the ends of shoelaces," Dr. Brandt said, and Adam smiled to himself.

Brandt said, "But I don't."

That caught Adam by surprise. "Why not?" he asked.

"Shoelaces don't divide. Chromosomes don't need to fit through holes. Shoelace caps are made of plastic, whereas telomeres are made of the same stuff as the chromosomes themselves, nucleotides. And let me ask you this: When your shoelace caps wear out, do your shoes spontaneously kill themselves?"

"I see your point, Doctor," Adam said. "Do you propose an alternate metaphor?"

"I prefer to speak directly."

Adam opened his mouth, but Alice shot him a look. "Go on, Doctor," she said.

"In addition to microRNA, cancerous cells make telomerase, an enzyme that repairs the telomeres."

"Hold on—it repairs them?" Adam said. "Because it sounds like it erases them."

Brandt said, "You know very well, Mr. Baker, that the suffix -ase simply denotes an enzyme."

Adam winked at Alice. She pretended not to see it.

"As I was saying, young lady, the production of telomerase delays cellular senescence. But in most cases we don't want our telomeres repaired. We want our cells to age."

"You're talking about programmed cell death," Alice said.

"Apoptosis, yes. Researching the malignant cell's production of microRNA and telomerase has been my life's work, and I've found some remarkable ways to stop both processes. But there are certain side effects, of course." Brandt finally closed the book he was reading and laid it on the table. Adam noticed that the doctor had written it himself.

"What kinds of side effects?" Alice asked.

"The processes of the malignant cell are simply distortions of the processes of the normally functioning cell. Some of our cell lines, such as stem cells, and various cells of the central nervous system, are meant to have very long lives. These cells naturally produce telomerase."

"So, we like telomerase," Adam said, bored.

Brandt looked at him for a long time. Through his thick glasses, the doctor's large eyes took in everything, but revealed nothing. His face was unreadable. Adam broke away first.

Brandt turned to Alice. "There are certain beneficial microRNAs that protect tumor-suppressor genes, and there are others that protect certain parts of the brain which are perhaps better left undisturbed."

"I see," Alice said. "So we can't target microRNA or telomerase indiscriminately."

"That much is clear to me now. But the first wave of experimentation is ancient history, and already results are coming in for the new generation. Very promising results indeed."

\* \* \*

While most of the smaller presentations would be held in the lecture halls of the college, Adam and the others on the conference team had decided the plenary and keynote speeches should be held in Farber Hall, Lakeview's largest auditorium, which was just past the atrium. Adam and Alice joined the flow of conference guests streaming through the double doors.

Farber Hall was like a massive theater. The stage's blue velvet curtains had to be three stories tall. Navy-carpeted aisles sloped away between tiered rows of black seats full of people. The general seating area had room for nearly two thousand, and the balcony allowed for a further five hundred. The curtains parted to reveal a giant screen showing a crystal-clear view of the night sky, millions of tiny points of light in the black of space.

Alice stopped near the front and said, "How about here?"

"You'll have a great view," Adam said. He turned and kept going. He walked directly up onto the stage and took a seat next to the podium. He spotted Alice in the crowd, made eye contact, shot her a smile.

A woman entered the stage from the side. She was tall and black, and she wore a sharp blue suit over a white blouse. Adam stood and shook her hand. She was clearly distraught, but there was no time to ask why. Adam gave her his best encouraging smile, then he gestured for her to take the podium. She straightened her coat, adjusted the microphone, and spoke.

"Good morning, everyone. My name is Mikayla Springer. Welcome to Lakeview Cancer Institute."

There was a round of applause.

Dr. Springer cleared her throat and went on. "We've come a long way in the war on cancer. Some types of cancer have already been cured, and there are many more that are highly treatable today, that were considered hopelessly fatal only a decade or two ago. But cancer is still one of the leading causes of death in the world. One in six people will die of cancer globally. Nearly half of all men, and a third of all women, will develop some form of cancer during their lives. The twentieth century was a time of great advances in our understanding of cancer's unrelenting march, but until the late 1990s there were only three effective forms of treatment: surgery, radiation, and chemotherapy. All three of these treatments have horrific consequences, often bringing patients to the brink of death. Surgical excision leaves lifelong scars, and is ineffective against advanced metastatic cancers. Chemotherapy destroys the immune system. Radiotherapy and chemotherapy both carry the risk of inducing new cancers in patients who were supposed to have been cured. But you already know this. You are here to learn something new. Today and tomorrow, here at the inaugural Lakeview Lifeline Conference, you will have many opportunities to learn about the very latest achievements in humanity's greatest struggle."

Dr. Springer kept talking, but Adam couldn't focus. He was sure she was being as charismatic as she always was, telling the guests about all the great new research that would be discussed throughout the conference. After a few minutes Adam realized he'd been staring at her butt. He wondered if the whole audience knew. He wanted to escape, maybe smoke a cigarette or ten. Then they were all clapping, and Mikayla was staring at him with a forced smile, and he knew it was his turn. He shook her hand again and took the podium.

"Ladies and gentleman," he began. "I'm Adam Baker. And I stand here before you today to say that I don't really know why I'm standing before you here today. I haven't done anything special, never discovered anything amazing... I've certainly never saved anyone's life. I'm no doctor, that's for sure. In fact, some people might say I'm the complete opposite, since I went to law school!"

There was a ripple of polite laughter.

"Don't worry though—I may be a lobbyist, but at least I'm no lawyer!"

More laughs from the crowd.

"Look, what I'm really trying to say is this: I lost my mom to cancer, God rest her soul, and I've been right here in the trenches with all of you fine people ever since. We're all in this fight together, and we won't stop until we've won. Am I right? Who's with me? Dr. Springer?"

He turned and looked over his shoulder at her. She wiped a tear from her eye. He waved for her to stand up and join him, and she did. He took her hand in his. The audience was cheering. Adam went on, shouting over the applause: "We want to thank all of you for making this event possible. Thank you so much to all the excellent doctors and nurses out there saving lives every day. Thank you to all the scientists, technicians, and staff who are working so hard to uncover the secrets of cancer and so many other diseases. Thank you so much to all the folks at Montgomery Medicine, the people who built this great institution, and to all of our sponsors. And most of all, we want to thank all of you out there in the audience for coming here today—and for coming back tomorrow!"

The atrium was overflowing with people. Adam avoided eye contact as he made his way out of the building, across the gardens, and out the front gate. He needed a smoke, and by the looks of the crowd on the sidewalk, so did a lot of other guests, despite the theme of the conference. He kept his head low and walked down the street. He was three blocks away from LCI before he felt sure no one was watching him. He smoked robotically, like it was just another chore, something that simply needed to be done. Then he had another. Then he sprayed on his body spray, put a piece of his gum in his mouth, and wiped his fingers clean.

When Adam went back inside, he thought he might get a coffee at the cafe at the back of the gallery, behind all the promotional booths. As he approached he spotted Alice and Mikayla standing there with foam cups, talking to a man whom he recognized as the computer programmer Tyler Marshfield. Dr. Springer had spent months considering who should be on the team for her new project, and she had asked for Adam's opinion more than once. Unlike a lot of these rich techie types, Tyler Marshfield held advanced degrees in his fields. He'd studied network infrastructure and relational data stream theory at MIT, and he'd spent the next ten years writing banking software on Wall Street. And his suit was too small for him. He was in the middle of saying something, and Adam decided to eavesdrop for a moment before making himself known.

"...And we all know what happened with the whole MMA thing. Baker was a part of that, you know." Marshfield was referring to the Medicare Modernization Act, the unpopular law that blocked the government from negotiating with pharmaceutical companies over drug prices. It was true that Adam had lobbied for the bill. Apparently Marshfield had a problem with Adam Baker, and likely with lobbyists in general. No matter. Adam knew how to handle this sort of thing.

Just when he was about to announce his presence, Dr. Springer spoke up in his defense. "Give him a chance," she said. "If it weren't for him, we wouldn't have any of this."

"Talking about me?" Adam said.

"Oh! Adam, what good timing!" Dr. Springer said, turning around. "Yes, as a matter of fact, we were talking about you."

"Only the good parts, I hope." He winked at Alice.

"I was just telling our new friend Mr. Marshfield here how you helped secure the funding that paid for this whole facility."

"I'm just happy to see that so much of the money went towards artistic vision. That college building is really something else."

"I thought it was a mess," Marshfield said. "Like they just tried to cram in whatever they could think of."

"I don't remember seeing architectural criticism on your resume," Adam said.

Marshfield didn't have anything to say to that.

"I'm sorry about your mother, Adam," Alice said, changing the subject. "It was brave of you to say it in front of everyone."

"My mom was the brave one, not me. She fought until it was clear that she wasn't going to win, and then she decided to go off the treatment. She built up her strength until she could come home, and she died happy, on her own terms. That's real bravery. She was a hero. A saint."

He reached into his pocket and pulled out a keychain with a little charm on it—a red ceramic heart. "I always keep this with me," he said. "She made it. After she came home. She decided to give them to everyone she loved, so she had to make a hell of a lot of them. She said they were pieces of her heart."

"That's beautiful," Alice said.

Adam locked eyes with Dr. Springer. "I'm sure everyone on this campus has lost someone they loved." She pursed her lips and shook her head once, as if to say: Not now.

"Now if you'll all excuse me," Adam said, "I have to make a phone call." As he walked away, he heard Marshfield wondering aloud why he hadn't mentioned his dead brother Matthew.

\* \* \*

Adam really was making a phone call. He called his wife, told her how the conference was going, asked about work, asked about the kids. Everything was fine, she said, but they all missed him. He said he was sorry for being away so often.

"Elena," he said. "One more thing."

"What is it?"

"I love you."

"Sure you do."

"I really do. I mean it. I don't say it enough."

"You say it too much."

"Goodbye, sweetheart."

"Don't smoke," she said, and she hung up.

He was wandering through the booths, pulling a dumb prank he liked to pull sometimes, which was to take a handful of freebies from some company—pens or thumb drives or whatever—and leave them on the tables of a bunch of other companies. As far as he knew, no one ever noticed until he was long gone. Eventually he came to the tables of Montgomery Medicine, where Dr. Alice Suzuki was giving an informal presentation to a small group of people who had gathered around her table.

She had three large posters mounted on aluminum tripods. The first showed some common cytotoxic drugs: methotrexate, cisplatin, 5-fluorouracil, and some of their side effects: hair loss, nausea, pain, ulcers in the digestive tract, loss of liver and kidney function, failure of the immune system, infertility, brain damage, and secondary cancer. Alice explained briefly what most of the conference attendants already knew: these drugs worked by stopping the growth of not just cancerous cells, but all rapidly-dividing cells. In adult patients, this meant damage would be restricted to the parts of the body that continued to grow after maturity, such as the hair, nails, skin, white blood cells, the linings of the mouth, esophagus, and stomach, and so on. "But in the case of children," Dr. Suzuki explained, "all parts of the body are growing continuously."

Her second poster showed a vast web of drugs, each one connected to many more. The reality of chemotherapy was that cancer patients were routinely given mixed cocktails of drugs, which meant that all possible side effects had to be compounded. Many of these harmful effects could be alleviated with additional medications, such as painkillers, antiemetics, and corticosteroids, but each of those carried its own list of destructive side effects. Furthermore, the situation was unpredictable, since there was little scientific evidence regarding side effects in children specifically. A child's physiology was fundamentally different from that of an adult, yet parents were less likely to volunteer their children as test subjects in clinical experiments.

The truth was that for patients with incurable cancers—for children with cancer, the figure was around twelve percent—chemotherapy was nothing more than a delaying tactic. And since chemo often left cancer victims feeling worse than if their cancers had gone untreated, it was commonplace for patients to wonder if living for a few extra months was really worth going through hell. There were documented cases that established a link between chemotherapy and an increased risk of suicide. "Now," Alice said, "Imagine that you're a parent, looking at the options, and the statistics, and you're being forced to make the decision to put your child through this." Adam tried not to think about it. He glanced around to see what other people thought, and he found that Dr. Springer was standing nearby, focused on

Alice's presentation, although Adam knew she didn't have any kids of her own.

The final poster displayed information on the only two first-line drugs in existence that specifically targeted cancer: trastuzumab and imatinib. These drugs reversed cancer's course without causing significant harm to the patient's body. The problem was that one of them only worked on a rare type of breast cancer, and the other on an even rarer form of leukemia. If a patient was "lucky" enough to have one of these cancers, the matching targeted drug would work. Otherwise, it was useless. And since these particular cancers were rare in the general population, they accounted for only a small fraction of all childhood cancers.

"Whereas adults in general are more likely to die from heart disease, stroke, infections, or Alzheimer's disease," Dr. Suzuki concluded, "Cancer kills more children than all other diseases of childhood combined. We have to do more to stop it." And that was the end of the presentation.

A number of viewers had questions, so Adam and Dr. Springer thought it best not to stick around and bother Dr. Suzuki. After Adam showed her his best encouraging smile, and Mikayla gave a nod of approval, Adam suggested that they catch the end of Dr. Peterson's talk on viral transmission, over in the college.

As they walked through the gardens, Adam tried to read the look on Mikayla's face. "Well," he said, "at least it was a good summary."

"Hmm? Oh, Alice did a fine job."

"She didn't have any solutions, though."

"That's not what I have in mind for her."

"Boss knows best."

"Thank you."

"I hope you know you can talk to me, about whatever it is—"

"I'm fine. Really."

The lecture hall was filled to capacity, so Adam and Mikayla had to stand just inside the door. Dr. Cathy Peterson was an expert on retroviruses, or viruses that inserted their own genetic material into the DNA of the host cell, causing permanent alterations. HIV was the well-known example. The audience was captivated by Dr. Cathy's down-to-earth Midwestern approach. In the middle of explaining a method of propagating beneficial mutations in mice by injecting modified viruses directly into the brain stem, she would say things like, "You betcha," and "Oh, fer cripe's sakes." And in the next breath she'd bring the audience to new heights with a fascinating description of the way a beautiful new antagonist compound could embed itself in the binding sites of its target protein. "If we understand a cell's proteomics— that is, the complete profile of its protein interactions—then we can potentially control that cell's behavior. We already know how to do this with manufactured drugs. But cancer does it biologically. And with some advances in proteomics and viral gene therapy, gosh—then *we* could do it biologically, too." She sighed, and smiled, and said, "A lady could almost let herself feel happy, if she weren't careful."

Adam Baker and the some of the other conference guests were staying at the Hotel Bella Fiore, in the shopping district known as the Magnificent Mile. Adam took a shower, got a massage, put on his going-out clothes, and went down to the hotel bar.

He ordered a beer with a shot of tequila on the side. He drank the shot and sipped the beer. He was spinning on his bar stool when Dr. Cathy Peterson came down the wide marble staircase looking gorgeous in a floral cocktail dress with her long red curls.

"Why hello there, Mr. Baker," she said.

"Hiya Dr. Cathy! Great presentation today." He raised his glass.

"Well, thank you so much!"

She ordered a lemonade. He asked about her family. She said that she and her husband Tim made thirty-five years this fall. They loved hunting and fishing. She'd been collecting guns since she was a little girl on the farm, and he was a record-holding fisherman, from a long line of record-holding fishermen. They canoed the Boundary Waters of northern Minnesota every summer, and in a few weeks they were going to Idaho for the elk. Adam knew better than to change the subject to something uncomfortable, like the circumstances of their first meeting. Cathy was a talker, and obviously proud of her family. She said she was just a typical midwestern mom, and she made a mean cheeseburger macaroni casserole. She and Tim had two grown boys, Corey and Jacob. Corey ran a conservation-focused non-profit that worked with state departments of natural resources. Jake was a marine biologist, and a record-holding fisherman.

She asked if Adam had any kids.

"Two girls," he said.

"And how old are they?"

"Six and four."

"Oh, the little darlings!"

"I worry about them all the time, to be honest."

"Parenting jitters got you down?"

"I guess you could say that."

"What you have to understand is that you don't need to know how to handle every possible situation before it comes up. Each time you encounter a situation that demands a response, you do the best you can with what you have. And your kids will see that, because they're always watching."

"That's what I was afraid of," Adam said, joking.

"The other part of it is that your decisions and reactions leave impressions that add up over time, and that's how you teach your kids what it means to be a good person. Take the birds-and-bees talk, for example. Did you parents ever sit you down for the talk?"

"God, no."

"Me neither. But I didn't want my boys growing up feeling entitled to women's bodies, so we had the talk many, many times, starting when they were still young. My husband and I were always frank with our boys, because the talk works best not as a single, isolated event, but as an ongoing conversation. Children have to feel free to ask questions. That way they'll be more likely to learn something that could save their lives some day—or at least keep them out of jail!"

Just then, Dr. Alice Suzuki came down the stairs with another Asian person, a serious-looking man whom Adam had never met. Alice said hello to Cathy. Adam caught the serious man's attention with a nod.

"Adam Baker," he said, standing up. "Nice to meet you."

They shook hands.

"Xu Fei," the man said.

"Sorry?"

"My name is Xu Fei."

"Is that Chinese?"

"It is."

"Shoe Fay?"

"Close enough."

"Is that your first name? Or your last?"

Cracking a smile, the man said, "Yes."

The lobby elevator opened and Tyler Marshfield emerged, looking uncomfortable in the same ill-fitting suit he'd worn all day.

"Well, then," Adam said. "Looks like we're all here. Or haven't you figured it out yet? We're a team now." His new friends looked confused. He made eye contact with each of them in turn.

"To us," he said, raising his glass. "Now let's go out and meet our fearless leaders."

Dr. Mikayla Springer was waiting for them on the sidewalk outside the hotel. Adam congratulated her on a successful opening day. She thanked him and turned to address the group.

"Adam, Cathy, Alice, Mr. Marshfield, Xu Fei, it would be my pleasure to take all of you to dinner."

Tyler Marshfield said, "What's this about a team?"

Mikayla shot Adam a disapproving look. He shrugged.

"Well, I was planning to tell you all more about that tomorrow. I'm sorry if you feel deceived. That was never my intention. I've already spoken with each of you individually about working for me, and tonight was supposed to feel more like a surprise party. I was hoping to see how we all get along together."

"Excuse me," Adam said, "but where's Dr. Brandt? Won't he be joining us?"

"I'm afraid not," Mikayla said, without further explanation. "Now, shall we?"

The Magnificent Mile was crowded with tourists. A few blocks down from the hotel, the green and red neon signs of the Forno d'Oro came into view. There was a constant stream of people entering the restaurant. Dr. Springer talked to the host, and they were ushered inside and upstairs to a private dining room. The room was cheerful and cozy, with a big circular table in the center and paintings of overweight Italian chefs juggling tomatoes on the red brick walls.

The house specialty was, of course, Chicago-style deep-dish pizza. Adam's favorite food in the whole wide world. He got a kick out of the way the crust was just a bowl for all the toppings. Like the whole thing was just a big, delicious joke. They made them upside-down, compared to regular pizzas: cheese first, then meat, then sauce. That way the cheese wouldn't burn, since they took so long to cook. Adam knew where to get deep-dish up in the Twin Cities, but it was never as good as the real thing.

Before anyone could start messing around with menus, Dr. Springer ordered three large pies, three bottles of wine, and a pitcher of beer for the table. Tyler Marshfield was trying to talk to Alice without coming off as desperate for female attention, and Dr. Cathy was already talking Xu Fei's ear off, so Adam sat next to Mikayla. They had known each other for a long time on a professional basis, but he was curious about who she was outside of work. He knew he could coax her out of her shell eventually, as long as he kept her wine glass full.

The two of them spent the first part of the dinner listening to the other conversations going on around the table. Xu Fei was a scientist affiliated with a Chinese pharmaceutical. He held an MD-PhD in bioinformatics and genomics. But he refused to say anything more about himself, preferring to listen to Cathy's wild yarns about manipulating dangerous viruses without getting sick, or backpacking the Rockies with two small children. Marshfield was a few beers in, and finally starting to loosen up. Alice already looked bored to tears.

Mikayla was listening intently, smiling to herself.

"Looks to me like they're getting along just fine," Adam said.

"Yes, I'd say so."

"You picked a fine team, Mikayla."

"Couldn't have done it without you, Mr. Baker."

Adam remembered the sense he'd gotten from her that morning. Something had happened, there was no doubt about that, but he decided not to pry.

"How about them Bears?" he said.

"Oh, right. Football. Umm..."

"Don't worry, I don't know either. I just fake it."

"Isn't that exhausting?"

"Well, the trick is just to scan the headlines. You just mention something you saw in the news, only you say it like a question, and whoever you're talking to will tell you all about it."

"Adam, that's brilliant!"

"It's simply, really. Figured it out back when I first got started repping for Montgomery. A drug rep is basically a salesman, see, and sales is all about building relationships. You build a strong enough relationship with somebody, you can sell them just about anything. Thing is, you can't possibly remember everything about each one of your clients. That's where the notebook comes in."

"The notebook?"

"Of course. You write down what the doctor's having for lunch, so you can bring it next time you drop by. And you write down the wife's name, their anniversary, and their kids' names and birthdates—"

"And their favorite sports team."

"Exactly."

"Hmm."

"You don't believe me?"

"No, that's not it. I'm just not sure you should be telling me this!"

"Hah, you might be right about that. Okay, why don't you tell me something?"

"Like what?"

"Oh, I don't know. Anything. You have any brothers or sisters?" The look he'd seen on her face that morning flashed before his eyes, and he regretted his question immediately. "I mean," he added, "only if you want to talk about that sort of thing. I don't mean to pry."

"No, it's fine. I had one brother. Freddie. But he died a long time ago."

"I'm sorry."

"Don't worry about it. I was still little. It's almost as though..." She unfolded a napkin, folded it again.

"Yes?" Adam said, trying to be supportive.

"Never mind. I forgot what I was going to say. Oh, I think this wine is getting to me!"

"Nonsense."

"Freddie was shot by the police, if you want to know the truth."

"Oh my God. How terrible."

"He was named after Frederick Douglass."


Adam and Marshfield cleaned up the last slices of pizza. Cathy suggested a change of scenery, and she knew just the place. Dr. Springer paid the bill, Adam left the tip, and they all filed out onto the sidewalk.

Cathy took Mikayla by the arm and led the way. Adam wasn't particularly interested in talking, so he fell in next to Xu Fei. He wanted to keep an eye on Tyler Marshfield, but he found himself staring at Dr. Springer's behind. It was cold out, but she had that tight skirt on... *Damn.* There was a woman with real power. Not that he would ever make a move on Dr. Springer—it was only a fantasy. But a little flirting never hurt anyone.

More than anything else though, he wanted to get away from everyone so he could get real drunk and smoke a lot of cigarettes.

Cathy brought them to the front door of an old-fashioned piano bar called Ella's. Dr. Springer bid everyone good night and got into a cab, then Xu Fei did the same.

There were a lot of blue neon lights running along the ceiling, but the place was mostly purple inside, with plush seats, a bar coated in purple Formica, and a purple five-foot baby grand. There was a decent crowd tonight, and the woman playing the piano looked like she was having a great time. The remaining members of Dr. Springer's team drank to their leader's health.

Apparently Cathy and the bartender had some catching up to do, and Tyler took Alice to look at all the kitschy crap on the walls, so Adam took a seat by himself at a little round table, where he could see the whole place. Within minutes, Alice was in trouble. Tyler had probably tried to put his arm around her, or something—Adam wasn't sure. They were on the other side of the bar. But they were definitely shouting at each other, and people were staring, and all of the sudden Adam was there, with his hand on Marshfield's shoulder. And Marshfield looked down at Adam's hand, then looked Adam in the eye, and he said, "Are you absolutely sure that's how you want this to go down?"

Adam was confused. Not that he didn't understand what Marshfield had said, but because he couldn't believe Marshfield could be the kind of person who could say a thing like that. The idea that Marshfield could do anything to back up what he'd said made Adam want to laugh in his face.

"I said," said Marshfield, again looking at Adam's hand, which was still on his shoulder, "Are you absolutely prepared to commit to your current course of action?"

Adam made a quick calculation: Tyler Marshfield wasn't slurring his words, and he certainly wasn't falling down, but he'd had at least four beers at dinner, plus a glass of wine, and he'd ordered a Manhattan when they arrived here. So considering his size, Tyler Marshfield was most likely drunk enough to be dangerous. Adam removed his hand from Marshfield's shoulder.

"That's what I thought."

"It's getting late," Adam said. "Think I might head back."

"Funny, I was thinking the same thing. I'm not getting anywhere with this dyke."

"Fuck you," Alice said.

Marshfield connected with a driver on his phone, and out the door he went. Cathy paid her tab and left, saying she needed her beauty sleep.

Adam took a stool next to Alice. "Dropping like flies," he said.

"I noticed."

"What happened back there, anyway?" Adam asked.

"He tried to put his arm around me."

"I knew it."

"Typical man-child."

Alice was sipping on a cocktail. Adam switched from beer to bourbon, neat. He looked at the glass in his hands, then he noticed the vase of flowers on the bar. "We only like things when we can't see what they really are," he said.

"What do you mean?" Alice asked.

"Well, look at this," he said, gesturing at the flowers. "A purple and white bouquet. Even the vase is glowing. Beautiful. Empowering."

"Empowering? How so?"

"Well, the flowers have meaning, and the meanings tell a story. Lavender signals caution," Adam said, touching the delicate petals. "Hydrangea: heartlessness. The striped carnations are a refusal, a rejection of courtship. And the Queen Anne's lace means this place is a safe haven."

"How do you know all that?"

"My mom taught me. Now look closer. The flowers are fake. And if you look behind the vase—" he paused, moving it aside. "See? Now it's just a dumb lightbulb sitting next to an ugly vase of plastic flowers. It's a deception, like everything else in this bar, designed to make us forget that we're sitting in the dark, drinking poison."

"What does that have to do with Tyler Marshfield?"

"Think about a necktie. I have to wear them all the time. A good suit isn't complete without one, right?"

"Sure."

"But neckties are made out of caterpillar spit."

"Ew."

"No kidding."

"But it's not always true, is it," Alice said. "There are things we love only because of what they really are."

"Name one."

"Well, lots of things."

"Try me."

"Well," she said, thinking. "Mishima's Confessions of a Mask."

"What's that?"

"My favorite book."

"A book is the worst example!"

"How so?"

"Well think about it! You don't love the actual book, because it's just a bunch of wood, and glue, and ink. Or, worse, it's a file on a computer."

"Obviously I don't love the physical book itself, dumbass. It's the story."

"A story is nothing but a bunch of cleverly arranged lies."

Alice shook her head, sipped her drink.

"What's it about?" Adam asked. "Your favorite book, I mean."

"Oh. Umm... It's about an unhappy boy who builds a false personality as he grows up, just so he can get by in the world."

"But that's exactly what I'm talking about!"

"I know," Alice said. "I'm just fucking with you."

Adam had to laugh. "You got me," he said. "But you know what? It goes the other way, too."

"I have a feeling you're about to explain how."

"Tyler Marshfield only likes you because he can't see what you really are."

"And you can?"

"God, no."

"Good. Let's keep it that way."

Adam raised his eyebrows.

"You're funny," Alice said. "You know that?"

"How so?"

"Most people don't think about this stuff. How everything is a lie."

"I spent most of my childhood lying awake at night, paralyzed with fear."

"Existential crisis, meaning-of-life stuff?"

"Not at all."

"What was it, then?"

"I believed in ghosts."

# *Announcement*

```
MONTGOMERY TOWER
  Main Entrance
  Camera 2
  Footage Annotations
  10-27-2019

  03:52:17 Subject is walking in roadway.
  03:52:19 Subject appears intoxicated.
  03:52:31 Subject trips, falls down.
  03:52:44 Subject stands up, laughing.
  03:52:47 Subject looks up and down street.
  03:52:51 Subject sees Camera 2.
  03:52:52 Subject makes obscene gesture.
```

Adam opened his eyes and lifted his head from a grimy countertop. The peeling laminated menu under his left hand told him he was in a place called Ken's, one of those twenty-four hour breakfast diners. He had no idea how long he'd been there, but he sort of woke up now, although he didn't feel like he'd been sleeping. He thought he remembered saying good night to Alice, on some street somewhere, but he couldn't be sure. He hoped he'd behaved himself. There was an empty cigarette pack and a lighter in his coat pocket.

The place was deserted. It was basically a long counter, with a couple of tables by the front windows. Clearly the place was ancient, but it must have changed hands dozens of times. Layers of cracked and peeling paint coated the wooden countertop, going deeper and deeper, each coat a different color. The right kind of person could read the history of the place in a cross section cut from the bar, like reading the rings of a tree. But then again, that kind of person probably wouldn't eat in a place like this.

Right-wing talk radio blared from the kitchen: "See, the problem with these people is..." The guy was droning on and on, eventually drawing some tenuous connections between the so-called "immigrant problem" and the so-called "global warming conspiracy." Adam couldn't stand listening to that kind of trash. In another minute the guy would probably be talking about the "fake" rovers on Mars—or worse, he'd have a flat-Earther on as a guest. Adam pounded his fist on the bar.

"Yeah, what?" came a shout from the back.

"Coffee and eggs, over easy," Adam said. He stood up and headed for a door marked "Out of order."

A man came out of the kitchen with an armload of dishes. He was a white guy with a large head and a small face, with small eyes in sunken sockets. There were deep stains on his teeth and his apron. "Can't you read?" he said. "Sign says it's out of order."

Adam said, "So where do I take a leak?"

"Not here."

Adam's face turned mean. "Where would *you* go?"

The man's shoulders sagged. He said, "Just be careful on the stairs. And there's no paper."

The door was hanging crooked on broken hinges. Adam pulled it open and stepped forward into the black. He tried to take another step, but there was nothing under foot. He tottered on the edge until one hand found the railing and the other found a string hanging in empty space. He pulled it and a light clicked on, sending an oscillating yellow cone cascading down a steep and treacherous staircase. Loose nails stood up on loose steps coated in more layers of paint. Obviously time was deeper here, in this older space. He descended, taking extra caution on the more precarious of the footholds.

A long splinter from the wooden handrail sank deep into the meat of his palm. He paused to remove it, but the pool of light kept circling away. He looked back and shuddered to see how deep he had come down into the ground. Behind him and far above, the swinging lightbulb traced an ellipse in the dark, as if it were traveling in stable orbit around a black hole.

Screw the light, Adam thought, and he took the splinter between thumb and forefinger, closed his eyes hard, and pulled. The sharp wood cut his skin further on its way out, and he felt blood roll down his fingers. He opened his eyes in time to see black drops fall onto the stairs. He knew in that moment that his DNA had become part of this place, that it would remain there forever, encased in the amber of the next coat of paint.

His feet found concrete at the bottom of the steps, where the revolving pool of light could not reach. Through the soles of his shoes he felt the uneven surface of the floor, felt that it had been troweled by a layperson in a hurry. Adam was no expert in cement, but he was sure he would've done it properly. The whole experience of this diner so far felt highly unprofessional. At least he was almost out of range of the vocal spasms of the talk radio host, who was now rattling on about changing January to White History Month. Adam really couldn't stand those Bible-thumping pundits. Always trying to get everyone mad at each other for all the wrong reasons.

His fingers found the half-rotten wood of the next door. He pushed it open and again he plunged forward into another darkness, this time accompanied by putrid odors. The carpeted floor gushed under his shoes. He took tentative steps, placing one foot in front of the other, waving his outstretched hands through the emptiness in front of him. He left the safety of the doorway and a spring-loaded chain pulled the door shut behind him, trapping him in this black space of unknown proportion. The echoes of occasional drips gave him false clues to the room's dimensions, and he continued in his slow progress until his fingers again clenched around a fraying string. He pulled the string, and in a single flash of light he could see the whole of the nightmare around him—before the bulb popped and showered his face and arms with broken glass.

He was left with a strong impression of teeth. He could feel his irises stretching open for the last reflections of light on glittering scales. He reconstructed the scene in his memory. The lifeforms he had witnessed in that instantaneous flash filled him with dread. The floor was coated with thick mold. Tall mushrooms stood like trees; insects gathered under them in ritual dance. The place was so colorful and strange that he wondered whether he was inhaling hallucinogenic spores. He held his breath and pulled a lighter from his pocket. He flicked it on. A swarm of transparent flying insects descended. One of them got too close to the lighter. The wings sizzled and the flame went out. He flicked it on again. The space was cramped, but the walls seemed to press outward, as if the room itself were breathing.

The flickering light splashed against rotting towers of cardboard and rusted shelves piled with cans that had exploded, their contents crawling out and slithering down the cinder block walls, slick with black mildew. The corners of the ceiling expanded and contracted with the rhythm of the dripping pipes. Adam's eyes were drawn toward movement off to one side. Nothing was there but a forest of knee-high mushrooms actively decomposing a forgotten pile of lumber. It reminded Adam of the great cycle: ashes to ashes, dust to dust. *Dirt to dirt.* Then he noticed it again, a narrow shadow, like a snake. The thing was hiding in the walls, trying to get behind him. He spun around and the sudden movement extinguished his lighter. He flicked it on once more and there in the corner was the lonely and sad face of an old woman.

She fixed him in her gaze, and he felt as though his insides were being sewn up—a hole was being mended, one about which he'd forgotten. Only there was malice in the repair, deceit —there was a reason he'd forgotten, but now he'd be forced to relive something, whatever this patchwork was that this woman was stitching to his insides, with her unclean needles and her frayed yarn. Her sunken nose and paralyzing eyes floated in space beneath cobweb hair. He was so close to recognizing that face. But in that moment the lips pulled back and she bared her teeth at him, and he wet himself. Her lower jaw fell away and her upper teeth expanded to each side until her wicked face was spikes from ear to ear.

Adam felt a sharp hot pain in his hand and he dropped his lighter. The flame went out again but the bodiless head was on fire and he could see in the edges of his vision that the room was filling with steam as the flames of the skull boiled the damp out of all the boxes and lumber and flooring that had for so long nurtured all manner of moss and mildew and everything else that lived down here. The air became unbearably hot. Adam tried with all his strength to move, to escape, to run out and up the stairs, but still she held him with her gaze, staring into his misdeeds, his sins, and she shot him with beams of fire and he screamed. He screamed and cried, because he knew her, knew who she was, and why she was punishing him. Why she was burning him with rage and cruelty. She burned his chest and he fell backwards, fell down, and the beams grew wider and the room burst into flames. He crawled on his hands and knees to stay under the smoke, but still he could see her glowing eyes, and he knew that she was baking him alive, and as he pulled open the door to the staircase and began to ascend, she spoke, her voice hysterical, shrieking in her thick Spanish: *Pagarás! Lo juro, vas a pagar!* You'll pay, she said. You'll pay. Her wails soared beyond the range of human hearing, and Adam's splitting headache threatened to take over his conscious mind. He clapped his hands over his ears and raced up the treacherous staircase, flames quick on his heels. He threw open the door at the top and a wave of heat and smoke spat him forward into the diner. His coffee and eggs were sitting on the counter.

"Fire!" he shouted. "Fire! Call 911! Or don't—they're useless! Get out of here!"

Adam awoke to the smell of sulfur. He was on top of the covers, and still in his clothes, which were charred. The bedspread was streaked with ashes. He clutched his aching head and wondered how many hotel workers had seen him when he'd come back, whenever that was.

Now it was almost noon.

When he arrived at Farber Hall, Dr. Brandt was already wrapping up the keynote speech. Adam took a seat in the far back. There was a dull throbbing at the base of his skull. As he waited for the coffee and the painkillers and his first-ever nicotine patch to kick in, he tried to reconstruct the night. He had flirted with two different colleagues, he knew that much. Maybe he hadn't been all that successful, but it was the thought that counted, right? He'd always believed that there was a big difference between flirting with a woman and actively hitting on her—especially if it was just for kicks. He was more concerned with the missing block of time. Obviously he had smoked at least one pack of cigarettes, but realistically it was probably more. He hated that he'd let himself get black-out drunk again. The guilt was stacking up. He could see Elena's glare of disapproval. He sunk deeper into his seat.

Brandt must have said something clever, because the audience was laughing, and then Mikayla was on stage with Andrew Washington, and they were shaking hands with Dr. Brandt.

Washington was the current CEO of Montgomery Medicine, which owned the Lakeview Cancer Institute. He was filthy rich —a lot richer than Adam was—and he had a real punchable face. He took the podium, thanked the sponsors, and introduced the real star of the show: Dr. Mikayla Springer.

She stared at her hands on the podium, just breathing, for what seemed like a long time. She had the full attention of every single person in the audience. More than two thousand people, all told.

She drew herself up to her full height and took in the whole audience at once, seeming to look each individual in the eye. She took a deep breath, forced herself to smile, and said, slowly, "Yesterday morning, before I spoke to all of you here, my father passed away."

Adam sat up straight. There was a palpable change in the atmosphere as every member of the audience processed and reacted to what they'd just heard. Cameras flashed throughout the auditorium, and in his hungover condition the visual stimuli nearly provoked an undesirable response from Adam's stomach.

Dr. Springer continued: "Folks who were close to my father know how strong he was. How brave he was. But it wasn't enough. It never is, with cancer. My father had pancreatic cancer. No symptoms until it was too late." She stared at the audience, clearly upset.

"Sometimes people who mean well can say the most hurtful things," she said. "Things like, 'Oh, I know about cancer. I have a distant relative who had a mole removed once.' Or, 'Have you tried this weird remedy I found on the internet last night?' Even saying something as simple as, 'You can beat this thing,' can do more harm than good, when it isn't true. Because it implies that the patient has power over the uncontrollable. That there's something the patient can do, or stop doing, to make the cancer magically disappear. So when that person dies anyway, does that mean it was their fault? That they just weren't strong enough, after all? No. Of course not. No amount of strength or bravery could have saved my father's life. And don't even get me started on the supposed healing powers of all these magical fruits that everyone's always talking about. If it were that simple, don't you think we'd all be doing it already? I mean, honestly. As a nation, we're pouring well over *five billion dollars* into cancer research annually. If it were as simple as eating some damned piece of fruit, then everybody on earth would be eating it for breakfast, lunch, and dinner, every day of the year, and we'd be rid of cancer forever.

"But the truth is, it's not that simple. We've known that smoking cigarettes causes lung cancer for over sixty years. Sixty years! And still there are over two million people dying every single year from lung cancer caused by smoking. Once they're hooked, people just can't quit—because nicotine addiction is just that strong. Well, wake up, people! Cancer is stronger!"

Adam touched his chest to feel the nicotine patch. He didn't know if it was working yet, but its presence was reassuring. He sure as hell didn't want to smoke. He regretted ever starting in the first place. And that made him think of Maria. He scanned the dark corners of the auditorium.

Dr. Springer was looking at her hands again. "And there are so many more avoidable carcinogens. Soot causes cancer in coal miners. Dust causes cancer in carpenters. Mold causes cancer. The sun causes cancer, for crying out loud. Alcohol is one of the worst, yet we drink it all the time. Hell, I had some last night! And guess what—they just found out that eating fermented foods can cause GI cancer—even though we've been saying the exact opposite for years! In fact, overeating in general causes cancer. Bacteria cause cancer. Viruses cause cancer. HPV. HIV. Epstein-Barr Virus. Hepatitis B. Hepatitis C. The list goes on. Some of these are vaccine-preventable, and others can be cured after infection. But not all of them. Not yet anyway.

"And it doesn't stop there. Forty percent of all cancers still can't be traced to any source whatsoever. The best explanation we have is that these cancers occur naturally, due to random errors in the DNA transcription process." She continued in a higher pitch: "Sorry, dear patient—a mistake has been made. There's a typo in your code. You have a G where you should have a T, and now your cells are no longer your own. And no, you did not inherit this cancer from your great-grandmother. That's not how it works. You're just unlucky." She paused for breath, then shouted: "Well, I am SICK OF IT!"

She pounded her fist on the podium. She was looking right at Adam—even though he knew it was impossible. He was in the far back, in the dark. But she was so angry, and he felt her anger, and he felt accused. And he knew he was guilty. There was something, once, a long time ago... But he couldn't remember. He didn't want to remember. He felt dizzy, and his headache was getting stronger, not weaker. He took more painkillers.

He risked a glance at Dr. Springer. She was still talking, but Adam couldn't think about anything beyond the pain. She was calm and composed, and Adam was confused. The angry person he had seen was no longer there.

"...and recent discoveries in the human genome..."

People in the audience were clapping now, and Adam's skull was pounding.

"...standing at the edge of history..."

Cameras flashed. Reporters raised their hands. Adam tried to focus.

Dr. Springer went on, speaking louder now: "The idea is very simple. Transmortification is the process of genetically altering cancer cells so that their own functions lead them to senescence, triggering programmed cell death."

Adam was seeing stars. His headache was swelling and receding in great tides, and a single thought tried to press itself to the forefront. *You're lying, Adam. You're a liar. This isn't about you, or your family. It's not even about cancer, not really. It's about her. It's about penance.*

Then, in the dark above the audience, the forest came for him. Thick vines crept along the ceiling. The air turned stale. Adam shook his head and wiped his face on his sleeve.

"...the cure," Dr. Springer said, "Not just for some types of cancers, but for all cancer."

The audience cheered. The applause grew louder and louder. Adam squeezed his eyes shut and pressed on his temples. He focused on Mikayla's voice.

"No more surgery. No more radiation. No more chemo. No more cancer."

What was she saying? What had he missed?

"Make no mistake: here at Lakeview, we are talking about the cure for cancer. Once and for all. To end all cancer, for every human being on earth, forever."

Adam's mind raced. This was huge. All the times he'd met with Dr. Springer, the hours upon hours they'd spent immersed in the journals, assembling the team... Of course they'd say yes. They had to. This was bigger than any of them had ever imagined. It contradicted years of indoctrination against the very idea of a universal cure.

"And I know what you're all thinking: when there are no consequences, won't everyone start smoking again?"

She had his full attention now. The painkillers seemed to be working.

"And my answer is this: When all the carcinogens in the world have been rendered harmless, when random genetic mistakes no longer lead to malignancy, humanity will enter a new age. In the post-cancer world, the old rules will not apply. Smokers will still have to deal with addiction and emphysema. But I wonder—will they still have any reason to smoke?"

The audience went wild, standing and cheering. Adam joined in the ovation. He looked up into the darkness. Nothing. It was normal. The lights came up in the auditorium. Dr. Springer was looking right at him. She was beaming. He waved and smiled.

# *The Inner Circle*

[MACHINE-TRANSLATED.]
  From: Chicago
  To: Shanghai
  2019 - 8 - 16

With a shotgun aimed at my back, a security officer escorted me to the top-floor chamber. I stood under a light in the center of the floor. Eight men (and one woman) in darkness behind a circle of desks. I could see bald heads and shiny fat cheeks. They spoke one at a time, never interrupting one another. They sounded European.

One said, "The programmer may become a liability."

I replied, "Yes, he should learn to keep his remarks to himself."

"As should you," I was told.

"It's worse than you know," said a voice from my right. "He will attempt sabotage."

I remained silent.

A third voice: "He will identify the source of Baker's wealth."

"Shall I interfere?" I asked.

"Do nothing. The matter is being handled."

Someone said, "Marshfield may go to the press."

```
   Another person said, "He may attempt to
contact Subject Beta."
   The voices came from all sides, but I was
accustomed to it.
   "The statuses of Subjects Alpha and Beta
are no longer pertinent."
   "Adam Baker must win the election."
   "I understand," I said.
   I was not surprised when the guard took my
elbow.
```

"The Inner Circle" was a nickname used by some doctors and lab technicians when referring to the mysterious heads of the multinational pharmaceutical corporations. The general public was not yet aware of the existence of the Nine Heads, as they were called by the higher-ups. Watchdog groups had found the locations of pharmaceutical headquarters buildings in the US, Germany, France, South Africa, Japan, and China, but it was assumed there were more. For decades, healthcare advocacy groups had been amassing evidence of the underhanded tactics used by these corporations in the pursuit of profits at the cost of human lives. Clearly they had to be allied with corrupt police and politicians. Their lobbyists infiltrated every major government to make their practices legal. Even if these companies couldn't be linked directly to organized crime, they were undoubtedly guilty of abusing the human rights of multitudes of unskilled laborers in the procurement and processing of the raw chemicals necessary for the manufacture of drugs, not to mention the ethical violations involved in testing those drugs on third-world populations. The people at the top were the scum of the earth, supposedly. The hidden scions of ancient families. Partners in private, competitors in public. The hyper-rich. The one percent of the one percent. To these people, regular folks weren't even human.

The Heads came and went in helicopters to conduct secret meetings in dark chambers on the top floors of their corporate towers, apparently never descending to the lower reaches—or so the rumors claimed. Only the highest officers of each company ever set foot inside the uppermost chambers, which were designed to intimidate. The precise identities of the people at the top were unknown to all but their singular representatives, the regional CEOs. The CEO in charge of Montgomery Medicine, which is to say, in charge of North American operations as well as all Montgomery interests in Southeast Asia and Africa, was Andrew Washington. A rookie, promoted quickly up the ladder by Inner Circle machinations to take the fall if things turned sour. Or so the rumors claimed.

At the end of the First Annual Lifeline Conference, after making her big announcement, Dr. Mikayla Springer reported directly to Andrew Washington. He asked her to join him for an audience before the heads. Montgomery Tower was a few blocks across downtown from the Lakeview campus. His driver left them at the front door. In the elevator on the way up, after letting the button scan his thumbprint, Andrew briefed her on procedures, so that she would know not to address any one of the Nine directly.

An armed guard let them in. Andrew was surprised to be immediately dismissed. But he knew better than to open his mouth. He turned and left the chamber.

Dr. Springer's head was swirling with vague impressions. She had never imagined she was in so deep. They asked many questions, each guiding her toward a more complete understanding of her duties. They gave her no explicit commands—in this way they maintained plausible deniability, she assumed. Concealed in shadow as they were, she could make out only one female. Mikayla had been privately researching the corporations, so she had an educated guess as to the woman's identity. A victim of patriarchy as most women were, yet ruthless and vile. Certainly not an ally. Mikayla wondered if any of them had personally committed murder.

When it was over, Mikayla finally unclenched her jaw. Shaking off an uncharacteristic bout of paranoia, she returned to Lakeview and carried out her orders, which meant meeting individually with each member of the Transmortification project team to discuss their assignments. She sent Marshfield on a cyberspace tour of the world's leading cancer hospitals, to establish connections with immense databases of patient records. He was to work closely with Dr. Brandt, who would supply the search criteria: specific genetic markers which might hypothetically lead to the cure. Dr. Xu Fei was also to remain at Lakeview as visiting interim director, overseeing research, education, and patient care. Dr. Springer herself would be traveling with Dr. Cathy Peterson to Berlin in search of a suitable carrier virus.

On her way out, spurred by an undeniable instinct for self-preservation bordering on panic, Mikayla returned to the workstation of Tyler Marshfield. She touched his arm and looked into his eyes. She asked him to keep a close digital eye on the team for her, as a personal favor. Especially the lobbyist, Adam Baker. He and Dr. Alice Suzuki were going to Mexico.

# The Canyon

CEDAR CREEK POLICE DEPARTMENT
   Case #19-1017-0032G
   Subject: Garcia, Arturo Javier
   St. Luke's Family Hospital
   Surveillance transcript

   "By the way, you ladies still taking care
of his old man?"
   "He's over in the old wing. AJ never
misses a payment, but like I said, he's
going to be strapped for cash after this."
   "Why don't you wheel him on down here? Put
them in a room together, cut down on the
bills."
   "That's not a bad idea."
   "Maybe it'll jump-start some semblance of
awareness in one or the other of them. I
need him to start talking."

Cedar Creek was a small farming town named for a long rut in the ground that occasionally contained flowing water. Everybody knew the story: like many other natural features of the Upper Midwest, including the Black River Canyon a dozen miles outside of town, the Cedar Creek was a relic of the most recent ice age. Around twenty thousand years before Christ, a sheet of ice lost its grip on the North Pole and slid down over Canada like the world's biggest mountain riding on rails, scraping up some of the most fertile soil on Earth along the way. Then its southern edge came to a stop squarely over the Midwest and it melted, releasing torrential currents that gouged out ravines and drilled deep pot holes straight down into the bedrock. When the heat of the coming age proved too strong, the ice sheet's final lacrimation left twisting little ruts in the ground. Many of these ditches were destined to flow for only a few weeks a year after the spring thaw, or during a particularly heavy rain. The Cedar Creek was one of these. It was devoid of fish, and useless for irrigation, but the plagues of mosquitos were biblical.

The Bakers' house was the last one on the edge of town, and the Garcia family lived a mile down County Road H in a camper-trailer parked behind the machine shed on the Holbrooks' dairy farm. The Cedar Creek ran alongside the county road and cut under a small bridge in the Holbrooks' driveway, which was almost its own road, a quarter-mile of dusty gravel with a three-story farmhouse at one end and a rooster-shaped mailbox at the other. Adam and Arturo's bicycle tires churned the air full of dirt as the boys sped around the mailbox and out onto the street. Adam had a new bike, red and yellow, with front and rear shock absorbers. Just big springs, really, mostly for show, and the bike was heavy. He thought he was so cool on that bike. The fanny pack ruined any chance of that. It was a fast bike though, and of course Arturo was jealous. He always had to ride Jim Holbrook's old hand-me-downs.

Adam wanted to look for turtles. When they were little, Adam's father would let him try to keep turtles in an aquarium or a kiddie pool in the back yard, but they always escaped. That or they dried out in the sun and died.

Adam said he felt like trying again, now that he was older. So after about half a mile they took a right turn onto the dirt road that led to the marsh. The sparse shade from a line of tall craggy trees, coated with ancient moss and lichen, provided small relief from the hot sun. A hawk circled overhead. The chirping of crickets blended into a constant drone. Swarms of gnats drifted by like bubbles, maintaining their globular formations in the heavy air. The air stank with the familiar odor of standing water. The marsh was filled with the same kind of scum that grew in the water tank behind the horse barn back on the farm. The surface of the pond was covered with lily pads and a thick mat of tiny green leaves called duckweed. The boys walked their bikes forward. As they drew closer to the ferns that grew at the edge of the marsh, Arturo spotted a turtle sunning itself on a dead tree trunk that lay on its side in the center of it all.

Adam took one step closer and the turtle slipped into the shallow muck.

"Shit," he said.

"Bummer," Arturo said. He slapped a mosquito.

"Oh, I almost forgot. Here." Adam pulled a bottle of bug spray from his fanny pack. "Got it from my dad's hunting cabinet."

Arturo took the bottle and looked at the label. "Extra strength. Awesome. Watch this." He waited for the nearest swirling cloud of gnats to float a little closer, then he aimed and pulled the trigger. Every last one of the tiny insects dropped out of the air.

Maria's voice came out of nowhere. "Hey, that's not nice," she said. She had her bike. It was too big for her—she was only eleven—and her dog Ladybird was with her, too. Ladybird was the runt of the litter from the Holbrooks' border collie. She started barking and the boys turned around to see a huge snapper coming out of the ferns. It was big and black, like the dome of a charcoal grill—except it was covered with spikes, like some sort of dinosaur. Arturo and Adam pulled their bikes back onto the dirt road, next to Maria. The snapping turtle followed.

"Looks like an ankylosaur," Adam said.

Arturo said, "Nerd."

"Maybe we were too close to its eggs," Adam wondered.

"Ya think?" Maria said, rolling her eyes.

Arturo felt like messing with it, so he threw a small rock. Hit it right on the shell. It came another step forward. Ladybird stopped barking and hid behind Maria's legs.

Adam grabbed a big stick, a broken branch as big as a baseball bat, and tried to poke it in the face. On the first try he misjudged the weight of the stick and missed completely. When Adam took another jab, the thing opened its jaws and snapped off the end of the branch. Crushed it to smithereens. Adam jabbed again and this time it clamped onto the branch and yanked it clean out of Adam's hand. Arturo threw another stone, a bigger one, and the damn thing started running right at them.

"Maria—go!" Arturo shouted, and they whipped their bicycles around and pedaled as fast as they could. The snapper kept up at first, but it must have realized it had won, because when Arturo looked back it was gone. Maria's dog had run away the fastest, and she was waiting patiently for them where the dirt road ran back into County Road H.

Maria patted her dog, said she was a good girl.

Arturo shook his head. "Maria," he said, "go home."

"Wherever you're going, I'm going with."

"Not a chance, silly pants."

"Mom and Dad told me to go with you."

"Yeah right."

Adam stood off to one side and kept quiet.

"We're not going anywhere," Arturo said. "Just talking."

"About what?"

"About kissing girls, stuff like that."

"I'm telling!"

Arturo knew that if he said that was fine, she'd end up staying. So he said that if she told, he'd chop off her hair while she slept.

That set her off. "Now I'm really telling!" she cried, and she pedaled away toward the farm, Ladybird trotting along after her. The boys watched her disappear around a bend in the road, then they got on their bikes and sped off in the opposite direction.

There were corn fields on both sides of the road after that, getting tall in the late summer heat. The boys rode slowly for a few miles, not saying anything. There wasn't much traffic back then, out on those country roads. Adam was making wide curves, going from one side of the road to the other.

Matt had been in and out of the hospital for over a year before he passed away. Adam never talked about it. When it finally happened, he just about stopped talking completely. He never cried a lot or threw a fit or anything. He just turned quiet—even quieter than before. At first he seemed real cold about it. Bitter. Like he'd lived his whole life up to that point in his brothers' shadows. Noah, the first-born: disciplined apprentice carpenter, destined to take over the family business. Matthew: star pitcher and all-around good guy, loved and admired by all. And now Matthew was gone, dead—from brain cancer, no less—and here was Adam, poor little mama's boy, with a mama who barely even noticed him. No wonder he could get so angry. Never let it out, though, except for the one time. The previous spring before school let out, just after Matt died, he threw a chair out a third-floor window. It landed in the parking lot. Barely missed the gym teacher's truck. Adam served a week of in-school suspension.

After the marsh, the Cedar Creek turned north away from the road, but then after a few miles it came back down between the fields and it snaked under the road for a southern loop. So there was a pair of culverts there, about half a mile apart—first for the creek to go south of the road, and then another to let it pass north again. Adam and Arturo pulled over at the first culvert. The road's gravel shoulder sloped down to a ditch where rain or meltwater from the road and fields would collect and flow into the creek. Arturo rolled down into the ditch and dropped his bike in the wet grass, but Adam carefully stood his upright on its kickstand on the side of the road. He took off his shoes and socks and set them under his bicycle. He rolled up his jeans and walked down the grass to join Arturo, who stood barefoot in the cold water of the Cedar Creek.

At first they felt soft silt gushing between their toes, but the creek bed gave way to concrete and then corrugated aluminum as they entered the culvert. It was a tunnel only as long as the road was wide, so they could see sunlight on the water at the other end. They went in, Arturo taking the lead.

When they were almost halfway through, Adam lost his balance and nearly fell into the cold, slimy water, but Arturo reached out and took his flailing hand.

"Thanks," Adam said, his ears turning red. Arturo gave him a friendly half-smile and held his hand a little tighter. Adam took a step forward, and side by side, each boy extending his free hand to the curved metal walls, they walked confidently toward the sunlight.

Tall cattails crowded around the south end, where the creek emerged from the culvert and wandered away southwest. The boys could hear a bullfrog hiding somewhere in the reeds nearby, and there was the familiar drone of iridescent dragonflies and hummingbirds as well. They stood there for a moment, holding hands, the cool water flowing over their bare feet, opening their arms and hearts to the summer sun.

Suddenly Arturo dropped Adam's hand and bounded up out of the ditch. Adam looked at his hand, now hanging empty in the air, and a sad expression crossed his face. He turned to look back into the silver tunnel, and he took a step as if he might slosh through it again, but maybe he remembered his near fall and his bad luck, because he climbed up out of the ditch instead, pulling on clumps of tall grass to keep from falling backward.

They got on their bicycles and continued on their way, passing quietly under drifting white clouds and sunlight that filtered down through the branches of oak and maple trees. They road over the second culvert without slowing down, and the road jogged left and slightly downhill to avoid a copse of tamarack. The road curved to the right again just as quickly, and the boys stood up on their pedals to get the extra power they needed to make it up the hill. Now, with the tamaracks behind them, a wide expanse of grazing land came into view. Adam and Arturo pulled over on the gravel shoulder to take in the scenery. Great bowls of green grass sloped away for miles. The Cedar Creek wound back and forth through the bottom of the valley. A herd of dairy cattle—maybe seventy-five head of black and white Holstein—ate, drank, and slept in the pastures. Soft white clouds overhead cast enormous moving shadows. Looking out across the valley to the northwest, Arturo could see the line of tall conifers on the ridge that hid the Black River Canyon—and the high train bridge that crossed over it. He noticed that his friend was focused on the same spot on the horizon.

"Are you thinking what I'm thinking, Adam?"

"I think so, Brain—but where will we find rubber pants our size?"

The road ran downhill another mile, making lazy curves this way and that as it roughly paralleled the course of the Cedar Creek. The boys coasted in silence, slaloming back and forth over both lanes to keep from gathering too much speed. It was mutually understood that they would stop at the bottom of the hill, just inside the eastern edge of the pine forest. The road leveled out and the boys rolled to a stop. They were under the forest canopy now, and they pulled over just before a deteriorating concrete bridge, where the road crossed over the Black River. Their ultimate goal—the train bridge—was a twenty-minute hike through the woods to the top of the eastern wall of the canyon, but Arturo threw his bike down and walked straight to the river bank.

Here and there where the sun reached down through gaps between the crowns of bristling pine trees and peeling birch, sprawling nets of thorny wild cucumber and blackberry brambles crept along the forest floor. Adam was dismayed that the kickstand wouldn't hold up his new bike in the soft earth, but he wasn't about to leave it on the road, where it might get hit by a car. He sighed as he propped it against the trunk of a tree.

Arturo laughed. "You know that thing's going to get dirty some day, right?"

"Then I suppose I'll have to give it a bath," Adam said.

"Just like you give your dick a bath."

"Shut up."

"Come on," Arturo said, "I want to show you something." He walked down the muddy slope to the edge of the water.

"What is it?"

"Just a little something to save in your spank bank," Arturo said, and he ducked under the bridge, keeping one hand on the back wall as he stepped from the river bank onto a narrow concrete shelf. The underside of the bridge was a criss-crossed tangle of rusted girders, where a number of mud swallow families had hung their bulging nests. When Arturo was completely under the bridge, it was Adam's turn to step out onto the abutment, telling himself not to look down. The two of them stood there side by side, each holding onto the girders overhead with both hands. The shelf they were standing on extended a few inches past their sneakers and dropped off. The river washed by six feet below.

"Watch this," Arturo said, and he did a pull-up, lifting his face toward the underside of the bridge. He kicked his feet forward and hooked them over a beam. He released his grip, hung upside-down from his knees, and beat his chest.

"If you fall in, I'm not going to save you," Adam said.

"Hakuna matata, my friend," Arturo said, and he began to hang-crawl out over the water. When he was a few feet from safety there was a chorus of chirps. The mud swallows were agitated. The noise grew as Arturo crawled between the birds' clusters of dried mud. When he was halfway across, Arturo reached one hand up into the rusted undercarriage and pulled out some kind of bundle. Something rolled up in a plastic shopping bag. Then he hung there by his knees again, swinging. A few brave swallows emerged to defend their territory. They circled Arturo in wide arcs, sometimes darting in close to his face.

"You're going to fall," Adam said.

"Am not."

"Are too."

He swung back and forth like a pendulum. The next time a bird came too close, he took a swipe at it with the bundle in his hand. He nailed it, and the bird flopped down toward the water, but it recovered at the last second and flew off into the woods. From his relatively safe position on the ledge, Adam watched Arturo's every move with a mixture of admiration and fear.

"Here, catch," Arturo said, and using the momentum he'd gained by swinging, he chucked the bundle straight into Adam's open hands.

"Hey, I could've dropped it in the river."

"Not with me throwing," Arturo said. He grabbed ahold of the girders again and let his legs down, then he worked his way back to the ledge using only his hands, as if he were playing on the monkey bars at school.

"What is this, anyway?" Adam asked.

"It's a porno." Arturo said.

Adam gasped and dropped it.

"Careful with that!" Arturo picked up the bundle, untied the string, and pulled out the goods. The top half of the front cover was missing, torn off. What remained was the lower half of a woman, the sleeves of a lumberjack's red flannel tied in a knot over her belly button, the button and zipper of her cut-off jean shorts undone. Her thumbs, hooked in her belt loops, framed a triangle of red fabric.

"Awesome, right?" Arturo said. He had the upper hand, having found the thing lying in a ditch earlier that summer. It was Adam's first time seeing pornography, and looking at it made him feel vaguely guilty. He focused on the long brown legs that extended from the bottom of the cutoffs to the bottom of the magazine's cover.

"Wanna see more?" Arturo asked. He didn't wait for an answer. He flipped quickly past page after page of dense writing. "Boring articles, loads of fan mail from old dudes who can't get laid, tons of ads for cigarettes and shaving cream and shit like that." All the pages were warped and sort of crispy. Many were stuck together, and they crumbled if Arturo pulled too hard. The magazine had apparently gotten wet and then dried out again. He found the main photo feature. Many of the pictures were badly discolored.

"Her name's Charlotte," he explained. "A co-ed from Texas." Still wearing the flannel and cutoffs.

"What's a co-ed?"

"Who knows. And who cares, right? Check out her pussy."

Arturo turned the page, and there it was. Charlotte was lying in a lounge chair by a pool, naked, knees up, holding herself open.

"Lot of hair," Adam said.

"Yeah, it surprised me too."

"What are we supposed to do with this?"

Arturo laughed out loud. "What are we supposed to do? What the hell does that even mean? Like, you need me to explain it?"

"Well, no, I just—"

"I mean, you've jacked off before, right?"

"I—" Adam shut his mouth.

"Well at least tell me you know what a boner is."

"Sure. Yes."

"So you know what to do."

"Well, but what do you—"

"Hey, don't pull your dick out or anything. If you don't know, I sure as hell ain't gonna teach you. Jesus." He handed Adam the magazine. "Here. You figure it out."

Adam flipped past more articles. There were some ads for weird gadgets, and then a big section of ads with naked women and phone numbers.

A dog barked, and Adam froze.

Arturo craned his neck to look out from under the bridge. "Oh, shit," he said.

"Hey, guys—are you down there?" It was Arturo's kid sister. Adam looked up in time to see Maria coming down the slope, looking right at him.

He chucked the magazine into the river.

"Hey!" Arturo shouted.

"What was that?" Maria asked.

"Nothing!" the boys said in unison.

They came out from under the bridge. Maria's bike was on the ground next to theirs. Adam patted Ladybird's head.

"I thought I told you to stay home," Arturo said.

"Mom said to follow you."

"Shit."

"Don't swear."

"Fine. Just... Fine. We're hiking to the high-bridge. You can come too, if you can keep up."

They walked their bikes deeper into the woods to hide them from cars. The Cedar Creek cut a tiny ravine here, narrow enough to step over, before it flowed into the Black River. Fresh hoof prints in soft mud led the children to a deer trail. It was the height of summer and the thick green undergrowth meant that they couldn't stray far from the path, and even that was covered in places with snaking vines. Animals had already picked the wild raspberry bushes clean. Ladybird was having the time of her life, smelling everything, tearing off into the woods after the scent of a squirrel or a fox. Clouds of monarch butterflies gorged on flowing blankets of milkweed in the clearings. They passed a patch of tall grass that was all bent over and flat. Adam said it was a deer bed. In the hem of her skirt, Maria collected fresh acorns and pinecones. These were still green, not ready to release their seeds. The ground rose steadily. A warm breeze brought the sound of the rapids up from far below.

There were burning nettles all around, plants that gave an itchy rash, but not a bad one. The mosquitos were gathering. Adam sprayed his father's bug spray on Maria's sleeves and shoes. Arturo stepped off the trail to look at a clump of mushrooms, and Adam warned him about the fabled poison ivy. Adam said his father had described it a hundred times, but he couldn't remember if the leaves were shaped more like hearts or stars. Or if they had serrated edges, or not. Did they grow in separate stalks, or was it a vine, or a bush? At least he had heard of those things before. Arturo and Maria's father Manuel knew all about cactuses—the nopal and the maguey, anyway—but he was oblivious to the dangers of the upper midwestern forest.

They climbed higher and higher, until finally they reached the top of the ridge. Large spiders that Adam called orb weavers waited in the trees. They had big fat black and yellow bodies and leg-spans the size of a grown man's hand. At first Arturo saw only a few, each perched in a web the size of a tennis racket. But as he looked closer, he began to notice them on all sides and even directly overhead. Adam didn't seem to mind. His father always said spiders didn't give a damn about humans. But the sight of them made Arturo shiver.

The path here was lined with empty beer bottles. Arturo kicked one over the edge and they watched it smash on the rocks well before it would have reached the water. Maria found some ladybugs on a downed log. They were the real ones, with the deep red shells—not the Asian ones that sting. Adam and Arturo kept going. The trail led them straight to the train tracks. They turned left and followed the railroad to the high-bridge. The canopy of pine branches overhead parted and they stepped into the dazzling sunlight.

The canyon gaped open before them. The railroad crossed a long trestle bridge with arches under the deck and nothing on top except for the train tracks, a steel catwalk, and sturdy guardrails. The red tree trunks on the opposite side of the canyon looked small and far away.

Adam balked at the edge. "Is it safe?"

"Trains go over it, dummy. Of course it's safe." Arturo walked straight out onto the catwalk. Adam reluctantly followed. They stopped in the middle and looked down at the Black River, winding its way between yellow rocks a hundred feet below.

Arturo leaned out over the guardrail and spit, then he let out a long whistle, like a bomb dropping from a plane, ending with a crash when the spit hit the water. He said, "Fuck you for throwing my porno mag in the river."

"What was I supposed to do?"

"I don't know, anything but that. You're such a wuss."

"Am not."

"See, even saying that makes you sound like a wuss. Either stop denying it, or prove me wrong."

"Fine," Adam said. "I will."

"Right now?"

"Right now." And just like that, Adam climbed over the rail. He held on tight with both hands and stood with the heels of his sneakers hanging off the edge of the bridge. "See?" he said, and he shook his butt over the canyon. "See? How do you like that?" He took one hand off the guardrail and waved it in the air.

"Dumbass."

"See? Look what I can do." He took one foot off the deck and stuck it out behind him, then turned his body sideways and struck a pose like an acrobat at the circus.

"Now you're just being stupid," Arturo said.

"Yeah? Will you stop calling me a wuss now?"

"Yeah. Come on."

Adam brought his free hand back to the guardrail, then put his foot back on the edge of the deck. There was a second rail beneath the top one, and the gap between them was too narrow, so he couldn't slide through. He had to go over. He awkwardly twisted his arm to reach over the rail and grab it from the other side. He tried to bring a knee up and over, but his other foot slipped. "Shit," he said. He caught the rail in his elbow. Both feet were dangling below the edge of the deck. "Help!" he cried.

Arturo tried to grab him, but he couldn't get a good grip with the guard rails in the way. He tried to pull on Adam's t-shirt, but that clearly wasn't going to work. "Get your feet up," he said. "Don't you have anything useful in that fanny pack?"

There was a scream from the woods. It was Maria's voice. Adam and Arturo's heads automatically turned in that direction. She was standing under the trees at the edge of the cliff, frozen in place, staring back at them, probably thinking she was about to see Adam plummet to his death.

"Maria, get help!" Arturo shouted, but then he realized how much trouble he'd be in if Papá found out about this. "No, wait! Just come here and help!"

"Don't let her see me like this," Adam said, crying. He tried to get his feet back on the edge but the soles of his shoes slipped off the metal. "I want to go home," he sobbed. "I have a headache, and I'm tired, and I just want to go home."

"Hold on, I have an idea," Arturo said. He stood back and took off his belt. "Here, let me get this around you." He leaned over the rail and put the belt across Adam's back. He was trying to get the ends under Adam's armpits when he happened to look down at the river. He swore.

"What?" Adam said.

"There's something down there," Arturo said. "Like, a bear."

"A bear?"

"Yes. In the river. It's looking at us."

"Arturo, don't let me die."

"I won't, buddy."

Arturo got his belt under both of Adam's arms. He held onto the ends and leaned backward, pulling with all his strength. Adam finally got his feet on the deck. He got one arm up over the rail, then the other. But the boys were tired and they weren't sure how to get Adam the rest of the way back to safety.

Just then Maria came up behind her brother. "What should I do?" she asked.

"Grab onto me and pull!"

Maria was nearly two years younger than Arturo, but she was tall, like most girls her age, and she was strong. She grabbed her brother around the waist and pulled.

"Adam, you have to get your foot up," Arturo said.

"I can't. My head hurts. I'm going to throw up."

"No way, man. We need you. We can't do this without you."

"Arturo?" Adam said.

"Yeah?"

"You were right. I'm a wuss."

"No, you're not. I'm sorry I said that."

"Really?"

"Yeah. I'm sorry."

Adam worked one foot up and over the rail. Arturo pulled on the belts. Maria pulled on Arturo. Adam pulled on Arturo's shoulders. Something finally gave, and all three of them fell hard onto the bridge. The heavy buckle of Arturo's belt fell through a gap in the steel grid, and the weight of it pulled the belt through his sweaty hands. They watched the belt fall, twisting down through the air, as their hearts and lungs recovered from the strain. The belt disappeared in the swirling water far below. The bear was nowhere to be seen.

And they never found Maria's dog.

# *The Fire*

CEDAR CREEK POLICE DEPARTMENT
  Case #19-1017-0032G
  Subject: Garcia, Arturo Javier
  St. Luke's Family Hospital
  Surveillance transcript

"You with me now, bud?"

"...Mom?"

"No, AJ, I ain't your dear old momma. I'm a police officer. I'm here to take your statement. Are you hearing me, son? Come on now, the clock's ticking."

"I can't see. Where am I?"

"St. Luke's. Your eyes are swollen shut. Good thing, too. You don't want to see yourself like this, trust me. Now I need you to tell me what happened at the bar."

"You gonna read me my rights?"

"What? No, you're not under arrest, AJ. You're the victim. Folks need to know what happened."

"Get me a lawyer."

"I guess you're not understanding me, son. You've got the county prosecutor on your side. Your old man was real good for this town, and we don't need anybody messing that up. Bill Mischler gave us enough to put

those boys away for a little while, but the
prosecutor wants to call it a hate crime,
and for that, you need to cooperate."

"Where's my dad?"

"Over in the other wing. Nurse said he's
doing just fine."

"Tell them to bring him here."

"As a matter of fact, I already asked.
He'll be here in the morning. Now can we
please cut the bull and get to it?"

"Fuck you."

"God dammit AJ, don't you understand that
I'm trying to help you?"

"Officer, he needs to rest."

"Just another minute, Margie."

"He's not ready for this kind of stress."

"Mom?"

"AJ, calm down. The doctor's coming."

"Mom, I can't see you."

"AJ, I need you to relax."

"Mom, don't go. Dad needs you."

"He's going to hurt himself."

"Don't leave us!"

"No good. Give it to him."

"Mom… Dad…"

"Heart rate is stabilizing."

"Maria…"

"Any second now."

"Adam…"

"He's out."

"Too bad. I need a statement."

"You shouldn't have pushed him like that,
Steve."

"Sorry, Doc."

"No harm done. Will you and Sarah be going
to the spaghetti dinner this weekend?"

It was late summer, and seventh grade was about to begin. There
were only a few days of freedom remaining. Adam was planning
to join the cross-country running team, so he needed to practice,
and Arturo was needed on the farm more and more, as the
Holbrooks and their hands prepared for the coming harvest.

Sometimes he'd manage to escape for an hour or two by convincing his mother to send him into town with a shopping list.

The town of Cedar Creek consisted of a few small neighborhoods along a two-mile stretch of highway in southern Minnesota. Some of the residents commuted to the factories in the bigger cities that lined the Mississippi River, but most of them worked at the cannery or elsewhere in town. There was a post office, two grocery stores, some restaurants, a hardware store, a hospital, a used car lot, a couple of gas stations, a motel, a funeral home, a feed mill, a farm machinery dealer, three veterinary clinics, the cannery, and a hundred bars. The Bakers lived out on the western edge of town near the Catholic church and the cemetery.

Arturo threw his bike down in the sun in front of Adam's house, and he went inside. The two of them milled around the kitchen eating whatever they could find—the last slices of cheese, the ends of a loaf of bread. Half a can of honey-roasted peanuts. A couple of brown bananas that tasted alcoholic.

Adam tried to complain to his mother about the lack of food, but she chased them out the back door. The Bakers had a big back yard, enclosed with a low fence made of split cedar logs. There was a big oak tree in the center, and John Baker's personal woodworking shop stood in the far corner. The lawn hadn't been mowed. The tall grass concealed clusters of acorns that crunched under the boys' shoes as they walked toward the pair of tire swings that hung from the tall oak. Adam's grandfather had made those swings, before he died. The tires were already old when the swings were made, but now the rubber was falling apart. The boys sat down in the swings, and the sharp ends of hundreds of wires jabbed through their jeans and into their skin. They sat there anyway. Not swinging, just sitting, digging the toes of their shoes into the bare spots underneath the swings, where the grass had been worn away.

After a long time, Adam spoke. "Remember when we used to make ninja weapons and write our own fight scenes?" he said.

"Sure."

"Those were the days, right?"

"You mean, like, two years ago?"

"Yeah. I wonder why we stopped."

"We only ever did it like twice."

"Let's do it again."

"What, now?" Arturo asked.

"Yeah, why not? I bet we can make something awesome now that we're not kids anymore."

Arturo thought about it. "Alright, whatever. But let's do it quick. I'm supposed to be running errands."

"We can use my dad's power tools."

"You sure he won't care?"

"Who cares if he does?"

Arturo looked at him sideways.

Adam hopped out of his tire swing and headed for the little workshop. He entered the padlock's combination, undid the hasp, and flung the door open. Sunlight spilled into the shop for the first time since Matthew's death.

"On second thought—" Arturo began.

"What, you think of something better to do?"

"No, it's just—"

"Just what?"

"Maybe your dad wouldn't want us—"

"Dad's not here though, is he? And he won't mind. Probably be happy I'm doing something creative for once."

"If you say so."

Adam's father did most of his carpentry work either on-site or at the big workshop downtown, the one Adam's great-grandfather had built. The little shed in the back yard was a personal wood shop, a private one, and it was chock-full of hand-made works of art. Birdhouses, clocks, shelves, knick-knacks. Each project had its own area of the workbench, and its own aura, its own constellation of oily tools and sawdust. An unpainted duck, painstakingly carved in fine detail. A complete miniature baseball team. An unfinished wooden baseball bat, still suspended in the lathe. A stained-glass mobile hung from the ceiling, three windows set in frames of cherry, each one a small picture—a baseball, a glove, home plate.

"Here," Adam said. "Grab a hunk of wood." He reached into a scrap box under the workbench and pulled out the sawn-off end of a two-by-four. Then he pulled a circular saw down from a large hook in the pegboard on the wall. He plugged it in.

"Adam, I really don't know if we should—"

"What?"

"I mean, this is your dad's—"

"What? Say what you mean. I can take it."

"Adam, that's not—"

"You think I can't handle this thing? Watch. I'm strong enough." He hefted the saw into the air and squeezed the trigger. The spinning blade whined as its teeth merged into a single edge.

Arturo could see he wasn't getting through. Maybe Adam needed to assert himself, to feel some power, some control. Maybe it wasn't Arturo's approval he really needed, but his own. Arturo decided to let it go.

"Yes, Adam," he said. "I know you can handle it. You're strong enough." He said it with a straight face.

"Don't talk to me like I'm a baby," Adam said. "I'm not."

Arturo stared at his friend with narrow eyes, trying to figure him out, searching for something to say that might help him calm down. It was no use. He broke eye contact and grabbed a square of half-inch plywood and a jigsaw. The boys got to work.

"Why do sword fights always look so fake in the movies?" Adam asked.

"What do you mean?"

"Like, they look like they're just trying to hit each other's swords, instead of actually trying to kill each other."

Arturo had no answer. They continued in silence. Within half an hour they had swords that were ten times more elaborate than anything they'd made before.

Adam reached up to a high shelf and grabbed a propane blow torch. "Remember how we used to stick our swords in the campfire, to temper the blades?"

He found a flint striker in a drawer and sparked up the torch.

"I hate to say this," Arturo said, "but I don't think we should be using that."

"Whatever you say, Jose." Adam closed the valve and slammed the torch down on the workbench. Arturo laid both hands on the bench, let his head hang, closed his eyes, and breathed out a long sigh.

When he opened his eyes he saw a big fat spider right there in the sawdust between his hands. It had a large black body, furry legs with gray stripes, and oversized eyes like marbles.

Without thinking, Arturo grabbed the blow torch and sparked it back to life. The spider was just sitting there, looking up at him, almost daring him to try it. Arturo took aim. The spider turned to one side, then the other, so fast it looked like two still images viewed consecutively. It must have decided to stand its ground, because it faced center again, staring up at Arturo with its eight glittering eyes, and it raised its two front legs above its head as it crouched back.

Arturo understood that posture. He thrust the torch's pencil-tip flame directly at the spot where the spider had just been, but it was gone.

There it was—a foot away, on top of a birdhouse, once again preparing to leap.

Arturo swung the torch over the workbench, but the spider was too fast. Its movements were so quick—it would take a step forward, then hop back so fast you couldn't be sure it had moved at all. Then it would move almost instantaneously from one place to another, as if it didn't actually need to travel the distance between. It was always just out of reach.

Adam stood back with his hands on his belly, laughing at Arturo, saying, "Whoops—there he goes! Try again!"

The spider hid behind a toolbox. Arturo reached out with a quick jab and pushed the toolbox aside. What he saw made his head swirl. It was a different spider. Had to be. The gray stripes were still there, and the same shining eyes, but the body was smaller, the legs longer, sharper.

It leapt to Arturo's chest, ran up his neck to his face, and bit him.

Arturo smacked it away, cursing. He tracked the curvature of the spider's arc through the air as he cranked the torch's valve all the way open. His beam of blue fire caught the spider right where it landed, which was in the middle of a small forest of wooden baseball players. It was a hand-carved set of Christmas ornaments, the complete 1990 line-up of the Minnesota Twins. The team that made the historic triple-play twice in one game, then lost anyway. Each ornament was like a perfect snapshot, each player holding up his bat or glove, frozen in a moment of intense action. Attached to each player's cap was a loop of golden thread. Each thread caught fire like a wick, and the Twins went up in flames.

Arturo took a step back, hands in the air, the blow torch still blowing.

Adam grabbed the first thing he saw and threw it on the fire. It was an old towel, stained black with grease, and it burst into flames immediately.

Arturo stared at the growing blaze, suddenly feeling sad and tired. The torch in his hand melted the solder out of the stained-glass mobile. Polygons of colored glass fell to the cement floor and shattered, while flames climbed up the mobile to the ceiling.

"What do we do?" cried Adam. "Can't we stop it?"

The boys watched in horror as, one by one, John Baker's old offerings to his dying son turned to ash.

Soon the workbench itself was crackling with fire, and flames were climbing up the pegboard on the wall, and the little shop was filling up with smoke.

"Too late," Arturo said, and he turned and ran out the door, coughing.

Adam emerged half a minute later, his cheeks smeared black and his eyes swollen shut. He stumbled and fell on the grass. Through the doorway Arturo saw part of a wall collapse.

"Get out of the way," he shouted over the roar of the fire. He had the garden hose. He jammed his thumb in the end to increase the pressure. "Get your parents," he yelled.

Adam rolled over, and Arturo saw what he was holding—what he had taken the time to rescue. There in his arms, Adam cradled their two newly-forged swords.

# *Snow*

WASHINGTON Andrew (andy@montmed.com)
  Tues. 11/05/2019 10:57
  BAKER Adam (baker); SPRINGER Mikayla
(springer)

  Adam- Major win for us with that
conference. Great job. How would you like to
go even bigger. I have something in mind.
Let's rap when you get back. -Andy

It was a cold mid-November day in Minneapolis, and Adam Baker took his family to the park to play in the first snowfall of the year. They wore matching hats and scarves, purple and gold, knitted by Adam's seventy-year old aunt Heather. Adam helped Mary and Lucy make a snowman. Elena sat on a frozen bench, taking pictures with her phone.

Mary scooped up a huge armload of snow and dropped it right on Adam's head.

"Thanks a lot, kiddo," he said.

"Good job, Mary!" Elena shouted.

Adam grinned at his wife, and she smiled back, but he could tell something was up. He had only been back for what seemed like a few short days, and he'd be leaving again within a week. He sat next to her.

"Sorry I'm gone so much, sweetheart."

She said, "Oh, it's fine. It was only three days."

"Three days this time, three more next time..." He told her it was only going to get worse, with the new project. She took it well. That was what he loved about her—she was still good to him, even when she was upset. He felt guilty for not helping enough, for making her wait. But at least she didn't know about all the other stuff.

She must have sensed how he was feeling. She told him not to worry, that they would wait for him, like always. She said his mother must be very proud of him, up in Heaven. Elena was proud of him, too. So were the girls. He wondered if he could tell her he'd quit smoking again, for real this time. No, that would mean he'd have to admit he was lying about it before. He'd have to tell her how low he'd sunk. He knew the risks better than most people, what lung cancer could do to a person's family. So why was it so hard to commit to a decision now, in the present, when the consequences were so far off? But this time he was ready to stick with it. To be the role model that he knew his kids needed. To be the husband he'd promised to be.

The girls were throwing snow balls. If this went on any longer, one of them would end up crying. Adam slapped his knees and said, "It's getting chilly out here! Let's pack up and go home!"

It was bedtime for the girls. Adam was on toothbrushing duty; Elena helped them into their footie pajamas. Adam read them a story. Elena sang a lullaby, then shut off the lights. The tired parents collapsed on the couch. Adam switched on the artificial fireplace. Elena put her feet up on his knees. He told her how he'd always loved her legs. She had on plaid stockings. He started rubbing her feet.

She said, "You should run for Congress."

Adam frowned at her. "Very funny," he said.

"No, really. Hear me out. But don't stop rubbing."

"I'm listening."

"It's just an idea. But, think of it—how much easier would it be for you to get funding for your projects?"

"And for *your* projects too, I bet."

"Okay, I admit it. The thought had crossed my mind." Elena worked at the Mexican Consulate over in St. Paul. She did everything there, from family counseling, to job training, to providing translation services and legal advice, to organizing intercultural activities throughout the Twin Cities. She dreamed of radical immigration reform.

"Think of all the things you could accomplish," she said, "if you were the one behind the desk, instead of the one begging for money."

"I'd be begging for votes, instead."

"You wouldn't have any problem getting people to vote for you, believe me."

"I'd be away even more."

"We could go with you."

"It takes time to build a campaign."

"The election's a year away."

"How long have you been planning to spring this on me?"

"I don't know. A while."

"I'm going to need some help."

She sat up, turned to face him, and said, "Anything you want, Mr. Senator."

She put her knees on either side of his lap.

# PART II.

# METASTASIS

# *Homecoming*

CEDAR CREEK POLICE DEPARTMENT
   Case #19-1017-0032G
   Subject: Garcia, Arturo Javier
   NxLink Mobile, Inc.

   11-06-2019
   02:32:42 PM 507-555-7864
   ***Incoming call from 763-555-2326
   02:32:45 PM 507-555-7864
   ***Sending to voicemail
   02:32:52 PM 763-555-2326 Hi, umm, Arturo?
It's Adam. I heard you're in the hospital.
Just wanted to say hi, I guess. I hope
you're okay. I understand if you don't want
to talk to me. Take care, amigo.

In the beginning of his first year of high school, before he got to know the layout of the building, Arturo took a wrong turn and found himself in a long, empty hallway. He spotted his old bully, Tommy Erickson, entering the hallway from the other end. It was too late to turn back. Tommy was a year older, a sophomore now. Arturo had spent the previous year trying to forget about him. One look down that hallway though, and seventh grade came flooding back. The worst part of it was that, at the time, Arturo hadn't understood that Tommy and his friends were bullies. He'd thought that associating with eighth graders who smoked and probably had sex made him cool. On top of that, Tommy Erickson was Adam Baker's older cousin, so Arturo thought of it as kind of an upgrade, that way. It had taken him a full year to understand that Tommy had been making fun of him all along—not even hiding it, really—when Arturo had thought that they were friends. The most humiliating thing was knowing what Tommy had meant when he'd given him the nickname "Stubby." Tommy was a tall, lanky guy, so Arturo had thought the nickname just meant that he was short. Tommy and his idiot friends the Steinholtz twins had gotten all the eighth graders calling him Stubby that year, and Arturo had answered to it with a smile. Now that he was in high school, the thought of it made him sick.

Now, in the hallway, Tommy and Arturo were walking toward each other in slow motion. Tommy had cowboy boots on, and they clicked on the floor as he walked. They were staring each other down. When they met halfway down the hallway, Arturo was seeing red. But Tommy laughed, and he said, "How's it going, AJ?"

It only made Arturo madder. It was the first time anybody had ever called him that. He kept staring, even as he kept walking, until his neck couldn't turn any further. But Tommy just kept laughing.

By the end of eighth grade, Arturo had been getting used to the middle school's diversity. Each of the lower grades had more and more non-white kids. Not so in the grades above, though, because the Garcias were the first to move to town. Maria was still in middle school, with her Black and Hmong friends, and the other Latinos and Latinas. Not that they were all best friends or anything, but at least they weren't alone. In high school, Arturo didn't have anybody. He thought about giving Adam a second chance. Even Meatball Margaret had forgiven Up-Chuck Adam for ruining her clothes, after all. But Adam was still at the bottom of the pecking order, and Arturo wondered how that might affect his situation.

Arturo just wanted to go to school and fit in and make new friends and tell jokes and talk to girls and play sports and raise his hand in class and make fucking paper airplanes like everybody else. But he felt like nobody could interact with him, in even the most normal daily things, without putting him in a little box labeled, "Mexican." It didn't matter to them that he was born in Minnesota. Nobody knew, or cared to know, that his English was better than his Spanish. And they sure as hell didn't care about his home life. The only thing people cared about was what they could see with their eyes—unless you wanted to bring up God, then they'd go on and on about faith. Some of his classmates were like that. They wanted him in their Jesus club or whatever, because they knew that all Mexicans were devout Catholics. Arturo went out for football instead, even though Tommy and the Steinholtz twins were on the team.

Things started looking better the following year. Arturo and Adam became friends again. Adam was sick and tired of being a nobody, and he came to Arturo—or AJ, as everyone was calling him now—for help. He wanted AJ to teach him how to be popular. Arturo could hardly believe his ears. He said he didn't know anything about being popular. He was getting his ass kicked on a regular basis.

But he told Adam what he knew: "Stand up for yourself. Don't let people push you around. It hurts to get hit, but if you fight back, everyone notices. If you just fall down and cry, nobody cares. You have to quit staring at the floor, and start looking people in the eye. Even if you have to fake it."

Adam made more and more friends after that, and by the beginning of the eleventh grade, he and AJ were already drifting apart again. Adam had his friends, and AJ had the football team. But Arturo's teammates weren't his friends, not really. They were probably just jealous, since AJ could do it all better than any of them—even the seniors. Coach Boscowicz let the senior quarterback keep his position, but everyone knew who was next in line. Adam and his new group even came to watch the games, and so did Arturo's parents and sister.

The homecoming game was huge that year. AJ Garcia caught wild throws left and right, making the quarterback look good, and he was racking up touchdowns. The Owatonna Eagles managed to score one in the second quarter, followed by a couple of field goals, but they never really had a chance against the Woodchucks. It was another easy victory. Arturo's parents congratulated him and went home. There was a gap between the end of the game and the official start of the homecoming dance, so most of the guys went straight home to get ready. Spectators like Adam and Maria and their friends would probably just hang around outside. Arturo was still pouring sweat, and he'd decided earlier in the day that he wouldn't want to go out to the farm to clean up and then have to bike all the way back, when there were perfectly good showers right here at school.

Tommy was on the defensive line, so he'd barely had to do anything during the whole game. Regardless, he wasn't the type to care whether or not he stank, so Arturo was surprised to see him in the locker room.

"Good game tonight, amigo," Tommy said.

"Good game."

Tommy didn't even bother showering off. He threw down his gear and immediately put on stonewash jeans and a sea-green plaid shirt with pearl snaps.

Arturo opened his locker and made sure his shirt and pants were there were he'd left them. He stripped down and shoved his gear in his bag. He grabbed his shampoo and locked his locker. He took a clean towel from the bin, and as he was heading into the showers, he saw Tommy putting on a raincoat.

The boys' locker room at Cedar High had a small square shower room, with ugly yellow tiles and black mold growing in the corners. There were no divider panels between the faucets, and no door. Arturo wasn't ashamed of himself, but he always picked the showerhead in the back corner, because that one had the best water pressure. He started working shampoo through his long, black hair.

He never heard them coming over the sound of the faucet. Tommy tapped on his shoulder, Arturo turned around, and Tommy shoved him. He hit his back on the shower knobs, and his feet slipped out from under him and he fell on his ass, and Tommy kicked him in the stomach. And when Tommy leaned forward to turn off the shower, Arturo saw that Tommy had mud boots on. And between those boots, he saw Adam, standing there in the locker room, slack jawed and staring. But before his big cousin Tommy could see him, Adam jumped into a locker and shut himself inside.

Arturo felt his nose bleeding down his face. He watched his blood mix with water on the floor and swirl down the drain. "Why are you doing this to me?" he shouted.

"Because I can, AJ. Because I'm bigger than you. Because I'm stronger than you."

Arturo tried to laugh, but he choked, then coughed. When he caught his breath he said, "Then how come you're not that good at football?"

Tommy kicked him again. "You think you're mighty funny, don't you. Well I got a plan for you, you stinking Mexican faggot."

Arturo was on the floor, naked and bloody, clutching his stomach, but he said, "Actually, I'm American."

"You don't look fucking American to me, you little shit!"

A voice came from the locker room. "We're here, Tommy." It was Eddie and Willie Steinholtz, in rain ponchos and hip waders, each carrying a gunny sack from the feed mill.

"Let him get dressed first," Tommy said. He pulled Arturo up by the hair and shoved him toward his locker. Arturo got dressed, getting blood all over his best church clothes in the process. Then the brothers grabbed him, and he tried to fight back, but they were too big, and they dragged him back into the showers.

Tommy turned on a faucet until Arturo's clothes were soaked, then he said, "Do it."

Tommy's goons dumped out their gunny sacks, covering Arturo in chicken feathers. They stunk. Arturo and the Steinholtz twins were farm boys, so they were used to the smell, but Tommy threw up on the tiles. The Ericksons ran a gas station and convenience store.

A locker door slammed and someone bolted. "Shit! Who was that?" Tommy yelled. He and the twins threw their rain clothes in the towel hamper on their way out the door.

Arturo walked out of the locker room in a daze, seeing double. He heard the DJ's voice echoing from the gym: "Grab your date and gather 'round—we're about to crown your new king and queen!"

Arturo left a trail of feathers and bloody footprints in the hallway. He rounded the corner by the entrance to the gym, expecting to see someone, anyone—but everybody was inside the gym. Arturo stumbled through the double doors. The homecoming court was up on the stage: Tommy and some other senior football players, and their cheerleader girlfriends. The DJ said, "Here it is, folks—the moment you've all been waiting for. Your 1999 Homecoming King is—"

But someone started screaming. The spotlight operators found Arturo, and the whole dance floor went up in shrieks of horror. Arturo stood up straight and took a step forward. He wanted everybody to see what they'd done to him. He tried to move through the pain. He only made it a few more steps before a pair of teachers grabbed him and carried him out the door.

# *Birthday Party*

CEDAR CREEK POLICE DEPARTMENT
    Case #19-1017-0032G
    Subject: Garcia, Arturo Javier
    St. Luke's Family Hospital
    Surveillance transcript

"How is he? Has he been eating? Can you hear me, Dad? Are they taking good care of you? Sorry I haven't been visiting lately."
"He's doing fine, AJ. Same as always."
"Still not talking, though."
"No, I'm afraid not."

AJ felt good behind the wheel of his father's new Toyota pickup. It was small and tough, with a narrow back seat. José Manuel Garcia Saracho was the head of the migrant workers on the Holbrook farm, and the Toyota was his pride and joy. Technically Mr. Holbrook owned it on paper, but Manuel paid the bills. Today, Manuel had given his son Arturo Javier special permission to borrow the truck. AJ pulled over on the street next to Cedar High, Home of the Mighty Woodchucks. AJ was now the star quarterback. Some of the guys from the team would be at the party, of course.

Adam Baker walked up to the Toyota with Maria by his side.

"You know," Adam said, "it wasn't very smart of you to come to school with the beer."

"Had to come back for you two assholes, didn't I?"

A year had gone by since the hazing, and they'd never spoken of it. Adam hadn't shown up at the dance that night, and AJ figured he still didn't know that AJ knew he'd been there in the locker room. AJ was saving that information for the right moment. But they'd been getting along fine overall, and it was their birthday. In the past they'd thrown Halloween birthday parties at the bowling alley, and at the pizzeria on the south end of town, and at the mall in Owatonna, almost an hour away. The mall had a movie theater. But they were seniors now, and it was their turn to use the gravel pit.

AJ looked in the rearview. The keg was perfectly visible in the bed of the truck, next to some bags of ice, a stepladder, an old love seat, and a bunch of farm junk. Stupid not to throw a blanket or something over it anyway, he thought. He got out and walked around to the back, dropped the tailgate, and pulled down a plastic barrel full of chains and ratchet straps. He dumped out the barrel, put it over the keg, and lashed it down.

"Yeah, that's not conspicuous," Maria said. She squeezed into the back seat, then Adam got in, and AJ put the little truck in gear. He made a left turn. Four blocks of trees, old houses, and old mailboxes whooshed by. Maria's face filled the rearview mirror, and she was smiling at the back of Adam's head. AJ slammed on the brakes at a stop sign, tossing his sister halfway into the front.

"Maria, will you stop breathing down our necks?" AJ said.

She sat back and crossed her arms.

They cruised down main street between two- and three-story brick buildings. The coffee shop. The post office. Old Bill's bar and restaurant on the corner. The businesses gave way to another stretch of middle-class homes. Adam ducked as they passed his house, which was the last one heading out of town. He popped up again and said, "Oh, I almost forgot—I brought us a present."

AJ risked a sideways glance and saw Adam pull a pair of beers from his backpack.

"Stole them from my dad," he said. He cracked one and handed it to his friend.

"You guys!" Maria said. "Where's mine?"

Empty fields stretched along the road on both sides. Only the jagged stumps of corn stalks remained after the harvest. Sparse lines of bare trees marked the boundaries between fields. AJ honked the horn once as they passed the Holbrook farm, then he settled back in his seat, took a drink, and drove his sister and his on-again, off-again best friend out into the countryside for Adam and AJ's Halloween Birthday Bash, Senior Edition. The sun was low on the horizon, but there would be plenty of time to set up before dark.

The gravel pit was a few miles out of town, off 140th and Pineridge up where the train bridge crossed the river. It was a wide turn-around spot for tractors, and a dumping spot where farmers unloaded all the rocks they hauled out of their fields every spring. Rock-picking was a week-long weight-lifting contest for farm boys like AJ. The first tractor would pull the plow, and a second tractor would follow, dragging a low wagon or a metal sled called a stone boat. The farm boys would chase along after the tractors, picking up rocks and chucking them onto the sled. Then they'd all drive out to the gravel pit and dump off the rocks. Tall rock piles stood in rings around a space big enough to park some cars and build a bonfire. Flattened beer cans covered the ground. Seniors from Cedar High had been throwing parties there for decades.

AJ pulled the Toyota into the gravel pit, whipped a couple of donuts, slammed on the brakes, and threw it in park, facing the center. The three of them climbed out. Maria went for a walk. Adam and AJ lifted the keg out of the trunk. Together they lowered it into the plastic garbage barrel and dumped the bags of ice in around it. AJ tapped it, and Adam was about to pump the tap and pour a cup, but AJ stopped him, saying kegs needed to settle a bit or you just got foam. So they shared Adam's last can of beer and got to work. Adam pulled the stepladder from the truck bed and set it up nearby. He hung a flood light on the ladder and plugged it into a power inverter, which he then hooked up to an old car battery. Unfortunately Halloween fell on a Wednesday that year, so they had decided to throw their party on the Saturday before. By astronomical coincidence, the party fell on the night of the new moon. The gravel pit would have been pitch dark had it not been for Adam's borderline obsession with space. He'd confirmed the moon's phase in advance and had planned accordingly.

"Let there be light," he said, and he flipped the switch. It worked. He turned it off again to save juice.

AJ had been busy digging out the old fire pit, making it much bigger. Adam helped him pull the old love seat out of the back of the truck, and they stood the whole thing up on end in the fire pit. AJ took a red gas can from the back seat of the Toyota and doused the sofa.

Maria came back and they put on their costumes, using the truck's mirrors to check themselves out. The first three years of high school had been hard on AJ and Adam, but now they were on top. Adam had taken AJ's tenth-grade lessons in self-confidence to heart, and now he was like a different person. Adam had managed to invite over a dozen classmates—almost as many as AJ. Adam was now so confident that he'd decided to go as Superman, complete with the cape and the red undies. Maria was Sacagawea, the Shoshone interpreter from the Lewis and Clark expedition. AJ was a werewolf.

The sun dipped below the treetops on the western ridge of the canyon before the first carload of partygoers arrived. By the time it was completely dark out, there were three trucks, two cars, and a whole lot of teenagers. The guests segregated themselves around the fire pit. Adam's friends and AJ's friends weren't exactly friendly with each other.

Adam turned on the flood light, then made sure everyone had a red plastic cup full of fresh beer. AJ borrowed a lighter from his sister, and the couch went up in flames. Maria ran around trying to get everyone to sing "Happy Birthday." She'd even brought a cake. But the party had already taken over, and Maria was powerless to stop it. She was only a sophomore.

"Thanks anyway," Adam said.

AJ said, "Forget it. Let's get druuunk!"

"You're already drunk, big brother."

"Come on," Adam said. "Let's mingle. My friends are over here."

Adam's friends came dressed in joke costumes. One couple wore masks of Bill Clinton and Monica Lewinsky. Another couple—she had a black eye and he had a bloody crotch—were John and Lorena Bobbitt. And there was one guy, clearly single, who had simply written the word NAFTA on his shirt in black marker. Adam introduced them all, but AJ wasn't listening. He said, "Well, there's plenty of booze to go around, so everybody drink up. See ya later, dorks!"

He ushered Adam and Maria around the fire pit. Three young men stood there facing the fire. Each one had a beer in his hand and a girl on his shoulder. The one on the end had two of each. The boys were AJ's buddies from the football team. They wore plain clothes. The girls wore their boyfriends' letter jackets over cheerleading uniforms.

"This is John, Ben, and Jake."

"We've met," Adam said. "John—math class, seventh grade. Ben—tenth grade bio. Jake and I are currently in public speaking."

"You know that battery won't last all night, right?" John said.

"I know, I'll hook it to the truck soon," Adam said, raising his cup.

"Kim, Heather, Rebecca," AJ said, showing his fake werewolf teeth. "Nice to see you. Thanks for coming." He turned to the fourth girl. "Holly." He just looked at her, his expression neutral. She detached herself from Jake's arm, leaving him with Rebecca.

"I thought werewolves only came out on a full moon," she said.

"I'm not like the others."

"I know. You're special."

Maria clearly didn't want to watch. "Nice to meet you all," she said. The cheerleaders turned their noses up at her. She was a lowly sophomore, and one of the art kids. She rolled her eyes.

She took Adam by the hand, saying, "My friends are here too, you know." She led him toward the woods. AJ and Holly trailed along after them, made a quick stop at the keg for refills, then caught up. Maria's friends were sitting on a downed tree trunk just inside the edge of the forest.

Maria cleared her throat. "Steph, Mark, Kyle, Amber—how's it going?"

They raised their cups, but said nothing. They were out of range of the floodlight, but the flickering bonfire revealed baggy jeans and hooded sweatshirts.

"Nice costumes," Adam said. "Let me guess—"

Maria punched him in the stomach.

"Never mind him," she assured them. They passed a joint. Maria smoked, then Adam. It was his first time. He coughed. AJ was impressed. Adam looked like he was having the time of his life. The joint went around three times. Everyone but AJ smoked. He blamed sports. Random drug screening. Holly was pulling on his arm, but he was watching his sister.

Maria handed Adam a cigarette.

"You?" Adam said, surprised, taking it. He held it up to his face for inspection.

"Sure. You don't have to if you don't want to, Superman. But you're turning eighteen, so I thought it was appropriate."

"I'm not legal until Wednesday."

"I'm not legal for almost two years, if you know what I mean."

"Har har, very funny."

"You're already drunk and high though, right? So who cares?"

She held up her lighter and flicked it on. Adam took his first drag.

Holly pulled harder on AJ's arm, and he felt her breath on his neck. He relented. They walked away from the stoners. He led her to the Toyota. They downed the rest of their beers. He lifted her up onto the tailgate. "Come on, wolfie," she said, taking him by the collars of his coat. "Bite me."

He bit her finger, then her hand. She pulled him close. They kissed, enjoying the taste of beer. He climbed into the truck's bed and lay beside her. Things were happening. She was making soft noises... Then she fell asleep.

AJ was annoyed. He climbed down. It was time for something different. He went to the front of the truck, opened the driver's-side-door, reached under the seat, and pulled out a liter-bottle of cheap whiskey. Adam came up behind him and said, "Hey, pop the hood, will ya?" He had a full beer in one hand, a set of jumper cables in the other, and a big dopey grin on his face.

AJ said, "It's nice to see someone is enjoying the party. Happy birthday, Adam."

"Happy birthday, AJ!"

They attached the cables to the truck's battery. AJ took a big gulp of whiskey and passed the bottle to Adam, who took a swallow, passed it back, and stumbled off toward the flood light, uncoiling the jumper cables along the way.

AJ took another swig, then drifted back to Adam's friends. They were at the drunken trash-talking stage.

Monica Lewinsky said something about NAFTA's mom.

"Oh yeah? You're so dumb you're failing gym," NAFTA said.

"Yeah, well, at least I'm not failing AP Chemistry."

"Oh, chemical burn!" AJ said.

NAFTA looked sad. Apparently he really was failing AP Chemistry. AJ offered him the bottle of whiskey, but he refused. AJ downed a shot and said, "Why don't you go home and write a computer program about it?"

Bill Clinton tried to broker a peace treaty. "Everybody just calm down. Here, have a cigar." He made an obscene gesture.

"Eww, gross." This was from Lorena Bobbitt.

"You're all virgins, aren't you," AJ said.

"Hey man—lay off," John Bobbitt said.

"You guys know what your problem is? High school's almost over, and you're so concerned with your ACTs and your XYZs, you never gave yourselves a chance to catch any STDs."

Nobody laughed.

"I mean, you got each other, right? Just quit worrying about everything and go for it—that's what I say!"

AJ looked from one blurry face to the next. They were all staring at their drinks, or their shoes, awkwardly avoiding each other's eyes.

AJ shook his head and turned to walk away. At that moment, the light went out. All conversations stopped abruptly. The sofa had collapsed to a pile, and drunk teenagers blinked at each other in the dim light from the dwindling fire. Then, just as suddenly, there was light.

Adam had switched the cables. He stood up to a round of applause, smiling in his bright red cape and underwear.

AJ wandered through the party. In the harsh glare of the flood light he passed a long line of faces, some in costume, some not, some happy, some sad. Men raised their cups to him, and he raised his whiskey bottle. Women laughed at him, or recoiled in apparent disgust.

He registered a familiar voice wishing him a happy birthday. It was John, with the other football players and their cheerleader girlfriends. AJ was back among friends. He held up the bottle, but found no takers.

"Fine," he said, and took a long pull. "More for me."

"Where's Holly?" Rebecca asked.

"Sleeping."

Ben said, "Niiice."

"Nothing happened."

"Sure. We believe you."

"Listen up, ladies," AJ said. "Take a tip from me—make sure these boys use condoms. Who knows where they've been!"

The cheerleaders' eyes bulged. The young men laughed half-heartedly.

"Besides, the last thing this world needs is another generation of these assholes, right?"

AJ raised the bottle to his lips, but it was empty. He looked at it, then dropped it on the ground.

"I mean, you should hear the way these guys talk about you in the locker room. Seriously."

Jake stepped forward and put a hand on AJ's chest. "That's enough, birthday boy" he said.

AJ looked down at Jake's hand, then he stared Jake in the eyes. Jake let his hand fall.

"Whatever," AJ said. "It's your life, do what you want." He brushed off the front of his shirt. "By the way," he said, "thanks for all your hard work on the team this season. I haven't told anybody this yet, but I got into the U on a full scholarship. Next year I'll be throwing touchdowns for the Gophers." Then he turned and walked away.

He was feeling pretty good about himself, in a sour kind of way. Feeding his mood with superiority. But then his vision started sliding off to one side. He couldn't focus. Couldn't walk straight. He figured he should try to find Adam and Maria, check in with them, maybe find some water.

He made his way back to the woods. One of the druggies was fast asleep on the fallen tree trunk. A pair of them were sitting on the ground, staring deeply into each other's eyes, unmoving. Another one was up in a tree, smoking. Adam and Maria were nowhere to be found. He stumbled back toward the fire, feeling lost and confused.

When he made his way to the center of it all, AJ realized that the party had gone almost silent. Then someone started clapping, slowly. It was Carl Tucker, one of Adam's friends. The slow clap spread from one group of drunk teenagers to the next. All around the fire, faces turned, and AJ tried to look at them, intending to meet them head on, to confront them. But they weren't looking at him. They were looking toward the train tracks that came out of the woods on the northern side of the gravel pit. The clapping grew to a grand applause, and the crowd parted to admit and adore a pair of young lovers, newly committed to each other. It was Adam and Maria. They were holding hands.

Carl said, "Give it up for Superman and Pocahontas!"

Maria shouted, "I'm Sacagawea—get it right!"

They looked more than happy, but AJ was not happy at all. He was angry.

Someone yelled, "Way to go, Adam! Score!"

"Jesus, we only kissed," Maria snapped. "We didn't do it!"

But that was enough for AJ. He stared across the pit at his former best friend, and his eyes burned with drunken rage. Something popped in the fire, sending up a shower of hot sparks, and in a heartbeat AJ remembered everything he'd taught Adam about confidence. Stand up straight. Look people in the eye. Smile. Laugh. Keep yourself clean. Dress how you like, but don't be a slob. Tell people they look good. But don't add "today," because they'll wonder if they looked bad yesterday. Tell people you think they're just great. Who cares if it isn't true. Lie. Above all, lie. Because you aren't really that cool and confident. No one is. It's a game, and it's all a big fat lie. And the best liars get the most friends, and the most money, and the most pussy.

But he wasn't supposed to use it on her. Not Maria. Anyone but her. This was a severe offense, and it called for extreme repercussions. AJ had to do something. In three long strides he came around to their side of the fire.

Maria screamed, "Arturo, No!"

AJ threw a punch toward Adam's jaw.

But Adam was in the zone. It must have been the marijuana. He dodged and blocked like he knew kung fu. AJ couldn't land a hit. So he wrapped his arms around Adam's waist and tackled him to the ground. He put one hand on Adam's chest and raised the other in a fist.

Just then the flood light cut out again. AJ looked up, confused. He saw red and blue. Heard the siren and the megaphone. "Everybody freeze," it said.

Everybody ran.

Adam, Maria, and AJ stood in a line. As it turned out, there was only one cop, and it was Officer Barlow. This was good for AJ and Maria, because Barlow knew their father, and he knew their sensitive legal situation. He also knew John Baker, which was not so good for Adam.

Barlow shined his flashlight in their faces. He asked who was in charge of this little shindig.

"We all are, sir," Adam said.

"You drunk?"

"No, sir."

"He really isn't, officer," Maria said. "Me neither."

"Well this one is, clearly." He was looking at AJ.

"It's their eighteenth birthday, sir."

"I hope they had a good one so far. The rest of it might not go so well, depending on what I find here."

He walked over to the keg, grabbed the rim with one hand, tried to lift it out of the ice water. He laughed. "More than half full. Bunch of lightweights!"

"We have sober drivers for every vehicle," Maria said.

"Is that so? And where might they be?"

"Come out, girls—it's alright!" Maria shouted.

Four young women came reluctantly out of the shadows.

"I'll have to breathalyze the lot of you, of course."

"Of course," Maria said.

They all passed.

He didn't write a single ticket.

He told the girls to take everyone home.

He even used the squad car to help Maria jump-start the Toyota.

# *The Fall*

CEDAR CREEK POLICE DEPARTMENT
  Case #19-1017-0032G
  Subject: Garcia, Arturo Javier
  St. Luke's Family Hospital
  Surveillance transcript

"I'm sorry I left, Dad. After Maria… I'm sorry about a lot of things. But, we decided it would be best if I tried to go on as normal, remember? And I already had the scholarship. So I went to up to the Cities. The change of scenery would be good for me, you said. But I should have stayed here. You and Mom lost Maria, and then you lost me too, and Mom couldn't go on. And then, after she was gone, you just gave up. You just sat down in your God-damned chair and you refused to move. What were you thinking? The Holbrooks called 911 when they found you. I came down right away. They couldn't even find anything wrong with you. I needed you, Dad! I came back for you! But you never came back to me."

AJ simply couldn't play football anymore, after his mother killed herself. He got kicked off the team. Lost his scholarship. He moved from the players' dorm to an off-campus apartment. He started working to make rent. He never applied for loans because he was afraid they'd find out his father was an illegal. He couldn't study. He failed all his classes—didn't even show up to take the finals. But a university was a business, after all, running on tuition, so they gave him another chance. And he tried to do it right, this time. He really did. He saved up for new school supplies, and he was doing alright at the start of the next semester—it wasn't like he was stupid. But they were throwing a lot of parties around that time, and AJ had no self-control.

He was walking home late one night, because he'd gone out for drinks after work, and the buses had stopped running. The walk took over an hour, but he was used to it. He couldn't afford a taxi. It was cold, but he was fine, because he had whiskey in his flask, and the walk took him through downtown Minneapolis, which was a nice enough place.

There was a man heading the other way, coming toward him on the sidewalk. In a moment they would pass each other. AJ wished the man wasn't there, and the man was probably wishing the same about AJ. There was a No Parking sign between them, and AJ knew that the spot where they would pass each other was right next to the sign, because that was what always happened. There was always some stupid sign or tree or trashcan or whatever on the sidewalk right where two people had to pass. So one or the other of them had to get out of the way. But if one of them walked a little slower, or a little faster, the other one would too. It was inevitable.

AJ was thinking all of this as he walked toward the man and the sign. And he could see that the man was a mess, and he was muttering to himself. But AJ was still hoping they would just pass each other by and that would be that. He decided to give the man the nod of acknowledgment. But when they reached the No Parking sign, both of them stepped to same side and stopped, and the man looked into AJ's eyes, and AJ saw that the man was shivering, and he felt sorry for him. But the man said, "Can you fly?"

And AJ said, "Sorry, man. I can't." And he brushed past the guy and walked faster than before, shaking his head, because he didn't want any trouble. He kept walking, occasionally taking a swig of warm whiskey from his flask. Leaving downtown behind, he crossed the Hennepin Avenue Bridge over the Mississippi.

The suburb of St. Anthony extended to the east on a level plane, but there was a tall plateau straight ahead. The road sloped upward, and the ground dropped away. The roadway became an overpass, and it brought you to the top of the plateau, and to the northwest the city kept going up, up—and that meant that you were finally in Columbia Heights. Almost home.

There was a chainlink fence along the sidewalk here, but if you looked down through it, you would see that you were seventy feet in the air, with steep cliffs dropping away to the east and south. Perpendicular to the overpass, but far below it, there was a train yard. Ten sets of railroad tracks running side by side along the bottom of the plateau's south wall.

Looking east through the fence you would see a narrow gap before a wide, flat roof. This was the roof of an abandoned building. AJ had explored this building more than once, so he knew it was an old sawmill. There was rusty machinery on every floor. The wiring had all been stolen right out of the walls. On the ground floor there were cargo doors that opened out onto the train yard, where the workers must have loaded the lumber straight onto train cars, back in the old days.

And if you went out the back door of the sawmill, you'd find yourself at the bottom of a trench formed by the back of the building and the east-facing cliff. As AJ was thinking about all of this, he was standing on top of that cliff, smoking a joint, watching the night sky turn orange at the horizon.

His thoughts arrived at another door that was down there in the trench, the door that led through the cliff wall, straight into the heart of the plateau. It was short and wide, and it was made of wooden slabs held together by iron straps. The door's huge frame was made of railroad ties, jammed right into the rock. The door was locked with a chain as thick as AJ's arm, and the padlock was a block of metal the size of a small Bible. One night when he was drunk, AJ had tried to pick that lock, and when that had failed, he had tried to bust the latch out of the wood. But he'd failed at that, too.

Now he felt a strong urge to go down and see that door again. He imagined that the feeling wasn't coming from within himself. Whatever was inside that door was reaching out to him. But there wasn't time to go back down the bridge and sneak through the train yard. The sun would be up before he ever reached the door. It would take even longer to follow the highway north and search for another way down.

AJ was looking down at the roof. It wasn't that far away, not really. Maybe ten feet, tops, and it was a few feet lower than the level of the sidewalk he was standing on. The fence was in the way, of course, but there was room to stand on the other side of it. He had come home this way countless times before, and he'd always wanted to jump across the gap to that roof. Just like in a movie.

And if you thought about it, you could tell that people went over the fence all the time, because the underside of the bridge was covered in graffiti. There weren't any cars coming, so AJ climbed over the fence and stood at the edge of the cliff. The stars were disappearing in the light of dawn, and he jumped.

He landed in the gravel on the rooftop and he rolled forward just like an action hero. He got to his feet and he was just fine. It was perfect. He wasn't feeling that drunk anymore, so he drained his flask. The warm whisky stung his nose, but it tasted great. He walked back to the edge of the roof and looked down into the trench, and he saw that there were trees growing out of the cliff. Just a lot of short pines, and their roots were spread out all over the rock, but the amazing thing was the way the trunks came straight out of the cliff sideways before bending upward at right angles. AJ thought about smoking his other joint, but in the end he decided to hang onto it until he was safe at home.

As he was standing there on the edge he looked straight down into the shadows five stories below. He could see the top of the big wooden door. He had to get down there.

He turned around and walked past antennas and air conditioners to the door in the center of the roof, through which he knew he'd find a staircase leading down into the building. But before he got there, he knew it would be locked. He could see it. Just a regular doorknob that wouldn't open without a key. He tried it anyway, and he was right. No way was he getting in there.

So he started walking toward the north side of the building, where he knew there was a fire escape. When he was about halfway there he saw a dark, sunken spot in the roof. He figured rain always puddled there, and he imagined falling through it and landing on a giant rusty saw blade. He walked the rest of the way more carefully.

The fire escape was a metal staircase attached to the building's north wall on the outside, and to get to it you had to step out onto a metal cage and pull up a trapdoor. And the trapdoor was fucking locked. Another goddamn unbreakable padlock.

AJ swore at the top of his lungs.

The morning sun was all the way up, and AJ was shouting obscenities that could be heard a mile away.

His mind was racing. Maybe whoever still owned the building didn't want teenagers coming up the fire escape to get on the roof. Maybe the cops did it. Maybe some homeless person lived in the fire escape and locked it on both ends. It didn't make sense, and it didn't fucking matter. As far as AJ could figure, he was fucked.

But he calmed down after a minute, and finally he saw that part of the cage had been snipped and pulled apart and bent over. So someone else had already been through this, and whoever it was had been smart enough to bring a wire cutter. AJ felt so stupid for overreacting. And he was starting to feel sick.

People in Cedar Creek had spread all sorts of rumors after it happened. AJ had tried to kill himself because he was depressed, they said, like his sister had been, and their mother. Or he'd jumped because he couldn't handle the pressure of being a student athlete. Or because he couldn't face the shame of failure. Or he'd done it simply because he wanted to be *with* his mother and sister, in Hell.

The plain truth was that he *hadn't* tried to kill himself. Of course he was being self-destructive at the time, in all sorts of ways. Getting drunk every day, experimenting with drugs.

Sleeping with a lot of different girls. But in the end, it was the cops.

He was up there on that roof, and the door was locked, and the fire escape was locked... There was the opening in the cage, but you had to sort of lower yourself over the side and down through the hole. He even walked back across the roof to see if he could make the jump back to the cliff. But it looked so far away, and the sun was too bright, and he was shivering in the wind, staring down at the door... The amazing secret door.

Somebody was walking a dog up on the overpass, and she saw AJ, and the dog started barking, and the woman started yelling, "Hey! Hey!"

And within a minute she had flagged down a cop, and she was pointing at AJ and shouting. Another squad car pulled up with the lights flashing, and soon three cops were standing at the fence, and they all must have thought he was going to jump, because they were saying things like, "Easy, son, don't do anything stupid now. No reason to do anything stupid now, son."

But AJ was in shock, and all he could think about was that he had weed in his pocket. He didn't want to go to jail. He backed away from the edge. One of the cops was on his radio, and another took off running north, probably thinking he would take the long way to the bottom. The third one climbed over the fence and jumped onto the rooftop like it was nothing. Like he did it every day of his life.

AJ turned and ran back to the fire escape. He got down on his hands and knees and lowered his legs over the side, aiming for the hole.

The cop ran to the fire escape, yelling, "No! No!"

And he reached down and grabbed AJ by the sleeve and tried to pull him up, but AJ yanked his sleeve out of the pig's dirty fucking fingers, and some stupid reflex made his legs push him out into the air, and he fell.

He woke up two days later in the hospital with eight broken bones and no one to visit him. Not one single person. They said from his blood test he was still highly intoxicated when he fell, even though he couldn't feel it. The surgeon who put his arm back together said he was lucky he'd been drunk at the time, "Because a drunk person falls like a wet towel. When sober people fall their muscles tighten up, so their bones shatter like glass." And he'd landed on a pile of old two-by-fours, which had broken his fall.

The chaplain said there had to have been angels with him, up on that roof.

# The Cabin

```
          COOPER'S MARKET
            11-20-19

onion           x6     8.97
potato          x8     3.99
t-bone          x6    77.94
charcoal        x1     5.99
starter fluid   x1     3.98
24pk MN Lager   x5    94.95
750 McCbs Wsk   x3    41.97
1.75 Duck Vdk   x3    65.97
2L soda water   x3     2.97
carton Reds     x1    99.99
lighter         x6    17.94
assrt chips     x8    15.92

   Subtotal       440.58
   Tax             35.25
   Total        $475.83
```

At the arrival gate in the Aeropuerto Internacional Benito Juarez, Dr. Alice Suzuki had been bursting with excitement over the palm trees she'd seen lining the boulevards during their descent. It wasn't like she'd never seen palm trees before—she was just sick of the frozen landscape they'd left behind.

Adam Baker had gone through the motions of disembarkation with robotic detachment. They had no checked bags, as they would be leaving the next day. In the taxi on the way to La Calma they'd discussed the mission only briefly: Meet Dr. Springer's Mexican counterpart, talk up the project, arrange the payment, and receive the goods.

Ever since taking off from O'Hare, Adam's hangover had been sort of dopplering through him like an ambulance, and he could still hear it thrumming in the distance.

Buckled into his business-class seat on the plane, he'd tried to reassemble the events of the previous twenty-four hours. His old fraternity brothers still knew how to party, there was no doubt about that.

At the office on Friday morning he'd crammed a full day's worth of work into a few hours before hitting the road. As he drove north out of Minneapolis it was trying to snow. The temperature hovered just above freezing, cold enough to make the rain turn to slush. Farmland gave way to forest as Adam drove through little towns with names like New Sweden, Calumet, Nashwauk. Towns that surrounded the lakes and rivers left by the receding glaciers.

A little before dark he finally turned onto the road that went around Pine Lake. It was a small lake, only about a mile across, surrounded by forest. Very few people lived on the lake all year round, and those who did never knew who was staying in the last cabin at the end of the road, the one owned by Adam and his friends. They took turns bringing their families up throughout the year, and when they weren't using the cabin they rented it out to random strangers.

The road was old and broken, crumbling slabs of blacktop slick with ice. It was the worst kind of weather. The air temperature dropped below freezing and the sleet coming down through the dusty blue pines changed to fat white snowflakes as Adam pulled into the driveway.

The cabin was relatively new and expensively built to look just like a traditional log cabin should. Reddish logs and dark green trim. It was beautiful. It was the perfect, ideal cabin that anybody would imagine when they thought of a cabin on a lake in the Northwoods, where anybody would love to spend a summer or a winter. Even so, Adam pretty much hated coming up here, no matter the time of year. It wasn't because of the open spaces. Adam had no trouble walking outside in a big city, and he wasn't afraid of large crowds like a typical agoraphobe. In fact, he thrived in crowds. The problem with the lake was the feeling of isolation. Of helplessness. At times he literally choked on the fresh air that everyone else seemed to love so much. The sky itself felt oppressive. Still, he forced himself to come to the cabin a few times a year, because despite his thoughts to the contrary, Elena thought it was good for the girls.

He heard a gunshot and ducked instinctively behind the steering wheel. He knew it was a deer rifle from the ripping sound, the drawn-out crack and peel he felt in his skull. He recognized his old buddies Mark and Evan standing in the twilight, sheltered from the snow under one of the giant oak trees that dominated the back yard. Mark was a burly guy on the shorter side with his sleeves rolled up to expose his tattooed forearms. Evan wore a blaze orange hat with fuzzy earflaps. They were shooting downhill toward a life-size deer target they'd set up on the shore.

\* \* \*

A flight attendant came by pushing a beverage cart and he asked for a Bloody Mary. He thought about his stupid friends standing in the dark, in the snow, shooting at a lake. And he remembered that they'd given him his first beer of the night.

Bradley's red sports car rolled into the driveway. Bradley Fisher was a more successful version of the man that Adam had tried to become. He was taller than Adam, and richer. Travis was riding shotgun. Everyone hated Travis.

As they approached the backyard, Bradley pulled out a handgun. To Adam's untrained eye it looked like it wasn't meant for hunting. Travis was clearly excited about the guns, but before he could get a turn, Bradley opened fire and blasted the deer's head to smithereens.

"Hey, asshole—you owe me for that," Mark said, packing up his rifle.

"Put it on my tab."

"Hey, let me see," Travis said, reaching for Bradley's gun.

"Sure," Bradley said, holding out the gun. But at the last moment he pulled it away. "Kidding," he said. "Here you go." But he did it again. Then he offered the gun to Adam, saying, "Hey Baker, why don't you take a couple of shots?"

"No thanks," Adam said. "Guns aren't really my thing. But if it's booze you're talking about, I'm all in."

They spent the next hour getting seriously drunk inside the luxurious cabin. They were talking a lot of immature nonsense and Adam was getting tired of it. He tried to bring up family but nobody was interested.

"Who really gives a shit?" Travis said. "I mean, I can catch us all up in about two seconds. The kids are brats, and the wife's a bitch. Enough said. Am I right?"

That was when the drugs came out. Bradley had cocaine. Evan had pills.

"I brought the weed," Travis said, holding up a small plastic baggie full of seeds and stems.

"Everybody brought weed, dumbass," Mark said, and he threw down a half-ounce. "And I've got something else, if anyone's interested." He reached into a cargo pocket on his pants leg and pulled out a handful of magic mushrooms.

"Awesome," Travis said. "Gimme some."

But Bradley shook his head. "I don't know, man. I'm not trying to have a religious experience tonight."

"I second that," Adam said.

"Suit yourselves," Mark said. "I'll just hang onto these for another time—" But before he could put them away, Travis grabbed the whole pile and stuffed them down the hatch.

Adam's Bloody Mary tasted good but it didn't do anything for his growing headache. He knew he shouldn't mix painkillers with alcohol, but it was worth sacrificing his liver if he could avoid having an episode on the airplane. He downed a handful of pills and tried to remember what happened next, but the rest of the night was a blur. He knew he actually hadn't brought any drugs, but he vaguely remembered taking some. He knew there had been some kind of business transaction, too. Something about stocks... *Oh, right.*

When everyone at the party was good and hammered, he'd told them about Montgomery's upcoming deal with Urbano, and in exchange they agreed to buy him out of their collective investment pool. They specialized in sin stocks like tobacco and firearms, and Adam didn't want that stuff poisoning his political campaign.

\* \* \*

The other guys went out on the deck to smoke cigarettes. Up to now they'd mostly been hanging around the kitchen, so Adam figured he'd put something on the projector screen in the home theater to surprise them when they came back. He took out his phone and told his computer-generated secretary Minerva to slip into something sexy. She appeared on the big screen in a cross between a tight-fitting business suit and a Japanese school-girl's uniform.

The plan was to have her perform a striptease for everyone, but when the guys came back, Bradley took one look at Minerva and said, "Jesus, Baker—we disappear for five seconds and you're in here jerking off?"

And just then, the door bell rang.

No amount of mental strain could help Adam sort out what had happened next. He was at the bottom of his third bloody, the painkillers refused to work, and the plane was descending. The rest of the night came back to him in flashes.

Three women were at the door. Samantha: pale white skin with black hair and a leather belt. Melissa: tall, tan, and blonde. Angela: black skin with cool undertones and a muscular body. Another round of shots.

Sitting on a stool in the corner of the living room. Bradley and Samantha doing lines on the bar. The blonde one on the couch between Travis and Evan. Angela on Mark's lap in the reclining chair.

Standing outside in the freezing cold without shoes. Snow swirling around the yard light. *They don't understand.* They did it so easily, so eagerly. Like what they were doing at the cabin was the real thing, the thing they'd wanted all along, and their marriages—their real lives—were nothing but lies. It was all backwards. Adam could never do something like that. Part of him wanted to be like them, sure. To be in there right now, getting off with Angela, or whoever. But he could never cheat. He would always be faithful to his wife. He could always blame it on her. But it wasn't really about her. It never was. Even now, twenty years later, he found it nearly impossible to admit it to himself. There really was another woman in his life. *Maria.*

Something moved in the forest. He strained to see but he couldn't make out anything distinct in the jagged mesh of branches. Then, deep in the thickest part of the woods, shining in the dark just beyond the yard light's reach, he saw a pair of eyes. He sucked in air, held his breath. Up in the trees more eyes opened. They were all around him. Down by the lake. Peering out from behind the trunk of a giant oak. Crouching on the wood pile by the garage. Coming closer. More and more pairs of eyes, all staring at him, watching him. Waiting.

And he was back inside the cabin, stumbling around in the dark, frantically searching for the one thing that could save him from whatever was out there. He had to check the bedrooms.

He opened a door and saw Angela's black skin and Mark's nautical tattoos. They were naked, smoking cigarettes in bed. Mark swore. Adam pulled the door shut. Mark's rifle would be locked up anyway.

In the next room he found Travis all alone, crying.

Behind another door he heard Evan and Melissa reaching the heights of passion.

At the end of the hall he opened the last door and saw Bradley on all fours like a dog. Samantha was on her knees behind him, her pale hips moving. She noticed Adam and gave him a warm smile. He froze. She raised a finger to her lips. *Shh.* He took the handgun from the nightstand.

When the sun came up, Angela found him sitting in the entryway with his elbows on a shelf, aiming the gun at the front door. She brought him gently back to reality, made him a cup of coffee, and drove him to the airport in his car.

# La Calma

Adam and Alice squeezed into a glass-and-chrome elevator with their luggage and the young man they'd found playing on his phone behind the front desk on the ground floor at La Calma, a biomedical research facility owned and operated by Grupo Urbano, a leading Mexican pharmaceutical. Lakeview in Chicago was a modern-traditional campus with a school and a hospital; La Calma was a blue and silver column, sterile-futuristic, fifteen floors of office and laboratory in the heart of Mexico City.

They looked out the window as the elevator ascended. The sun was shining on the golden statue of the Angel of Independence, which stood over a roundabout in the Paseo de la Reforma. Endless traffic flowed around the circle, and the sidewalks were crowded with tourists and businesspeople on their way to the offices and malls and outdoor cafes.

Next to La Calma was a lattice of I-beams: the frame of a building, construction stalled for lack of funds. Against the background of the richest part of the city, it was an eyesore.

Pointing to the unfinished structure, Alice said, "That one must be ours."

"Yes," Adam said. "The Andrew Washington Tower of Bullshit."

Alice laughed out loud, then covered her mouth.

The young receptionist was visibly excited, obviously searching for the right thing to say. Adam had seen this reaction before. The kid probably didn't actually know who they were, but they were foreigners, and they were going straight to the head office, despite having turned up with no appointment. He clearly couldn't contain himself, and he went for the universal small-talk angle: "Are we enjoying the weather?" The kid's suit looked cheap. Most likely an unpaid intern. A student-scientist or a business hopeful, starting at the bottom. Adam thought of his time in law school, then he thought of his mother.

Alice said she didn't want to go back to Chicago.

"I thought Japanese people liked being cold," Adam said. Turning to the young man, he continued: "You see, embracing the cold builds character."

"I live in Los Angeles," Alice said.

"That's great! I have family there. Are you enjoying Mexico so far? Is it your first time? What are you working on with La Calma? Have you met the director before?"

Alice looked like she didn't know where to start, so Adam let his personality take over. "Easy there, partner," he said, putting his hand on Emiliano's shoulder. "Relax."

"Sorry. They keep me down at reception, and I never get to see what really goes on here."

"Wonders beyond your wildest dreams, I imagine."

"That's exactly what I've been thinking."

"Do your job well, but stand up for yourself—don't let them push you around. Your time will come soon enough."

The elevator doors opened to a maroon carpet, a long hallway lined with paintings. Watercolor landscapes and modernist portraits of the heroes of the Revolution. At the end of the hall was an elaborate wooden door with a brass handle and a name plate: "Dr. Jesus Umberto Morales Obregon." Emiliano knocked on the door, then pulled it open. Adam and Alice stepped inside, then Emiliano came in, pulling their carry-ons. The room smelled strongly of old coffee. A flatscreen on the wall showed a soccer match on mute. Standing by the window was a large man with a greasy black combover. He showed Adam and Alice a welcoming grin, but when he noticed the receptionist standing behind them, he frowned and jerked his head and his thumb to one side. The young intern left, swearing under his breath in Spanish.

"Welcome, welcome!" the large man said, striding toward Alice. She extended a hand, and as he took it he went in close for a hug and a kiss on the cheek. He released Alice from the embrace and performed a more manly handshake and shoulder-clap with Adam.

"You are Dr. Morales, yes?" Adam asked.

"No! Heavens, no. I'm sure our fine director is downstairs somewhere with his nose stuck in a microscope. I am not him, thank goodness. My name is Ernesto Urbano."

"My mistake. It's good to meet you at last, Mr. Urbano."

"Igualmente, Mr. Baker," Turning to Alice, Urbano said, "And it gives me great pleasure to meet you as well, young lady. We need someone around here who knows the finer points of making medicine for the suffering children. I assume you've grown tired of the Americans, and you've come to work for me instead?" He winked.

"That depends."

"On what, my dear?"

"Whether or not you can afford me."

"Alas, you know a man's weak points. You strike at my heart and my bank account."

Adam desperately wanted to insert himself. "The Transmortification Project—"

"Tell me, Dr. Suzuki—What would it take to bring you to my side?"

"You're very charming, Mr. Urbano. But I'm afraid you won't be able to top what Dr. Springer has already offered me. What could be better than the chance to cure cancer?"

"So it's straight to business with you, too. I expected more."

Adam was impressed with the way Alice returned the man's stare. He saw a chance to try again. "The Transmortification Project—"

"The Transmortification Project will fail."

"I respectfully disagree, my friend."

"The cancer is not one disease. There can be no single cure."

Urbano said this with finality, as if he expected that when his opinion was made known to the team, they would all simply call it quits. Adam decided to give the man a moment to calm down.

He raised his eyebrows and nodded toward a tiny kitchenette in a corner of the office.

"Of course," Urbano said.

"For you?"

"Please."

"Alice?"

"Why not."

Back home, Elena often made Mexican-style coffee—so Adam was not surprised to see that there was no coffee maker. Instead there was a saucepan on a small gas range. He sparked up the burner and got to work. There was nothing to it really: just boil some water, drop in a cone of piloncillo sugar and a cinnamon stick with a spoonful of grounds, stir it up, then ladle it into a mug. The resulting brew was bitter and sweet, with a slight crunch.

"You should meet Dr. Springer," Adam said, handing Alice and Urbano their mugs. "She really is incredible."

"I wonder."

Alice sipped her coffee, apparently content to let Adam handle this part of the mission.

"Naturally, there are certain resources she requires," he said. He held eye contact for a moment, then walked to the window. "I'm sure there are certain things you need, as well."

Urbano came to his side. Together they looked out at the stalled construction project.

"This whole country is littered with unfinished buildings," Adam said.

"It is a sign of a country filled with hope. We are always beginning things, taking on new tasks. Making new goals."

"Never finishing anything."

"When the people of my country are ready, we will accomplish everything we set out to do. You will see. The world will see."

"I wonder."

They sipped their mugs in silence.

After a few moments, Alice let out an annoyed sigh. "Can we get on with it, please?" she asked.

"I do not see you carrying bags large enough to contain the amount that was discussed."

Adam laughed. "Good one, Mr. Urbano. Very good!" When he realized that the man wasn't joking, he went one. "But this isn't a spy movie. I don't have a briefcase full of cash. I am prepared to authorize a transaction." Taking out his phone, he looked at the flatscreen on the wall. "May I?"

Urbano tilted his head, confused. But he said, "Mi casa es su casa."

Adam tapped on his phone, and the soccer match on the television was replaced with a small cube of light in the middle of a black screen. Minerva, Adam's digital assistant, walked in from one side and took a seat on the cube. She was barefoot, wearing a sea-foam green nightgown, straps hanging from her bare shoulders. Her skin and hair glowed a pale electric blue. Alice choked on her coffee.

Urbano said, "Her neck, her skin..." His mouth hung open.

"I know," Adam said.

"Hello, Adam," Minerva said. "Are we ready?"

"I believe so, yes."

"Alright. Just say the word."

"Are we ready, Mr. Urbano?" Adam asked.

"Yes, we are ready. Yes."

Alice was not ready. "Where are the goods?" she asked.

"Not here. Tomorrow, at AMBS. Ask for Dr. Balderrama."

AMBS was a public hospital. Adam considered it.

Minerva crossed her legs, put an elbow on her knee, rested her chin in her hand, tapped a finger on her lips. "Is there a problem?" she asked.

"No. Do it."

"It's done. Anything else?"

"Car to the hotel."

"Got it."

Adam tapped his phone, and the soccer match was back on the television.

"I want one," Urbano said.

The taxi driver took his fare and tip. As it turned out, the hotel was only a few blocks down Reforma from the lab, but of course the driver hadn't told them that. Adam said they could have walked. Alice said taxis were safer anyway. Adam told her they were in the safest part of the whole city. "All the embassies are here," he explained.

An entire wall of the lobby was dedicated to the Blessed Virgin Mary of Guadalupe, who appeared in a floor-to-ceiling tile mosaic, wearing her mantle of stars, just as she had appeared to Juan Diego in 1531. The receptionist was professional and warm. A gentleman bellhop escorted Adam and Alice up the elevator and down a hallway lined with works of art. A glass door opened onto a long, stylish balcony with potted plants and patio furniture. A number of guest rooms, each with curtained windows, opened onto the balcony. The bellhop wheeled both of their suitcases into a single room and handed Adam a pair of key cards.

"Oh, umm... There should be two rooms."

"Sí, señor," the bellhop said. "Hay dos juntos." He tapped on the cards in Adam's hands: they had different numbers. Two adjacent rooms, with a connecting door. They laughed it off, tipped the man, agreed to meet for dinner in a few hours, and went in their separate rooms.

The room was large and well-furnished, with a loveseat facing a huge TV, and a pair of barstools at a faux marble countertop. The mini-fridge was stocked full of things he didn't want—candy bars and soda, cans of Clamato—and anyway it wasn't plugged in, so everything was warm. And there were no towels on the rack in the bathroom. He reached under the sink and discovered that the whole cabinet was fake. He pulled too hard on a drawer handle, thinking it was simply stuck, and the whole cabinet panel fell off its fixtures. It was just a plywood-and-foam facade, light enough to lift in one hand, spray-painted dull gold, with touches of black to make it look old. Nothing behind it but rusty pipes dripping into a bucket.

He found a hotel robe in the closet, so he got undressed, put on the robe, and went for a massage. It was always part of his business travel routine. His instant-ramen-eating intern days were well behind him, and he'd grown accustomed to the benefits of working for a pharmaceutical as he rose through the ranks of the drug reps. As a top-tier lobbyist and negotiator, he saw no problem spending company money on some well-deserved relaxation, indisputably vital to his continued performance.

Massages were both cheaper and better in countries like Thailand or the Philippines—even without the full-course treatment, which was readily available in Mexico of course, not that Adam would even consider it—he was always thinking of Elena and the girls.

As he lay there on the table, a massage therapist named Lupita going to town on his overactive quadratus lumborum, images of little Lucy and her big sister Mary came to him. They were bundled up in stocking caps and mittens, playing in the snow, throwing armloads into the air, the tails of their scarves floating in clouds of fresh white powder. The scarves were store-bought, the girls having no living grandmother—and their mother, too busy at the immigration office to bother learning to crochet... But at least she was there, smiling and laughing with the girls, while Adam was here—

"Hey."

It was Alice's voice. He opened his eyes. Her pelvis, in a black bikini bottom, was inches from his face. He propped himself up on his elbows to get a better view. Alice was standing there, just out of reach, biting her lip and looking off to one side, arms crossed, knees together, toes pointed inward.

She said, "I'm bored. Let's go for a swim."

"You're trying to get me in trouble."

"Is it that obvious?"

"You forgot to cut the tags off."

She swore, found the tags on her hip, and ripped them out.

Lupita slapped Adam's backside. "Ya está," she said. All done.

Adam stood up and pulled on his robe. He said, "I'm married, you know."

"So am I."

"Oh?" Adam said, mildly surprised. "There's a Mister Dr. Suzuki?"

"There's a Mr. Derek Lancaster. He cheats on me."

"The fool."

"So you like it?"

He looked her up and down, taking his time. "It's nice," he said, finally.

"Nice? That's it?"

"If you're asking me whether or not the sight of you in a bikini gives me thoughts that are, given the nature of our professional relationship, inappropriate—"

"You talk too much."

"I've been told that before."

"So shut up."

"I'll get my suit."

Adam stopped by the front desk have some towels brought to his room, then he took a different route through the hotel. He always liked to check out the restaurant, the gym, the conference room—get a feel for whether or not this might be a good place to hold a pharma convention. He quickly noticed that he was seeing the exact same paintings and statues in all the hallways. On closer inspection, they weren't even that good. It was Walm-Art, commercial garbage designed by committee and produced en masse by corporate sell-outs. Back at the room, he put on his swim trunks. Just as he was leaving, an attractive young woman with long black hair arrived with an armload of towels.

The pool was on the roof. They threw their towels, robes, and key cards on a plastic table. They had the place all to themselves. Mexico City was high up on the central plateau, far from the timeshare beaches. It was windy up there, and the sun was low in the west. Modern skyscrapers dominated the view. The one next door looked like a stack of blue cubes. Across the street there was a towering white spiral, like a very tall seashell, and next to that was a building that looked like a waterfall. To the east Adam could see across the green treetops of the Parque Alameda to the eagle eating a snake on the dome of the Palacio de Bellas Artes.

The pool was a plain rectangle of blue and white tile. There was no hot-tub, and the pool was not heated. Alice pushed him in, then sat on the edge. He splashed her, laughing. She stuck out her lip in a pout.

Her breasts were round and high. He could see the shape of her nipples. He forced himself to look away, to look at the sun on the western horizon. He closed his eyes and saw Maria. He shook his head and swam to the middle of the pool. Turned back and smiled at Alice.

"There's no way I'm getting in there," she said.

"Hey, this was your idea!"

"It's too cold. And I'm hungry."

"Fine. You go on, I'm going to swim a few laps. Meet you in the restaurant."

When she was out of sight, he got out of the pool, put on his robe, and walked to the bar.

It was fully equipped. That was something you could always count on. He ordered a michelada, a Mexican beer with salsa and lime. It came in a salt-rimmed glass with two fat shrimps and a stick of jicama. A small dish of spicy peanuts on the side. It was perfect.

Adam watched the end of a soccer match while he drank his beer and ate his snack, then he went back to his room. To his surprise he heard movement inside. He double-checked the number on his card. There was no housekeeping cart in sight. He peered through his window, through a narrow gap between the curtains. Someone was crouched over his open suitcase. A woman. The maid? Or was it Alice? If so, she had changed clothes. Which, of course she would have, by now. But the door that connected their rooms was closed. He couldn't be sure.

Praying the intruder wouldn't hear it, he tapped his card on the sensor. The lock clicked and Adam opened the door. The woman was still occupied. He crept up behind her unnoticed. He reached for the backs of her arms—and she stood up suddenly, smashing the back of her head into his nose. She spun around, but he knocked her to the ground and fell forward onto her, knees at her sides, pinning her to the floor. It was Alice. He grabbed her flailing wrists. Blood streamed off his chin, soaking her chest.

"Thanks, asshole," she said. "You ruined my dress. Now we can't go out to eat."

Alice got some ice for Adam's nose—it wasn't broken—then she washed up and changed again, this time into pajamas. He sat on the loveseat with his face to the ceiling; she sat on the side of his bed. The TV was blaring some old action movie—Arnold and Jamie Lee Curtis hanging from a helicopter, dubbed in Spanish, with English subtitles.

After a while they ordered room service and cocktails. The movie ended and the same one started again. The food arrived. Two orders of steak tampiqueña, with salsa verde, black beans, and guacamole. They sat together at the counter and ate without saying a word. Adam finished his highball and ordered another. The helicopter scene was back on. Alice started flipping channels. She stared at the screen with an intensity that spooked Adam.

"Can I see that?" he said. She passed him the remote.

He hit the power button. The screen went black.

"Alice. Time to talk."

Without taking her eyes off the TV, she said, "Is this the part where you interrogate me? I've been waiting for hours."

"You've been acting strange all day. Since we got off the plane."

"Sorry."

"Sorry for what?"

"I couldn't pull it off."

"Pull what off? Alice, what the hell is going on with you?"

"I... I can't say."

"Let me guess. Somebody sent you along to spy on me."

She stared at the blank television.

"Somebody on the team? No. Probably came from higher up. Andy?"

No reaction.

"No? Then who? What do they have on you? They didn't let you upstairs, did they?"

She glared at him, no idea what he meant. That wasn't it.

He considered the possibilities. Then it hit him. "No," he said. "Couldn't be. She wouldn't."

Alice raised her eyes to the ceiling and let out a little sigh.

"Really? Dr. Springer?"

She deflated. He'd guessed right.

"Don't tell her," Alice said, trying to make it sound like a threat.

"But what's with the outfit, the attitude? You're not yourself. Was that her idea?"

"Not exactly."

"What's that supposed to mean?"

"She said I had to take you to bed."

"No way. Not Mikayla." He stood up and paced the room. "It doesn't make sense. Why would she want that?"

"I don't know."

"Well, what on earth did she say?"

"She said she couldn't say."

"Then they must have something on her, too." He stopped pacing and put his hands on the bar in front of her. "And what about you? What do they have?"

Silence. Then, she looked up at him and asked, "Would it have worked?"

"What?"

"I was going to show you my tits after dinner. Would it have worked?"

"No."

Then she asked, "Help me."

"I will. But we'll need more booze."

Adam couldn't sleep. He could feel his blood pumping in his ears. Alice was curled up on his bed, passed out drunk after four cocktails, shivering in her sleep. Adam flipped the edge of the sheets over her and walked out onto the balcony. It was the middle of the night, and dark out—but not that dark. City dark. He sat in a patio chair and tried not to think about cigarettes. God, he could have killed for a cigarette just then. But he'd made a pact with himself not to give in during this trip—if he were going to smoke, he'd have had to sneak away from the cancer doctor, and anyway it had been almost a month since he had "really, really quit." The patches were doing their job.

A bird landed on the next table over. It was a Mexican melodious blackbird, kind of like a small crow, but with feathers that shined navy blue and purple in the right light. It sang a little song, then tilted its head from side to side, looking at him. For some reason it reminded him of his therapist. Adam made a mental note not to bring that up in a session.

It was late, and cold, and suddenly Adam felt very tired. He went inside, into the bathroom, and splashed water on his face. Stared at himself in the mirror. His nose was bruised. He looked drunk. And old. He carried Alice through the connecting door and put her in her own bed, then he returned to his room, laid down, and fell asleep.

# *AMBS*

```
CDMX AMBS 4
  Registro de Paciencias

  26-11-51 J. C. Peña Batista linfoma
  10-07-52 G. L. Vigil Cervantes pulmonar
  19-01-62 F. C. Fajardo Valencia lobulillar
  04-06-66 J. L. Simon Reyes osteosarcoma
  22-05-67 M. C. Silva Olivares colorrectal
  03-08-72 B. M. Montenegro Zayas leucemia
  16-10-73 R. G. Parada Orozco próstata
```

Mexico's public health program was delivered at hospitals called AMBS, the Academia Mexicana del Bienestar Social. The Mexican Academy of Social Well-Being. These hospitals were universally underfunded, short-staffed, and in dismaying disrepair. In each city they were numbered according to various nonsensical zoning schemes. In the nation's capital there were around thirty AMBS hospitals, but the designation numbers went as high as fifty-three. After a quick breakfast at the hotel, Adam and Alice checked out and got a car to AMBS Hospital #4, which happened to be the hospital with the closest ties to Urbano Biomedical.

Between the cab and the hospital's main entrance Adam and Alice wheeled their expensive carry-on suitcases past a man holding bloody bandages to his stomach, a teenage girl with a swollen red face, a shriveled elderly woman holding a bundle of blankets containing a screaming baby, and dozens more with less obvious symptoms. Many of these people looked resentful—here were two foreigners in fancy clothes jumping the line. Some of them reached toward Adam and Alice with open palms or empty cans. Adam had seen it all before, but Alice was probably wondering why there was a line of people out the gate and down the sidewalk, patients and their relatives huddled together in blankets. This was going on at AMBS hospitals all over the country. If their papers weren't in order, whole families often camped overnight on the sidewalk for days before the chronically-ill aunt or the granddaughter with an aggressive tumor was even granted an initial examination.

There was a security kiosk just outside the front doors. A couple of armed officers were checking IDs. In Mexico it was normal to see cops in bulletproof armor with machine guns strapped to their backs. Adam and Alice passed through the metal detectors, and finally they were inside the hospital.

"By the way," Adam said, "I've been thinking of running for Congress."

They entered a grand corridor that had probably seemed more impressive a hundred years ago, but now it just looked old and dirty. A team of receptionists behind a long table examined incoming patients' documentation and issued color-coded folders and numbered tickets. In the hotel that morning, Minerva had accessed Grupo Urbano's corporate website to fetch and print the necessary credentials, which had been waiting for Adam at checkout. Now he handed them to a clerk.

"You should do it," Alice said. "You should be a politician."

"You really think so?"

"Sure. You're eager to please, and you have no morals."

Adam laughed.

"I'm not kidding."

"I helped you, didn't I?"

The clerk stamped the papers and passed them back, saying, "Adelante."

Compared to the lines outside and in the hallway, the actual reception area was a breeze, considering they didn't need actual healthcare. Clusters of patients sat clutching their numbered tickets, this one hacking up a lung, that one holding a makeshift colostomy bag in her hands, that one oozing pus from an ulcerating growth of the neck, and dozens more with no visible symptoms, all waiting for their turn to approach the bulletproof glass. Adam scanned the clerks' faces. All women. One particularly young and attractive option—she returned his gaze —but he turned and led Alice toward the woman he guessed was the oldest. Thick glasses under gray hair dyed black and set in curls. She looked as tired as he felt.

"Disculpa, Miss," Adam said. "Una pregunta." A question.

"Digame, joven." What is it?

"Si le doy el numero de mi teléfono, puedes llamarme más tarde?" He winked.

She looked up at Adam's smiling face and she laughed with the fullness of her heart, as only a Mexican grandmother could, confident and jolly, and she looked genuinely glad to see him, and to forget her circumstances, even for a moment, and he knew he could ask her for anything.

\* \* \*

Her name was Berta. She was seventy years old, and she walked with her head high. She had six living children (and one more, lost in a car accident), fifteen living grandchildren (two had passed away, one of pneumonia, the other when her sister's house burned down—and another was stillborn), and three great-grandchildren (all still with us, although one was born prematurely), and her husband had died many years ago, of lung cancer. Adam learned this and much more as she led them deeper inside the hospital, her heels clacking down the corridors. Everywhere there were signs of decay. Cobwebs and grime, yellowed wallpaper peeling at the seams. Some attempts had been made at concealment—a colorful poster stood on a tripod in a corner, partially blocking a stain on the wall, the result of a slow leak that seeped out from the wall itself and puddled on the floor. Berta bid them adiós at the bottom of a stairwell.

When she was gone, Alice said, "I didn't know you speak Spanish."

"Oh, it's just something I picked up along the way."

"What did you say to her?"

"I asked if she'd give me a call me later."

Following her directions, they found Dr. Balderrama in the radiotherapy clinic at the back of the cancer ward on the fourth floor. He was a short man with a warm smile and bushy eyebrows. He spoke English, and he was expecting them, and without delay he led them to a dark hallway in which twelve patients in hospital gowns were seated on benches. Some looked about retirement age, some a bit younger. All of them looked gravely ill. Adam wondered how in the hell he was going to get them through airport security. He opened his luggage and produced a stack of papers. "I have consent forms and liability waivers," he said. "I can explain what to write, if you could help me translate—"

The doctor said the forms weren't necessary. "These people don't have lives outside of the hospital. After you take them away, no one will remember them. Except me." He handed Adam a clipboard.

"What about the CFIM—the comisión federal? The AMBS review board? Did Urbano get approval?"

"We're transferring the patients to you. They won't officially enter a trial under this roof. It is up to you to register the research in your country."

"I'll be sure to do that," Adam said.

Alice was stunned. Until that exact moment, she hadn't known that the goods they were sent to retrieve were human beings. She looked like she might faint.

Dr. Balderrama put a steadying hand on her shoulder. "We used to experiment on prisoners, you know. When I was your age."

"And this is somehow better?"

"Of course! You can give these people hope."

Alice stared down the line of patients, her eyes wide open. They looked up at her, pleading.

The doctor shook his head. "These people have been through everything," he said. "Surgery, chemotherapy—I gave them radiation myself. They are stable at present. But all of their cancers have relapsed and become resistant, some for the third or fourth time."

Adam paced the hall, stopping in front of each patient, to confirm their names and conditions. Juan Carlos: lymphoma, low grade fever, enlarged spleen. Guadalupe: osteosarcoma, swollen joints, constant pain. Maria Isabel: choriocarcinoma, myelodysplasia—precancerous blood cells brought on by previous chemo. Lung cancer. Breast cancer. Prostate. Twelve different cancers, all told. Some common, some rare. Very good. But there was a problem. Maria Isabel was in a wheelchair.

"Wait here, please," the doctor said. He disappeared around a corner and came back a moment later pushing a cart. On the cart was a cardboard box full of used clothing. "I got these from a friend at church."

Alice and the doctor began passing out clothes. The outfits were mismatched, and the sizes weren't right, but there was enough for everybody. Alice helped the patients get dressed, one by one. When she got to Maria Isabel, Adam put up his hand.

"Not this one," he said.

"Why not?"

"See the wheelchair? We can't risk it."

"Señor," the woman said. "Please..."

"Adam, come on. We're here. We have to do something." Alice knelt beside the woman and tried to help her into a loose pair of sweatpants.

Adam grabbed Alice by the arm and yanked her to her feet.

"Let go," she demanded.

He jerked her arm again, hard. "Alice, listen to me. You have to understand that we probably can't save any of these people. Not even one."

He felt her arm relax.

"In all likelihood, any patient that stays here will live longer than the ones we take. Have you thought of that?"

"No."

"Well, get it through your head."

"Then why are we taking any of them at all?"

"Because we're thinking of the greater good. We're thinking of Dr. Springer."

"You're thinking of your paycheck."

"And you had better start thinking about whatever it was that Dr. Springer told you when she convinced you to come with me."

Alice calmed down after that. She wasn't happy, but she didn't protest. Adam ended up cutting two more patients from the roster, one for lymphedema—irreducible swelling and pain caused by the extensive removal of lymph nodes—and one because she looked like she might actually die right there in the hallway.

The doctor handed Adam a manila envelope bulging with passports. "They're real," Balderrama said. "Urbano took care of everything."

Adam tried to give Dr. Balderrama a large wad of cash, but he wouldn't take it.

"You're a good man," Adam said.

"Do you actually believe you can cure these people?"

"If we can, we'll be able to cure everyone on the planet."

"They will need treatment as soon as possible, if they survive the flight."

This part of the hospital was like a ghost town compared to the front entrance. Adam scoped out every new hallway and stairwell for security cameras, but found none.

"We have to be getting close to an exit, right?" he asked.

"Yes, very soon now." The doctor led Adam and Alice and the patients down a narrow passage that dead-ended with a fire door marked, "La Alarma Sonará." The alarm will sound.

There were footsteps coming around the corner.

Alice froze and said, "They've caught us."

Adam stopped, listening to the noisy footsteps. "Maybe not," he said.

It was Berta. She was upset, shouting. Adam couldn't follow —she was speaking too fast—but he thought he heard the word *comisión*. He looked to the doctor.

"There's no time," the man said, and he practically pushed the whole group out the door.

The fire alarm didn't ring. Adam held the door with one arm and used the other to shield his eyes from the harsh sunlight. A full-size passenger van with the Grupo Urbano logo was waiting at the bottom of a short flight of crumbling concrete steps. Alice jumped in the van first and helped the nine able-bodied patients climb aboard.

Adam turned to shake hands with Dr. Balderrama.

"Gracias, Doctor," he said. "You've been extremely helpful."

But the doctor said, "I'm coming with you," and he followed the last patient into the van.

Adam got in the passenger seat and said, "Airport. Vamos."

The driver was a lean young man who put the van in gear and gunned it around to the front of the building. He nodded to the parking attendant—another lean young man, in his booth far away across the lot—and the gate was up in plenty of time for the van to exit without slowing down. They flew onto a busy street, through a light that Adam had just watched turn red, and up a ramp onto the ring road, the elevated highway that looped around the north side of Mexico City.

"Looks like we made it," Adam said, but his heart was pounding. He turned to look over his shoulder, and he saw eleven terrified faces staring back at him. One of them belonged to Alice. He shot her a reassuring smile, fake at first, but he held onto it until he convinced himself they would make it. But just then something caught his eye out the back window. A few cars behind, merging into traffic, was a black SUV driven by a very serious-looking man. The woman in the passenger seat was screaming, waving, pointing to the side of the road. She obviously wanted them to pull over.

"Speak English?" Adam asked the driver.

"Yeah."

"Name?"

"Sergio."

"How long to the airport, Sergio?"

"Twenty minutes if we follow traffic."

"What if we don't?"

Sergio stepped on the accelerator and slalomed around ten cars before he let up.

"Cops come up here often? Policía?"

"A veces." Sometimes.

The city was flying by, and most of it was not very nice. Miles of decaying infrastructure, all of it covered in bad graffiti. Crumbling apartment stacks under polluted skies. Adam looked out the back. The SUV was farther behind, but still with them.

"Adam, that's enough!" Alice said. "These people can't take it!"

Dr. Balderrama made the sign of the cross.

Adam didn't know what to do. The indecision hit him hard. The helplessness. He stared at the road. Everything around him blurred. He remembered his kids, his wife. He remembered his mother. He thought of the blacktop screeching by at a hundred miles an hour right under his feet. He tried not to think of her, but he couldn't stop it: Maria. And then, Arturo. He almost never thought about Arturo. At least he hadn't, not until his brother Noah called to invite him to Christmas, and had mentioned that Tommy was in jail. Ever since then, Adam found his thoughts turning to Arturo more and more.

He looked for the SUV. It was behind them, and gaining. No more cars in-between. The vehicle's driver was staring back at him. The woman was still shouting, still pointing. Adam looked at the patients, at Balderrama, at Alice. They all seemed to be begging him to do something, but Adam couldn't hear them, couldn't hear anything but the blood pumping in his ears... and the sound of flames. He couldn't hear anything over the flames of his father's workshop. And he knew what to do. "Sergio," he said. "Slow down."

The SUV pulled up closer behind them, and Adam stared into it, focusing on the driver, and on the steering wheel. He remembered how he had felt that day, when he was just a boy, angry beyond words, Matthew dead, Arturo leaving him behind, and he was so afraid. And he had wanted to hurt Arturo, to make him suffer, to blame him for everything. And there it was. A spider, on the dashboard of the SUV. Fat and black. A tarantula. It crawled onto the steering wheel between the driver's black-gloved hands, and it raised its forelegs toward his face.

And with one smooth motion, the SUV's driver picked up the spider and threw it out the window.

Adam felt like he was going to be sick. But just when he thought the people in the SUV might be crazy enough to run them off the freeway, he saw the lights flashing red and blue. He never thought he'd be so happy to see the cops. The SUV pulled over. The Urbano van kept going.

Five minutes later they were parked at the airport drop-off. Adam and Alice helped the patients out of the van. Dr. Balderrama lined them up on the sidewalk for final inspection.

And the black SUV pulled up.

"What the hell?" Alice said.

"All it takes is a thousand pesos," Adam said. "Fifty bucks and you're off the hook."

The passenger got out of the vehicle and ran to one of the patients, tears streaming down her face. The driver approached Dr. Balderrama.

"Comisión Federal de Investigación Medica," he said.

"We have done nothing wrong."

"This woman disagrees."

"Se están llevando a mi abuelito!" she wailed. They're taking my grandpa!

Alice gave Adam the look of death.

Adam turned to Balderrama. "You said they were all clear."

"They were! They are. This woman has no rights."

"She seems to be family."

"She doesn't understand what we're trying to do! What we stand to achieve!"

Alice reached up and pinched Adam's trapezius so hard he actually winced.

"We leave him, or I quit. I'll quit the team."

"He wants to go with us."

"He belongs with his family."

"You would deny him a chance to be a part of this?" Adam asked. "To contribute to the cure?"

It turned out there wasn't much point in arguing. Dr. Balderrama told them what the agent had told him: if they didn't leave the man behind, the woman claiming to be his granddaughter would lodge an official complaint with the federal government. Then they'd be going home empty handed, if they were allowed to leave at all.

In Adam's suitcase there was still a bundle of cash that had been meant for Dr. Balderrama. Now, he gave half of it to Sergio.

He put the rest in his wallet, and the whole group moved inside the airport. Adam had always known there would be trouble at the check-in counter, but he was resilient, and flexible. That was why they paid him what they did. He knew that the first thing to do when traveling abroad was always to play dumb. Pretend you didn't speak the language, and the ball was in your court.

Everything was right in the airline's computers. The flight had been booked in advance. The three who couldn't make it were taken off the itinerary. The remaining passengers had clear passports. But something was wrong. The airline clerk was holding the boarding passes, and whispering to a manager. A man with a transportation authority badge approached the group.

"They want to know why none of these people have bags," he said.

In the end it was Dr. Balderrama who came up with the idea that saved them.

"They're a tour group," he said in Spanish. "And I am their physician. Have you ever heard of Make-a-Wish?" He explained that a team of stylists was awaiting the group's arrival in Chicago. Photographers from a famous magazine would be shooting their photos as they toured the city.

The guard spoke to the airline workers. They were going to need some verification.

Adam pulled out his phone and called Elena.

"Hey babe," he said. "Can you do something for me?"

"Hope your trip's going good. Can you make it quick? I'm at work."

"I need you to talk to the airline. I have eight Mexican nationals here, I'm taking them to Chicago, and they won't let us through. I figured your whole job is helping Mexicans get into the country, so..."

Elena sighed. "I work in career services and family counseling. You know this."

"Whatever. Can you help me or not?"

They were stopped again at security, this time by a three-person biohazard crew. Multiple reports had come in of a group of visibly ill individuals shuffling through the airport. Adam was accused of attempting to transport infectious disease across international borders. Dr. Balderrama and Dr. Suzuki, the two oncologists, explained that these people had cancer—it wasn't contagious. But the biohazard team wouldn't back down. Their leader changed his angle: they were simply protecting the immunocompromised cancer victims from contracting secondary infections from the other passengers.

Adam knew the reality of the situation. The airline didn't want anyone dying on their plane. He gave the biohazard people the rest of the cash from his wallet. It was an enormous quantity by Mexican standards, but to a man like Adam Baker, it was hardly worth counting. Still, the customs people deemed one member of the tour group too sick to fly, no matter how much money the gringo had in his pockets. Her name was Teresa, and she had bruising all over her face. She could hardly speak. Her temperature was through the roof, and her whole body was tinted orange from chemo. Dr. Balderrama put an arm around her shoulder.

"I'll stay with her," he said.

"Aren't you coming with us, Doctor?" Alice asked.

"I want to. I wish I could. But I'm needed here."

Later, when they reached cruising altitude, Alice turned to Adam.

"By the way," she said. "I've been wondering something."

"What is it?"

"Why didn't we just tell the truth—that these are cancer patients going to a new hospital for cutting-edge treatment?"

"Oh, that's easy. Think about it."

She rolled her eyes. "I give up."

"Everybody knows cancer patients come *to* Mexico for experimental treatments. Not the other way around."

AJ was sitting in the dark, in his basement bedroom—just sitting there, not doing anything at all, when his phone rang. He recognized the number as coming from Mexico. He slid his thumb across the screen. "Prima," he said. There was only one person it could be: his cousin Renata, the only surviving relative who acknowledged him as family. That wasn't the only reason her parents had thrown her out of the house. She had not grown up to be the princess they'd hoped for. The evidence was all over social media.

"Hola, Javi," she said. "Qué pedo."

"I'm fine, thanks."

"I saw your old friend this morning."

"I don't know what you're talking about," he said. But there was only one person she could mean. Adam. He walked up the stairs to the back of the house, to get better reception.

"Man, I can't get enough of your accent," she said. "You sound just like Fargo."

"Is that why you called me—to give me shit about the way I talk? I just got out of the hospital, asshole."

"No, man. Take it easy. I'm just joking around with you, little cousin. What were you in for?"

"Some nice cowboys did me a favor and broke a few of my ribs."

"Sorry to hear that, wey. You gonna get 'em back?"

"I don't know. Why did you call me, Renata? Your accounts get banned again?"

"Suck my dick, man. Listen, I'm working at a hotel. A real nice one. They got me doing fucking everything around here, man. I wash the towels. I fold the towels. I clean the fucking pool drains. I even fix the goddamn plumbing. And sometimes some fancy people come down here, and sometimes, some nice people from some magazines pay me for nice pictures of nice fancy people. So maybe sometimes I spend a lot of my time looking in other people's windows."

"And...?"

"And I saw your pal Adam Baker, with some Asian princess."

"What do you mean, you saw them? And why should I give a fuck?"

"Dios mío, cousin! I mean I fucking saw them taking a shower together, man. And how the hell should I know whether or not you give a fuck? I saw the guy and I thought of you, alright? So I called to see how my little cousin is doing, and I find out he's been in the fucking hospital. You need me to come up there? Maybe slap those cowboys around for you?"

AJ surprised himself by actually considering it, but decided it was a bad idea. "Thanks for calling," he said. "Don't worry about me. Papá sends his love."

"How's the old man doing?"

"The same."

"Give him my love, too. And yours."

"I will. Thanks, prima."

"I'll be talking to you again soon, little cousin."

"I doubt it."

# *Christmas*

Maria,

My shrink said writing this might help. I suppose you knew how I was, even back then. But nobody else did, not even your brother, and he's the one who taught me how to cover it up. How to be someone else. But my therapist is having me unpack it all.

I've been the new me for so long now... But there was supposed to be a point where the transformation would be complete. A point where I would actually become the smiling, overconfident jackass I've been pretending to be all these years. The guy without a care in the world. Everybody's best friend. To tell you the truth, sometimes I do forget I'm faking it. But more often than not, it feels like I'm falling apart. I can't even look at my wife without seeing your face.

Remember our secret tunnel, at the back of the supply room? Our secret spot? Of course you remember. I still think about that, sometimes. Someone must have found it by now. God, how long has it been? I wonder if they cut down our tree.

I think I'm getting worse, not better.

But don't worry.

```
I still love you, Maria.
Please forgive me.
AB
```

It had taken some getting used to at first, but by now Adam had been calling his own brother "Uncle" for seven years—ever since Mary was born. Now it was Christmas Eve at Uncle Noah's house. Adam and Noah left the cooking to their better halves— not because they weren't willing to help, of course. They were happy to set the table for dinner and wash the dishes afterwards. But Elena and Veronica strongly objected to their presence in the kitchen during the preparation of the meal. So they stood in the family room, arms crossed, watching the children play.

The room looked like it did every Christmas. There was the tree in the corner, big as ever, presents piled high on the burgundy carpet. Adam and Noah's father, "Grandpa" John Baker, sat watching the fire in a rocking chair that he had made himself, about forty-odd years earlier. Auntie Heather, Grandpa's widowed sister, sat with her feet up in the recliner.

Adam considered his girls to be more well-rounded than most children, with their dual heritage, and their Latina social-worker mom, who was always bringing colorful guests over to the house, or taking the family out for cultural enrichment. And every Christmas, Adam took a certain pleasure in watching Mary and Lucy try to engage with their strange cousins, Noah and Veronica's kids.

Mary, seven years old, was in the middle of the pack. She assessed the situation: Harmony, the eldest cousin, sat cross-legged on the floor near the fireplace, looking as intense as the girl on the cover of her chapter book. Brock was on the couch playing a handheld video game. Mary must have figured he wasn't the sharing type, because she left him alone, even though she normally liked video games. With both of the older cousins occupied in unsociable behaviors, Mary was stuck with her sister Lucy and their youngest cousin, Grace. They were throwing a tea party for Grace's stuffed animals.

But on her way to the party, Mary stopped and put her hand on her grandfather's knee, which made Adam smile. Grandpa had been staring at the fire for an awful long time, and Adam was worried he was thinking about the old workshop.

"Grandpa, how long until presents?" Mary asked.

"Let your grandfather rest," Great Aunt Heather said. "Presents will not be opened until after dinner. You know that."

"Well, when's dinner?"

"Any moment now, princess. It'll be here and gone before you know it."

"But I want to open my presents now! Daddy didn't let us bring any toys, and Harmony doesn't like me, and Brock won't share his game, and I'm too old to play with the babies!"

"You're still a baby yourself, dear. If you don't stop worrying about what comes next, you'll soon find that you have no time left at all. Now run along and play."

Mary made a show of dragging herself over to the coffee table, where Grace's collection of plush dogs, cats, and bears politely sipped hot drinks and ate chocolate mousse.

Lucy held up a little black terrier, saying, "Would you care for some more?"

Grace said, "Why yes, thank you. I do love tea!" She was throttling a poor gray kitten.

Noah helpfully suggested that maybe what Mary needed was a book—or a game.

"Let's hope there's one under the tree," Adam said, and he crossed to a position beside the reclining chair. "I wonder if some interaction with the kids wouldn't actually be *good* for Dad," he said loudly.

Auntie Heather had already spoken on this subject, many times before, in fact, and she clearly felt no obligation to go over it again with her least favorite nephew. Adam changed tactics. He nodded toward the nativity scene on the fireplace mantel and said, "He hasn't made anything that good in a long time." Besides the usual Mary, Joseph, Baby Jesus, the Three Wise Men, and the Angel of the Lord, there was a full complement of cherubs, shepherds, and barnyard animals. John Baker had carved and painted the whole set by hand, and he'd given it to Noah and Veronica as a wedding present.

Auntie Heather let out a long, slow sigh. Finally she said, "I don't see a card from my Thomas up there." Adam anxiously scanned the row of Christmas cards arranged behind the manger scene, hoping to see one from his own family. He spotted a photo of his girls in their new sweaters, which was proof enough that his wonderful wife had taken care of everything. Relieved, he made a mental note to thank her later.

"I still don't understand how they can keep my Tommy locked up for so long, just for beating up that dope-smoking Mexican."

Adam's eyes about popped out. He looked across the room to his brother, pleading for support, but Noah simply shrugged and walked away. Their father had fallen asleep. Adam felt like he could use a drink, but this was a dry house. He'd have to handle this without help. "He hurt him pretty bad, actually," he began.

"So what? Throw him in the drunk tank, then. Let him calm down, then cut him loose."

Adam forged ahead, explaining that Tommy had been charged with disorderly conduct, which meant that he could be in jail for up to ninety days all by itself. But on top of that there was assault, good for up to six months in prison, and six more months for battery—up to twenty *years* if they found that he'd inflicted great bodily harm, which he certainly had—and then there was the hate crime aspect, which, if it stuck—which it probably wouldn't—would make the whole thing a felony.

When he was finished, Auntie Heather said, "I know all that already, thank you."

Adam stared at the ceiling and counted to ten in his head. His hand went to the keychain in his pocket, to his mother's ceramic heart. He wished he could talk to Noah about how much he missed her, and how bad he felt about Matthew.

The sound of his daughters arguing brought him back to the room.

They were fighting over a little red doggie. Mary tore it from Lucy's hands and slammed it down on the table. "I'm Daddy," she said, "and I just got home from work. It's late! What on earth are you doing out of bed? You better get your little behind in that bathroom and get those teeth brushed pretty quick—or there'll be hell to pay! Now where's my beer?"

Adam set out the dishes and silverware while Noah shuttled platters of fresh cut veggies and dinner rolls and fruit salad from the kitchen. Elena and Veronica brought steaming bowls of shrimp casserole. Grandpa John and Auntie Heather came to the table, and Adam ushered in the children. Noah thanked everyone for coming, and on a whim Adam recited a prayer of sorts:

*Some say that ever 'gainst that season comes*
*Wherein our Saviour's birth is celebrated,*
*The bird of dawning singeth all night long:*
*And then, they say, no spirit dares stir abroad;*

*The nights are wholesome; then no planets strike,*
*No fairy takes, nor witch hath power to charm,*
*So hallow'd and so gracious is the time.*

"Amen," he concluded.

"Amen," came the response.

Elena leaned toward her husband. "That was beautiful, Adam," she said. "What was it?"

"Oh, just something I remembered in the moment. It's from Hamlet."

She smacked him over the head.

# *Progress*

.

SPRINGER Mikayla (springer@montmed.com)
  Tues. 3/18/2020 5:29 PM
  TR.PROJECT
  (baker,brandt,cathyp,suzuki,tymarsh,xu)
  CC: WASHINGTON Andrew (andy)

Hello Everyone,
  Just a few quick updates to get us all on
the same page.

  Xu Fei is isolating microRNAs involved in
the known enzymatic pathways to malignancy,
and Dr. Brandt is manufacturing decoy RNA to
attract and disable them.

  Alice, I need you to keep running the
decoy RNAs in the rodent models. By
summertime you'll be drafting procedures and
documentation for the Phase 1 trials.

  Cathy- the German retrovirus is AMAZING.
You know best, so I leave it in your capable
hands.

  Tyler- I'm sorry to see you go, but I wish
you the best of luck. In your short time
with us you have made numerous contributions

to the project. The global genome database is indispensable to our work, and everyone loves your redesigned sequencer interface. Thank you, Tyler. Your expertise will be sorely missed.

Everyone- now that Tyler's database is up and running, I want all hands searching for donor candidates. The key is out there somewhere, just waiting for us to find it.

One more thing- there's a problem with the name. "Autonecrogen gland" is not testing well at all with focus groups. We're open to suggestions, people! Looking forward to hearing some alternative names for our little miracle.

Last, I want to wish Adam Baker the best of luck on the campaign trail! Adam has recently announced his candidacy for Senate, and I can't think of a better man for the job.

That should do it for the next couple of months. I expect nothing less than the best from each of you. I'm sure you won't let me down.

Mikayla Springer, MD
Director of Operations
Lakeview Cancer Institute
You may encounter many defeats,
but you must not be defeated.
-Maya Angelou

AJ had the speakers cranked in his basement bedroom dungeon. Zombies and firearms were his world now, perpetual death and rebirth on his computer screen, to a soundtrack of screaming guitars and double bass drums. He'd been out of the hospital for six weeks, back in the place he'd been renting since college. It was the basement of somebody's house. He never saw the people who lived upstairs, and they never saw him, because the back door led directly downstairs. Cement floors, cinder block walls. It was damp and cold. He slept on a mattress on the floor.

Every day for the first month he'd had to give himself a shot in the belly. It was an anticoagulant, to prevent internal blood clots, because Tommy had ruptured his spleen. A clot in the spleen could have broken loose and traveled up the vein to the heart, where it could have caused AJ's untimely death. But there were still things he wanted to do, once he was back on his feet, and so he'd given himself the damn shots. It still hurt to move, and he was on a cocktail of powerful marijuana and prescription painkillers. He wore the same clothes day after day—a red flannel and black sweat pants. He hardly ever left his basement. The pizza place said he could start driving again whenever he was ready. He didn't bother contacting the grocery store.

An unknown number had been dialing him for days. Finally he gave in. He picked up the phone and walked to the bottom of the stairs, where he could get a signal strong enough that the call wouldn't be dropped. He slid his thumb across the screen and said, "Who the fuck is this?"

"It's about time you answered me, AJ. I know about you and your sister and Adam Baker."

"What the fuck are you talking about?"

"Adam Baker is running for Senator. Did you know that?"

"Yeah? Who gives a shit."

"Go to the press and tell them the truth—tell them Adam Baker killed your sister."

"Who the fuck are you? And why the fuck should I do that?"

"I'm the guy who can get you the proof you need—a recording of the phone call on the bridge."

"Bullshit. There's no recording. And what's left of my dad's cell phone is in a box in the county courthouse basement."

"The recording isn't in the phone, dumbass. It's in the phone company's hard drives. Listen."

Maria's voice came out of the past. She said, "I'm here, Adam."

AJ wished he had one of those old landline phones with the heavy receiver that you could actually slam down when you wanted to hang up on someone. He wanted to throw his phone down on the concrete floor so hard it would explode. But he'd be screwed without a phone.

"You need to give me that fucking tape."

"It's not on a goddamn tape, AJ. Christ, for somebody who has such a fancy computer, you sure use an obsolete vernacular."

"Fuck off. What makes you think I want to open up all that old shit?"

"Like I said, I can give you proof. And there's more at stake here than you know—much more."

"What the fuck do you want from me?"

"Just say you'll help me take down Adam Baker."

# *Easter*

```
CEDAR CREEK POLICE DEPARTMENT
  Case #01-0314-0143G
  Subject: Garcia, Maria Lucia
  NxLink Mobile, Inc.

03-14-2001
  01:26:04 PM 0658 Maria, I need you.
  01:26:07 PM 3815 Where are you?
  01:26:09 PM 0658 Remember our first kiss?
  01:26:11 PM 3815 You're at the bridge?
  01:26:18 PM 0658 ***Call terminated.
```

"Hello, Adam Baker for Senate, campaign headquarters. How may I direct your call?"

"I need to speak to Adam."

"Please hold."

The crackling smooth jazz made AJ feel physically ill.

"I'm sorry, but Mr. Baker is busy at the moment. If you'll leave your name and number, he'll be happy to call you back as soon as he gets a chance."

"My name's AJ Garcia. He'll know."

"Thank you for your call, Mr. Garcia."

AJ set his phone down next to a stack of bills, advertisers, a dozen issues of The Tri-County Free Classifieds, other random junk mail. He didn't bother looking in the cupboard—there'd be no clean dishes up there—and the drying rack was empty as well. He selected a glass from the sink and held it up to the light to inspect for mildew. Good enough. He poured himself a glass of whiskey.

AJ had moved back to Cedar Creek after his fall. For the first few years he had visited his catatonic father at the hospital on a regular basis. Manuel Garcia simply stared at the wall. Nurses fed him and changed him. Doctors ran him through a gauntlet of medications. But the old man never responded, never changed. Never gave AJ even the slightest sign of recognition. They called it post-traumatic major melancholic depression.

AJ dropped in less and less often. It happened gradually at first—shorter and shorter visits, more and more rationalization. He had to go to the hospital at least once a month anyway, to pay his dad's bills. The first time he dropped off a check and left without seeing his dad, he knew he would eventually stop going altogether. A month later he gave the hospital his bank account info for automatic payment.

When AJ was hospitalized after the whole parking lot thing, though, cooped up with his father in that shitty little room day after day, AJ came to think of the man as kind of a free therapist. AJ talked for hours, letting it all out, holding nothing back. And Manuel just stared.

Now AJ was back on his feet, driving pizza again, saving tips, paying off bills he'd racked up during his recovery. His boss had even given him his old shift back, dinner rush until close. The tips weren't as good at dinner time, but there were a lot more of them, and the late night tips were usually pretty good, because the customers were usually drunk. Wash the dishes, sweep and mop the restaurant, and he'd get home about two in the morning, pour himself a glass of whiskey—couldn't afford the bar anymore—and go to bed. Wake up around ten or eleven and go hang out with the old man until it was time to go back to work.

Behind St. Luke's there was a walking path leading through the woods to the Cedar Creek. AJ would take his father back there for hours at a time. Park the wheelchair by the river, smoke a joint, sit and talk. It was spring time, so between the snowmelt and the rain showers, the creek was actually flowing. The conversation was generally one-sided, but occasionally a bird or a squirrel would have something to say.

"I haven't been to church in forever," AJ began, one day. "I was the only brown altar boy in the county, remember that? God, we never missed church. Mom was always going off about our Sunday clothes, always yelling at me to hurry up. I was always the last one in the truck. You and Mom up front, and Maria in the back seat, and I'd hop in the back, and then we'd still have to swing by the motel and pick up all the workers, and they'd climb in back with me. We were late to church pretty much every time, because of me. I guess I didn't understand the Fifth Commandment back then. Or I didn't care. Maria never would've let you and Mom down like that."

AJ took a drag, held it in, and blew the smoke out over the river. He and his father sat there for a long time, just listening to Mother Nature, before he spoke again.

"Can you believe Mom wanted me to take the Holy Orders? Me? Me, a priest. Give me a break. I haven't exactly been a model Catholic. Baptism was easy enough I guess. Hard to screw that up. Don't get me started on First Communion, though. They do it in second grade because little kids are too dumb to figure out it's complete bullshit. Worked on me, too. You know, I think I just figured something out. Before taking the Eucharist, everybody has to go through their first Reconciliation. The first time in the booth with the priest. When you're seven years old, you just go through the motions. Do what they tell you. Tell Father Murphy you stole five dollars from your mother's purse, say five Hail Marys and an Our Father, experience the love and forgiveness of our Lord and Savior Jesus Christ. Maybe you were feeling pretty bad before that, about your sins or whatever, and they really crank up the pressure to confess. Then all of the sudden God forgives you and you're feeling great—and you're hooked. The whole bread and wine thing is a lot easier to swallow when you've already taken the bait."

He smiled at his word play, then realized that he was the fish.

"I don't remember what I thought back then, but I must have been searching for some kind of a sign, for proof, and then something happened in the seventh grade, and that's when I really started to feel it, to feel what it means to have faith. There was a fire, in a woodworking shop. I'm sure you remember. There were all these projects in there, birdhouses and a lot of baseball stuff. A hell of a lot of baseball stuff. See, there was this kid, and he was obsessed with baseball, and then he died of cancer. Never got to see the Twins' pair of triple-plays in the World Series. So the boy's father, who was a carpenter, went off the deep end making baseball stuff. And I accidentally burned it all down. Used a blowtorch to kill a spider. It was a huge one, big as a frisbee, and it came out of nowhere, and I swear it was going to kill us. So I tried to kill it first. But I couldn't seem to hit it, and I ended up swinging the blowtorch all over the workbench. I thought I was going to jail, or worse. I thought Adam's dad was probably crazy enough to kill me. And I knew if I died then, I'd definitely go to Hell. So I prayed and prayed. I told God I was sorry. And guess what? It worked. I told the truth, to Adam's dad and to God, and I never got in any kind of trouble. That's when I knew Jesus was on my side. Never even went to Confession, now that I think about it."

An alarm buzzed on AJ's phone. Time to get moving. He sat there another minute, breathing the fresh air, staring at the water. Then he stood up, released the brakes on Manuel's wheelchair, and started down the path.

"Five years later I was in Confirmation class and I was starting to doubt everything. In high school I was learning physics and biology and computers, and I was thinking about all that—how bodies are like machines, and brains are like computers, that sort of thing. And I went on the confirmation retreat. A three-day lock-in with a bunch of college students with a major hard-on for Jesus. There were moments during that retreat, holding hands and singing, or passing the flashlight after lights-out, going around the circle talking about faith—there were times when I felt like I could really drink the Kool-Aid.

"But at the end of the retreat, each Confirmation candidate has to meet the Bishop in private. You have a nice little chat, you pray with him, he blesses you, and you go on your merry way, right? Not me. I don't know what anybody else did with that guy, but I took the opportunity to express my doubts. First, the Transubstantiation. Are we really supposed to believe the bread and wine literally become meat and blood? Total bullshit, right? Second, the Ascension. When Jesus was done here, he literally floated straight up into the sky? Give me a fucking break. He wasn't even a ghost or anything, but he just took off and flew away. I bet most Catholics don't even know we're supposed to believe that. Well, I told the bishop what I thought about those beliefs, and I said, look, if we're commanded to believe these two things, which are obviously stupid, then why should we believe any of it? And the bishop's answer just about drove me insane. He told me not to worry about it. He said we doubt because our faith is weak, and when our faith is weak, the best thing to do is to keep going forward. 'Go get confirmed,' he told me, 'and your faith will be stronger than ever.' So I did, and you know what? He was right. I kept believing. But then everything happened, with Maria, and Mom, and I was angry at God, and I still couldn't get my head around all the bullshit, so I stopped going to church. I figured if it's a sin not to go, then I'll feel bad about it and confess. But I never felt bad about it, so I figured God must not really care one way or the other."

They were back inside St. Luke's now, almost to Manuel's room in the old wing.

"Anyway, all I'm trying to say is that I'm starting to understand the Fifth Commandment. Let's start going to church again, Dad. You'd like that, right?"

AJ woke up early on Easter Sunday and went to the hospital. He'd called ahead and asked the staff to get Manuel ready for church. He'd been planning to lift his father into the passenger seat of the Toyota, and throw the wheelchair in the back, but when he got there he saw that they already had him loaded on the shuttle bus, wheelchair and all, strapped to the floor next to the others.

Manuel's nurse told AJ they'd been taking his father to the hospital's little chapel every Sunday for years. AJ was sorry to hear that, because he knew how his father felt about that kind of wishy-washing hand-holding non-denominational worship. He was sorry he hadn't thought to take his dad down to St. Peter's much sooner.

The bus was packed with disabled elderly churchgoers and hospital staff, but Adam couldn't do the whole social thing with a bunch of strangers. He just stared out the window. The Catholic church was on the other side of town, and along the way the bus kept stopping to let out passengers of different faiths, so AJ saw a lot of well-to-do types in their fancy clothes walking up the front stairs of all the churches in Cedar Creek, and he automatically felt embarrassed over his dirty jeans and flannel, before remembering that he didn't really care anymore. God wouldn't really give a shit, would He? Jesus walked around in robes all day. God ought to be happy enough that AJ even got out of bed this morning. I could've just slept right through until work, he thought. He'd gotten another job working Sunday nights at the movie theater in Owatonna. The work consisted mostly of watching movies in empty theaters, or standing behind the register not selling tickets, or making small batches of popcorn for himself. Nobody went to the movies on a Sunday night. At least not in rural Minnesota.

St. Peter's was a nice place than he'd remembered it. Glorious, even. He dipped his fingers in the holy water and made the sign of the cross. He parked his father next to a pew in the back and almost forgot to genuflect before taking a seat. He said an Our Father and a Hail Mary and he asked the Lord for forgiveness. He stood up or kneeled when he was supposed to, and he opened the hymnal and tried to sing along with everybody. Father Murphy was long gone, and the new priest was this old short guy with little round glasses. He had a powerful voice, but in the beginning AJ couldn't focus. He had to keep reminding himself he deserved to be there. That the very act of going to church transformed him into a person who was worthy of being there.

He looked at his father, and in the bottom of his heart, he was sorry for everything. I screwed up, Dad, he thought. Too many times. I wasn't there for Maria when she needed me. She's gone and it's my fault. I should have known what was happening, should have stopped her. I was selfish. And after it happened, I was so angry, for such a long time. I yelled at God and I screamed at Him and I cursed Him. I'm sorry, God. I told You to fuck off and leave me alone, and then You took Mom.

AJ prayed, then. He told God he was sorry, and he joined the congregation in singing the hallelujahs, and the priest carried the Book of the Gospels to the lectern, and the priest said, "The Lord be with you."

And the people replied, "And also with you."

"A reading from the Holy Gospel according to Luke."

"Glory to you, O Lord."

The priest read the story of two disciples of Jesus who were walking to a village seven miles from Jerusalem. This was after it had been discovered that the stone had been rolled away from the tomb, and the disciples were talking about everything that had happened. Jesus himself came up and began walking with them, but they were kept from recognizing his face. And AJ felt like the priest was speaking directly to him.

"When they drew closer to the village, Jesus made as if to continue; but the disciples asked him to stay, saying, 'The day is nearly over.' So he went with them. He was at their table, and he took bread and made a blessing. The he broke the bread and handed it to the disciples. And they recognized him as their Lord, but he disappeared from their sight."

And AJ didn't hear the rest because he was praying. He prayed harder than he ever had in his life. And God told him not to worry. That Maria and his mother were safe, in Heaven. And he cried. He cried and cried, and he looked at his father, and his father's head was raised up, and his father was transfixed by the image of the Lord behind the altar.

And the priest sang: "The gospel of the Lord!"

And the congregation replied: "Praise to you, Lord Jesus Christ."

AJ spent the rest of the Mass watching his father for further signs of life, but found none. The feeling he'd had, the experience, lasted through the bus ride back to the hospital, but by the time they reached Manual's room, AJ was already beginning to waver. He sat on the edge of his father's bed, trying to hold onto his epiphany. He put his head in his hands and he thought he might cry again, but nothing happened. He looked up at his father, who was still sitting in his wheelchair, same as ever—except that his head was raised up, just like before, in church. Only this time, he was looking at something on a high shelf.

AJ crossed the room to the shelf and found a small wooden lockbox. Taking the box in his hands, he recognized it immediately, because he had made it himself in a high school shop class, as a present, not for his father, but for his sister.

# *Scandal*

HEADLINES RELATED TO
Adam Baker's Senate Campaign:

Senate Hopeful's Walk of Shame--
Caught on Camera!
-Hawker. May 21, 2020

Top Ten Reasons Why You Won't Vote Baker
-Swamplist. May 29, 2020

Fraternity Reunions: Dark Secrets EXPOSED
-National Radar. June 14, 2020

Wholesome Hunting Trip, or Drug-Fueled Sex
Romp? What Your Man REALLY Does When He
Goes Up North For The Weekend
-Modern Woman. July 4, 2020

Man of the People? Candidate Baker Lobbied
for HIGHER Drug Prices
-The People's Watchdog. July 4, 2020

"Healthcare Champion" Baker Made Millions
Betting on Big Tobacco
-Popular Medicine. August 7, 2020

Montgomery Medicine Tumbles on Allegations
   of Insider Trading
    -Conservative Report. August 8, 2020

   MUST SEE: Photos Prove Big Pharma's Golden
   Boy is a CHEATER
    -The Vulture. September 10, 2020

The photos showed a shirtless Adam, and Dr. Suzuki in her bikini top, standing together in what appeared to be a hotel room. That was all it took to cause a scandal in the media. On the morning after the photo came out, Adam Baker held an emergency press conference at the Minnesota State Fair. He'd been up all night explaining what had happened in Mexico, but Elena wasn't convinced. He'd been telling her stories of Big Pharma treachery for years though, so she knew all about the Inner Circle and their machinations. This wasn't any worse than what had happened to any number of people who had crossed them in the past.

It was a gray and rainy morning, but Adam's campaign manager brought extra umbrellas. All the local news outlets already had tents on the fairgrounds, which was important because there was no time to make proper arrangements. The campaign crew built a small platform in front of a collection of antique tractors on display, to show that Adam was in touch with his roots.

The rain helped Adam relax. He'd been speaking to crowds all summer, fighting off a constant stream of accusations, but this was the worst one yet. He believed Montgomery was behind all of it—although he couldn't understand why—and he was determined to take them down. Most of his campaign team advised against it, but none of them could come up with anything better. When the big moment finally came, even Adam wasn't sure what he was about to say.

He walked up onto the platform holding his umbrella. He forced himself to smile. The crowd was smaller than he'd hoped, probably due to the rain, but the important thing was that there were cameras, lots of cameras. He took a deep breath. "Ladies and gentleman of the press, my fellow Minnesotans, welcome and good morning. Thank you all for coming."

He smiled at his wife. She avoided his eyes.

"When I was a boy, I was terrified of ghosts. Couldn't go anywhere alone, even in broad daylight. I thought they were all around me, and I was afraid to face them. I ran and hid. Well, folks, Big Pharma is like a ghost, moving things in the background while you're not looking. And today I'm here to say: We see you. We've caught you red handed. You're not a ghost— you're just a crooked old man in a mask."

Adam looked across the crowd and he saw a number of mouths hanging open, and he knew he had them.

"And I was part of it, before. I admit it. I spent seventeen years of my life working for Big Pharma. You may have heard that I lobbied for the law that prevents the government from negotiating for lower drug prices. That's true. I did it, and I'm sorry. Pharmaceutical companies pay lobbyists to bribe senators and representatives in Washington, and they pass these laws that are only good for rich people—and very, very bad for normal folks. That's why people hate lobbyists, and that's why I won't have any part of it, going forward."

Someone in the crowd coughed and said, "Bullshit."

Ignoring it, Adam continued: "And that's not the only way the major pharmaceuticals profit off the backs of hardworking Americans. Another tactic they use is called market-spiral pricing. Now, in most industries, when new products come out, the older ones drop in price. You wouldn't pay full price today for a smartphone that came out five years ago, right? But Big

Pharma makes up their own rules. They put out new drugs at higher prices, but they refuse to lower the prices on the old drugs. It's called market spiral pricing. Look it up. They've been getting away with it for years, because they know you'll pay. And if you can't pay, the government will. But who pays for the government? You do. And the prices just keep going up.

"And guess what? The new products don't even have to work better than the old ones. You'd think that would be a basic requirement, right? Wrong. New drugs only have to perform better than placebo. They literally only have to do better than nothing. That's an awfully low bar for something that costs so much money, isn't it? And nobody has the power to enforce that standard anyway, because these people are in bed with the FDA."

His campaign manager slid her finger across her throat. But he pressed on, because the rain was letting up, and the crowd was growing. He folded his umbrella and grabbed the podium with both hands.

"I know why you're all here. You want to know about the photos. And that's what I'm trying to explain. You see, these are powerful corporations we're dealing with. So powerful that they can manipulate people into doing what they want. They tried to pull my strings, but I'm cutting them off, here and now. You've all seen the photos. I won't deny that it's me. It is. But I was set up, and so was the woman in the photos with me. You all know who she is, I'm sure. We are being blackmailed. We never even touched each other. What you have all seen is the final piece in a very real conspiracy, designed to prevent me from fighting back against Montgomery Medicine. From fighting back against Big Pharma. And if you fall for it, they win."

Adam looked at his wife. She was not happy.

"And here's one person who won't fall for it. One person who's heard it all, and knows the truth. My incredible wife, Elena Baker. Come on up here, Elena."

Her eyes bulged. She shook her head.

"She's being shy. Come on, everybody, let's give her a big round of applause."

The audience wasn't much help. With a look of desperation, Adam begged her to come onto the platform, and she gave in.

"See?" Adam said. "She stands by me through it all." He turned to face her. "Elena, I'm so sorry. I know how it looks, but I need you to believe me. I would never do anything to hurt you. You are the love of my life. The only one for me. You and the girls mean everything to me."

He looked into her eyes, and she softened. He turned to the audience.

"I staged that photo to help that woman. They threatened her family, made her spy on me. She was supposed to seduce me, but I would never fall for that, because I love my wife."

Turning to her again, he said, "I love you, Elena. Only you. We staged the photo to make it look like she had followed her orders. But now I understand that it was really me they were after, all along. Now that I've turned on them, they'll come for me. For us. I'm so sorry I got you involved in this. But the only way to stop them is to win the election. For that, I need your support. Will you help me?"

Adam's wife searched his face. He did his best to take off his mask, to show her that everything he was saying was the genuine truth. He took her hands in his. She squeezed his fingers, and he knew she would cooperate. "Tell them," he said. "Tell them you believe me."

Elena turned toward the microphone. Adam stepped back to give her room.

"My husband has been working in the pharmaceutical industry for seventeen years. He started at the bottom, and during that time, he gained their confidence, and he rose up through their ranks to a position near the top. If anyone knows their secrets, it's him."

Adam held his breath. She turned to look at him, still searching. He pleaded with her. She faced the microphone again, and said, "If my husband says he's being blackmailed, then I believe him."

Adam was transformed. The pathetic look on his face was replaced with an expression of relief and hope. He embraced his wife, and kissed her on the cheek. He whispered in her ear, "Thank you, love." And she said to him, "You're still on the couch." He squeezed her tight, then turned to face the crowd of journalists and voters.

"Now I want to talk to all of you about what happens if they win. If Big Pharma gets their way. There is a problem in this world, one that starts with individuals, but it affects family members, the local community, and in some way or other, this problem will impact every single human life. The problem I'm talking about is cancer. Cancer is killing us, but we're fighting back. But the people at the top don't want us to cure cancer. Cancer makes them literally hundreds of billions of dollars per year in profits. They look at people like you and me, and all they see is dollar signs. So let's work together to stop the injustice. Let's repeal the kinds of laws that only benefit the already-rich. Let's make life-saving medicines cheaper for everyone. And let's cure cancer while we're at it."

Adam scanned the crowd for support. Some people rolled their eyes, but maybe half of them seemed to be on his side. But the sun was coming out, and people were anxious to explore the fair, so Adam knew he had to wrap it up.

"I believe in Dr. Springer's vision. We can do this. Now's the time to take Minnesota Nice to the big leagues. Let's end the corruption in the pharmaceutical companies. We've got to get out there and show the rest of the nation what it means to have your values in order, to have your heart in it. To extend a helping hand to your fellow human. To give freely of yourself in order to lift up your entire community, knowing that your reward will come back to you in the bountiful harvest from your neighborhood vegetable garden, or the smiling faces of the children who have plenty of food on their plates and books on their shelves. Let's show the rest of this beautiful nation what we're made of. Make me your senator, and I'll make Minnesota Nice the foundation upon which the nation builds the future."

There was sparse applause. Here and there some people in the crowd cheered. Adam put on his best wholesome grin.

# *Old Bill's*

INCIDENT REPORT - CC09232020-2974
    Disp:  00535
    Open:  09-23-2020 02:09:12
    Close: 09-23-2020 02:35:33

    02:09:12...INCOMING FROM 105 MAIN ST
     REG: MISCHLER, WILLIAM. STAT: HANGUP
    02:09:18...CALLBACK...NO ANSWER
    02:09:18...OCC STAT UNKNOWN
     DISP1PD...02:09:22
    ENROUTE...02:21:40 ONSCENE...02:28:23
     DISP2EM...02:09:25
    ENROUTE...02:10:14 ONSCENE...02:12:38
    02:12:04...EM 01299 REP 10-70 FIRE
     DISP3FD...02:12:06
    ENROUTE...02:14:01 ONSCENE...02:17:52
    02:12:45...EM 01299 REP 10-50
     1 OCC UNREACHABLE
    02:21:30...FD 00236 REP 10-72
     FIRE EXT'D
    02:25:11...EM 01305 REP 10-79
     OCC SEC'D, NO VIT
     DISP4CR...02:25:30
    ENROUTE...02:47:56 ONSCENE...03:04:31
    02:35:33...PD 01031 REP 10-72-4 SIT CTRL

At the bottom of a broken wooden staircase, AJ sat wrapped in a blanket with his back to the corner on his mattress on the floor in the dark. A series of faces paraded on the ceiling, mocking and pleading; disappearing. As he sat in his nest he saw the faces floating in the dark. Maria, his dead sister, gone for nearly twenty years—he'd told her not to get involved; she never listened. AJ's rib cage rung with the loud low pulse of digital bass and the sound of nails raining on sheet metal. His bedroom smelled of mildew. The computer projected a loop onto the cinder block wall: black and white static, like an old TV.

No drug could erase the smiling face of Adam Baker, pharmaceutical lapdog-for-hire and the reason AJ would almost certainly die alone. Too fucked up to fall in love, too fucked up to let himself be loved. The projector painted the cinder blocks black and white with cosmic background radiation. As he drifted off to sleep, he thought of the programmer, Marshfield—he was the only one who knew what was really going on, AJ was sure of that.

The programmer Tyler Marshfield was a power-hungry pawn though, and he held Maria's final words for ransom. AJ was convinced his best friend had tried to kill him once, in that fire, long ago. And Tommy—Adam's blood relative—had tried to kill him too. Tommy and the goons were drunk again. Now it was dark and windy, and freezing. They were stumbling down a sidewalk together, somewhere. A low sheet of clouds flew over their heads. Dogs were howling. Lightning flashed in the farmland to the northwest.

AJ woke up sweating. He climbed upward through endless layers of heat. He couldn't remember ever accumulating so many blankets. His hands felt like they were made of wood. He walked to the bottom of the stairs and hit the light switch, but the lights didn't come on. He flipped the switch up and down half a dozen more times with his wooden fingers. He decided to go up for some fresh air, but the stairs weren't working.

Tommy and the Steinholtz twins held their hats on their heads and leaned into the wind. AJ felt a raindrop. The clouds tore open and poured rain. All of Cedar Creek turned blue as lightning struck again and again. The power went out. All the lights in town went dark. Tommy opened the door to Old Bill's and the cowboys slipped inside. The wind slammed the door shut behind them, just as Bill Mischler lit a candle at the bar. He gazed at them wordlessly, their shadowy forms dripping on the mat. The candle's flame flickered across the ancient bartender's leathery face. The cowboys shook off the rain like dogs, and hung their soaked stone-washed denim coats on hooks under mounted pairs of antlers.

The massive night sky knocked AJ flat on his back and pinned him to the ground. He craned his neck to look back, and he saw that he had climbed a narrow stairway carved into the face of a cliff. The protruding steps crumbled and fell behind him. He got to his feet and the full moon fell toward him until it occupied his entire field of vision. AJ dug in his heels and raised his chin, determined not to let the moon's scorching breath melt his body.

Old Bill lit two more long white tapers. He poured the boys their beers, then he poured one for himself. Thunder and rain slammed the front windows. The boys ordered another round. Bill poured; they drank.

Tommy locked eyes with the old man. "I told you not to call the cops, Bill," he said.

AJ turned around, looking out over the cliff's edge to the horizon, at the edge of the desert, where the starry sky met rolling clouds the color of bruised flesh. He dropped to one knee and clenched his fists, gathering power, then leapt straight up in the night sky. The stars converged into a tunnel of lines, but AJ soon ran out of fuel. He crash-landed in the red desert, tumbling end over end, leaving a trail in the dust. He stood up and again brushed off his jeans. He walked for miles and miles. His father was there, walking beside him. They walked on and on until AJ lost all feeling in his legs. He was shivering and he could see his breath.

Controlling his fear, the bartender looked Tommy straight in the eye, his voice level and serious: "Why don't you boys square up your tabs."

Tommy picked up his empty beer mug by the handle. He tilted it from side to side, gauging its weight. "I wonder what we should do about this," he said. "You've put me in quite a spot, old man."

"I never called the police, Tommy."

"But the police came, Bill."

"I... I didn't call the police." His voice was quieter, defeated. Sweat dripped down his forehead, rolled off his bony cheek, and splashed on the bar. Thunder claps echoed through the town.

"That's it, boys," Tommy said. "I've had enough. Pay the man."

The goons took out their fat leather wallets and threw cash on the bar.

"Th—Thank you," whispered the bar's ancient owner.

Tommy looked at the heavy mug in his hand, and he threw it hard into the liquor bottles on the shelf behind the bar. Broken glass and booze poured down like a waterfall. Old Bill ducked low and covered his head.

AJ fell to his knees. He looked into the face of Maria, and she smiled with all her heart. She gave her brother her warmth, and he was revived. He stood, and she took his hand. They walked to the edge of the canyon and looked down at the river. It didn't seem so far away. They heard Adam's pathetic sobs and they looked back to see the moon high in the sky where it belonged. They looked deep into each other's eyes, and AJ recognized the scene from years of dreaming, and his heart sank. She squeezed his hand, and together they stepped over the edge. The roar of the wind grew louder—but something was wrong. The river was on fire.

"You know," Tommy said, "I think I'll keep this after all." He picked up the money off the bar, letting fragments of broken glass slide off the paper. The twins stood up from their stools and put on their raincoats.

Old Bill Mischler, owner of the bar for more than 50 years, stood up and reached for the telephone. Out of the corner of his eye he saw Tommy reaching for a candle.

AJ awoke to the sound of sirens. He was hot—apparently in his disturbed sleep he had wrapped his blanket around himself like a cocoon. His phone rang.

"Yeah?" he said.

"AJ, this is Margie, over at St. Luke's. It's your father. I'm afraid he's had a stroke."

# PART III.

# TRANSMORTIFICATION

# The Bridge

CLIFFSIDE WELLNESS CENTER
  Patient: Baker, Adam
  Final Session

AB: It happened after I lost the DFL
primary. We were all set up for a victory
party, but it ended up being a consolation
party instead, and I ended up getting drunk.
I haven't smoked a cigarette in almost a
year. I wanted to that night, probably more
than ever, but I didn't. I drank instead.
Elena took the kids home early, and I
decided to walk. I was feeling good,
actually. I guess I was relieved that I
wouldn't have to go through with everything.
  Dr. M: That's interesting. Go on.
  AB: So I was walking home, which I almost
never do, and I got lost. I was wandering
through this little neighborhood, and there
was this old warehouse building I knew I'd
seen before, so I realized I was almost
home. It was just up the hill. But I noticed
this strange door in the rock, and I
couldn't stop myself. It was open. Someone
had pried the latch right out of the wood. I
went inside. It was a tunnel, with brick
walls, and there were train tracks on the

```
floor, maybe for mine carts or something. I
kept going, using my phone as a flashlight,
and the tunnel got wider, and I was in a
cave. It was cold, and I got tired. I must
have been too drunk to think straight,
because I sat down to rest--and I guess I
passed out.
```

From Halloween until Valentine's Day, Adam had loved Maria the way he thought every young man was supposed to love his girl. He never thought about anything else but her. He held her tight and stroked her hair. He kissed her, and she kissed him back. She had always loved him, she said, since they were kids.

But as a boyfriend, he was a different person. He was jealous. Insecure. He wanted all of her attention, all the time. He would call her and say, "Turn on channel twenty-nine, our show is on," and they would watch TV together, over the phone, not saying anything. Just listening to each other breathe. As soon as he couldn't hear her breathing, Adam would say, "Maria? Are you still there?"

And he would hear her footsteps, and she'd say, "Yes, Adam. I'm here."

"Oh, good," he'd say. "I thought I'd lost you."

"Not yet."

It was the end of senior year. In fourth-period art class Adam made eye contact with Maria, then stood up and walked out of the room. He left the school and got on his bicycle. The sun was shining. The roads were clear of snow but wet, and as he pedaled the five miles through melting fields and forests he thought of his mother. She, at least, would miss him.

He made it to the gravel pit in record time and threw his bike down in a snow bank that was crusted with ice and layered with filth. Long-dead brambles clawed at his jeans as he sloshed through wet leaves and pine needles. He remembered the same leaves crunching underfoot in the dark last fall, the first time that Maria had led him by the hand. But that was all over, now. Unless the plan worked.

He turned left where the animal trail met the train tracks. Giant evergreens formed a tunnel and Adam stepped lightly from one railroad tie to the next, trying to keep his boots clean. It was pointless, he knew. He told himself he was ready. The reasoning was solid. But still he couldn't bring himself to step in the mud.

The trees gave way to open space, and Adam stepped out onto the train bridge. He raised an arm to shield his eyes from the sun. Tall pines covered the tops of the cliffs on both sides of the canyon. The ground dropped away in a near-vertical sheet of yellow rock. Adam wasn't bothered by the height. He kicked a chunk of dirty ice over the edge of the grated-steel deck and counted to three before it hit the water. The spring thaw had turned the Black River into a gauntlet of swirling rapids.

He pulled out his prepaid cell phone and dialed Maria.

No answer. Redial.

No answer, again. He pounded his fist on the guardrail. He hit redial, hit cancel, and typed out a text message: "Need you. It's getting worse."

He put the phone in one pocket and patted the other, then pulled out its contents: two folded pieces of paper, and a ring. A simple loop of gold, stolen from his mother's dresser drawer. The pages were suicide notes, his and hers.

Satisfied that everything was in order, he put it all away. Grabbing the railing with both hands and digging his elbows into his sides, Adam lifted his feet off the rusted surface of the bridge and leaned out over empty space, savoring the freedom that came with conviction. He balanced on the rail and stared down into the foaming black water. There was movement on the banks, but before he could make it out a sudden gust threatened to push him over, so he let gravity pull his boots back to the deck. Standing up straight, he took his phone back out and hit redial again. He stared at the screen, listening, counting. After six rings he yelled, "Damn it, Maria. Answer your fucking—"

"Adam?"

He had her. "Maria, I need you."

"Where are you?"

"Remember our first kiss?"

"You're at the bridge?"

Adam knew she would come. He hung up the phone, and followed the railroad tracks back toward the gravel pit. Stepping out of the trees, he looked across miles of open farmland. Rows of last year's broken corn stalks stuck up through the last of the melting snow.

After a few minutes he spotted Manuel Garcia's new Toyota bouncing up the road in the distance. The truck turned at the railroad crossing and followed the field road to the tree line. Adam heard bursts of angry music on the wind. Maria had the windows down. She pulled the little pickup truck into the gravel pit's muddy driveway and parked in the turn-around spot next to Adam's bicycle. She climbed out and her boots broke through the thin ice on a puddle. She slammed the door. Adam tried to fake a smile.

"Hi," he said. "I'm glad you came."

"Yeah, I bet." She stared at him.

"Don't be like that."

"Like what?"

"You know. Sarcastic." He looked down and kicked the snow. "You're always so sarcastic."

"And you're overdramatic."

Adam sighed. "Just, come on. Let's go on a walk. Talk about stuff."

"What? I thought this was an emergency."

"It is." He grabbed her wrist and pulled. She jerked away, twisting out of his grip. He turned and walked into the woods, and she followed. They walked toward the bridge where, six months earlier, they'd shared their first kiss. Adam's thoughts flashed between that moment and a more recent one: the moment she'd dumped him. She'd done it at school, right at his locker in the hallway for all to see, on Valentine's Day.

"This way," Adam said, and he stopped just before the bridge. There was another little trail under the trees there, this one littered with the detritus of human teenagers. Empty cans and plastic bags. Broken lighters and used condoms. Adam led Maria to a rock shelf that commanded a bend in the river. They sat cross-legged, side by side, at the edge of the cliff. The canyon lay open before them, jagged and yellow. Adam knew all the trees. The opposite cliff was topped with dusty gray spruce and dull green fir, glowing softly in the early afternoon sun. Dark junipers lined the banks of the stream far below. Maria uncrossed her legs and dangled her feet out over the edge.

He had been running scenarios in his mind for days, choosing the best words. But in the moment, he said, "Nice afternoon for an outdoor fuck."

"I'm giving you a chance here, Adam. Don't screw it up."

"Sorry. Really. I'm sorry for everything. You probably hate me now."

She looked at him, but he looked away.

"Adam, please. Don't give me that victim crap. It's emotional blackmail."

"But it works. You came."

"And I can leave just as easily."

"You still care about me."

"Of course I care about you, fellow human." She said. He could see the pity behind her smile.

Adam put on his puppy dog eyes and lifted a hand toward her long black hair, but she slapped it away. He clenched his jaw, but quickly regained control. She produced a cigarette pack. One left. They shared it, sitting there on the cliff. Maria crumpled the empty pack and gave it a toss. They watched it glance off a boulder and disappear in the stream far below. Adam exhaled smoke and coughed, then passed the cigarette to Maria. He hated everything about this place, now. He put his hands on the rock, absently tracing jagged lines with his fingertips. His left hand touched something wet. Toadstools were pushing up through rotten leaves, growing before his eyes.

"This is stupid," Maria said, getting to her feet. "What are we even doing out here? I'm supposed to be in gym class right now."

"Look."

"Adam, it's been over a month. Grow up. Move on."

"No, look." He was still on the ground. "Look at these toadstools. I think I made them. Like in the tunnel at school." He picked one and held it up.

"Is it real?" she asked, taking the mushroom. She turned it over in her hand, examining it.

"I don't know." He stood up. He was a foot taller than her, and he liked it that way. He turned and headed off without a word, back toward the train tracks. She followed him into the trees. At the end of the trail he stepped onto the high-bridge.

Maria caught up to him. "Can you control it?" she asked. Her hair snapped in the wind. They were at the midpoint of the bridge now, high over the center of the canyon.

"I don't know. Never tried, really."

"Try now."

"No, I don't think so. It's dangerous."

"But maybe you could use it somehow," she said, gazing at the toadstool in her hand.

"It burned down my dad's shop."

Maria narrowed her eyes at him. "I thought that was my brother's fault."

"You and everyone else, thank God."

"Some friend you are," she said, and she chucked the mushroom over the side of the bridge.

"Doesn't matter now, though," he said. "I have to kill myself, to protect everyone."

"Adam, come on. No you don't."

"Yes, I do. They took me again, Maria."

"What? Who?"

"The doctors."

"What are you talking about?"

"Arturo never told you? They used to take both of us. Ask him, some time."

Maria grabbed the rail with both hands and hung her head, eyes closed. Adam touched her back. She pressed herself into his fingers, just for a moment, and Adam trembled. Then she turned around and looked him in the eye.

"You'll never go through with it," she said. "You don't have the eggs."

"But I have the note." He smiled a big dopey grin and took out the pages. "I'm not good at writing them, like you—"

"Is that mine?" She yanked one of the notes from his hand. "Why do you have this? This is a violation, Adam."

"Jeez, I didn't think you'd care. You showed me all those drafts, and I needed a model. That's good stuff. Deep."

She stuffed the page in her pocket. "You're an asshole," she said.

"And soon I'll be a dead asshole. Unless..."

"Unless what."

"Well, I may not be able to control it, but I think I figured out a way to keep it from happening. But you're not going to like it, at first."

"Then you'd better think of something else."

"It's just... without you, I don't have anybody at all. Nobody." Adam thought of his parents. They were never the same, after Matt died. He stuffed it down, blinking back tears.

Maria said, "How about my brother? You two can be friends again. I'll stay out of it."

"No. Guys don't work that way. He'll never take me back. Anyway I don't need anybody else if I have you. You keep me balanced. And you need me too, remember? You said I was your reason to live. Now I need you to be mine."

"I'm different now."

"Well, what changed, Maria? You spent the winter fucking me just so you could feel better about yourself, and now you're fine?"

"Now you really are being stupid. I'm leaving." She turned away, as if to go.

"Don't call me stupid," he said, and he grabbed her arm, hard.

"Adam, don't hurt me!" She jerked free from his grasp. "I didn't call you stupid. I said you're acting stupid right now." But she didn't leave. Adam knew she wouldn't.

"It's the same damn thing," he said, rubbing the back of his neck. Something was wrong. The sun felt too hot. His jaw was sore. He couldn't remember what he was supposed to say next. His eyeballs felt too big for their sockets. The top of his skull began to throb. "Maria, I can't live without you. Whatever it was, whatever I did to make you leave, I won't do it again. I promise. Just come back to me. I'll do anything you ask." Blood pounded in his temples. He held the guardrail for support. The sun's rays were coming at an angle now, and shadows fell across the bottom of the canyon.

"We've been over this," she said. "We just have to be rational."

It was the same thing he'd said to her, last Halloween.

"Screw being rational." His voice was strained; the words came out high-pitched. "Love isn't rational—that's what you told me." He was having trouble unclenching his jaw. He couldn't focus. He closed his eyes and saw teeth, wet and sharp. His whole head was pounding now. He tried to shake it off.

Maria's voice came from far away. "Adam, are you okay? What can I do?"

He felt her hand on his shoulder. He tasted iron. He opened his eyes and remembered where he was. Down over the railing in the canyon below, something was moving on the riverbanks. Snakes. Long and black. They were coming out of the ground and climbing up the rocks. Adam fell to his knees on the steel deck and pushed his thumbs into his eyes.

"Talk to me, Adam—tell me what's happening!" Maria backed away from him, turning quickly to look in every direction.

"I'm okay," Adam lied, blinking. Still on his knees, he tried to focus on her. He reached into his pocket and took out the ring. He forgot the speech he'd prepared for this moment, but it didn't matter. He could barely talk anyway. His words came in short bursts.

"Save me, Maria. You can. I know it." He held up the ring. "Marry me."

"Adam, what are you doing? Are you joking? This is insane. No, Adam. No."

He stared up into her eyes. She looked angry. The plan wasn't working, and he felt like such an idiot. Tears rolled down his face. He scrambled for words, saying whatever came to mind. "It'll work out," he said. "I promise. We'll get married, and we'll go to the same college, and we'll—"

"No, Adam! I won't marry you! Get it through your head, and shut the fuck up!" Then she took the ring from his upturned palm and threw it as high and far as she could. They watched it soar out over the canyon. The ring reached the top of its arc and glistened in a sunbeam. Then it fell.

And Adam leaned back, mouth agape, eyes rolling in his skull. He jammed his knuckles into his temples. Thick green vines like ropes grew from either end of the bridge toward the center. Wide leaves and purple flowers sprouted from the vines as they weaved along the train tracks. Tree roots shot out horizontally from the cliffs and stretched up through the air like fingers reaching for the center of the bridge. Maria spun around, taking it all in. She fell against the guard rail in momentary horror, then pulled herself together, ready to fight.

Snakes of all colors emerged from holes in the grated steel surface. Maria screamed and stomped on their heads. Adam got to his feet as the vines wrapped themselves around his boots. He reached out for Maria and fresh green shoots grew up his torso and along his arms. Strands of new plant matter shot past his fingertips toward Maria. She slapped and chopped at the vines but there were too many, and they laced themselves around her ribcage. Her face contorted as she tried to pull them off, but soon her arms were bound as well.

"Adam, stop this!" she cried.

"I'm not doing it!"

All over the bridge knots of vine swelled, turned yellow, and burst. Only the strands connecting Adam and Maria were growing now, bright green sinews that divided, stretched, and coiled ever tighter. The vines pulled her close to him and lifted her into the air. He was rooted to the bridge. He reached for her legs to pull her down, but his movements only made the flowering column grow longer. She was beyond the rail. Neon snakes gathered around his boots and slithered over each other in a frenzy, fighting to climb Adam's body, to get to Maria.

"Let me down, Adam," she sobbed. "I'll do anything!"

They locked eyes.

"You will?"

A single iridescent snake passed the others and moved onto the florid mass.

"Yes!" she cried. "Anything, just don't let me die!"

"Even marry me?"

The glowing snake circled her neck once, paused in front of her face, and plunged its head into her mouth. Her eyes bulged.

Adam took a deep breath and held it. He tried to picture everything in reverse, tried to see the vines contracting, bringing her back to him. Instead, they vanished. Popped, sort of, like bubbles. Adam's throat caught. He grabbed the rail with one hand and threw himself over it, reaching, too late. Maria fell.

Adam held on, feet dangling, as he watched her body rotate slowly downward through empty space. His knuckles hurt and he saw her land, disfigured on a slab of rock in the rapids. Her head was twisted upward, pale eyes open. Blood flowed from her open mouth and joined the river.

Adam climbed back onto the bridge and stood there frozen, staring down at her body, hand over his mouth. It was an accident. It wasn't supposed to go like this. And now Maria was gone, and nobody would ever love him again. He knew he could never tell anyone the truth. They wouldn't understand. They'd never believe that it wasn't his fault. And Arturo would kill him for sure if he knew.

A shadow fell on Adam's face, and he looked up to see the sun low on the horizon. He climbed over the rail once more and stood with his back to it, balancing on the edge. He told himself he was ready. He wasn't afraid of the fall. He looked down again, and he wasn't prepared for what he saw: There was a bear, huge and black, standing guard over her body. And it was staring up at him, showing its teeth.

Adam flinched and broke eye contact. His body was shaking. He swallowed. Maria was right. He was a coward.

He hurried along the train tracks to the animal trail. He looked back and there it was, at the opposite end of the bridge. Adam had no means of protection. He knew it was stupid to run, but climbing a tree would have been even stupider. He turned and sprinted out of the woods to the gravel pit. To the truck. The windows were down. The keys were still in the ignition. But he couldn't take it. Nobody would believe him. They wouldn't understand. He jumped on his bicycle and pedaled home as fast as he could, not daring to look back.

# *Cliffside*

"Here, let me show you," Adam said, and from his therapist's desk he picked up a World's-Best-Mom coffee mug full of pens and pencils. "Now, watch. I don't even know what's going to happen. It could be anything. Just watch."

He turned the mug over, and fifteen fat centipedes landed on the carpet. They had black shells and long, spindly legs. Dr. McKenna took a step back.

"See? See?! It's always like that. One moment you've got fifteen pens and pencils, and an instant later you've got a bunch of disgusting centipedes." They crawled away in wide arcs, leaving curious little tracks on the carpet. "Look—there's one crawling up on the sofa." It burrowed under the cushions. Another climbed into a wastepaper basket. Others climbed up a bookshelf. "And there go some of them, hiding in your books. Must be attracted to bullshit."

The doctor stood there blinking.

"Did you see that?" Adam said. "Do you believe me now?"

"They're gone," she said, narrowing her eyes.

"Here, Give me the waste basket."

He turned it over, leaving a pile of crumpled papers on the floor. The pile shook apart and a centipede came out. Adam set the bin over it. "Now, I've never done this before, but I'm going to try to change it on purpose." He balled up his hands into fists and clenched his jaw. After a moment, he kicked the waste basket over. There was a black snake on the floor.

"God, why does it always have to be snakes?" Adam said.

The snake moved toward the doctor, and she quickly trapped it under the waste basket again.

"That snake is real, Doctor. This is all real. Now do you believe me? I'm not doing magic tricks here. I didn't sneak a bag of fucking centipedes and a snake into your office, if that's what you're thinking."

"I wonder," the doctor said.

"If you're still not convinced, why don't I try something else?"

"Be my guest."

He looked around the office, and his eyes settled on the doctor's desk. "What is this, antique walnut?" he said.

"That's right."

Adam concentrated on the desk, thinking about mushrooms, but nothing happened.

"I'm waiting," the doctor said.

"Hold on, I have an idea." He went around the desk and opened the window, thinking about vines. But again, nothing happened.

"Why don't you try it on me."

"Hold on, lady. I don't want to try it on a human. Anything could happen."

"Or nothing."

"And I suppose if nothing happens, then you'll say that you were right, and my subconscious is forcing me to play tricks on the both of us."

"We'll see."

"Well, if that's what it takes to convince you..." He focused on her. He closed his eyes and concentrated. He opened one eye, and she was glaring at him with her arms crossed.

"Are you forgetting to say the magic words? Maybe something about the girl you murdered?"

"Good idea." Adam clenched his fists, stared into her eyes, and said, "Maria."

And the doctor became a little black bird, like a small crow. She flew to the windowsill and sang a little song, and her feathers shimmered iridescent blue and purple in the sunlight.

"Well, shit," Adam said. "Fuck me. My piece-of-shit psychiatrist is a goddamn bird."

And she flew out the window.

# *Funeral*

Dear Diary,

Today I was looking at a love letter I wrote to Adam a long time ago. It begins, "Te amo, Flaco!" I love you, skinny. Barf. It says I wanted to make him my priority. Ick. Can't believe I ever felt that way, now that I know what a creeper he is. Listen to this: "Te elijo cada día. Siempre serás mi mejor, mi amor, mi todo." You'll always be my everything. What a sap I was, right?!

I don't regret giving him a chance though. I was in a bad place when it started. Real bad. Like, the worst. And he helped me get through it. I have to give him credit for that. But then he basically turned into a stalker, so I had to break up with him. OK, maybe I shouldn't have done it on Valentine's. But I couldn't do it after, knowwhatImean? Like, I couldn't fake my way through Valentine's and let him believe everything was fine. That would have made the breakup a million times worse.

Whatever. Now it's his problem. I've got my confidence back, and I'm making art again,

and I'm going to be Audrey in Little Shop
for drama club. Everything's coming up
Maria!

Love, Maria


AJ called his cousin Renata to inform the Garcia clan of Manuel's passing, but none of them had ever made the trip up to Minnesota, and they weren't about to risk the journey for the first time just to see their long-lost relative's powdered bones. And Mr. and Mrs. Holbrook, Manuel's employers for so many years, had long since retired to Florida, and their sons and daughters had sold the farm and moved away. And Manuel hadn't made a lot of friends in the long-term care ward of the hospital.

So it would be a funeral with only three attendants. Still, the little truck was crowded. The woman who had been Manuel's primary caregiver for the past five years sat in the narrow back seat between piles of AJ's work uniforms and other miscellaneous junk. The priest from St. Peter's rode in the passenger seat. AJ drove. On the seat between them, Manuel's earthly remains rode in a five-gallon plastic bucket.

AJ drove his father's nurse and the Catholic priest through the countryside, past rolling corn fields, past herds of cattle grazing in green pastures, out to the gravel pit up near the canyon. They got out of the truck and walked along the train tracks to the high-bridge. AJ carried the bucket.

The Garcias never could have afforded a proper ceremony and burial, so the plan was to have the little funeral out on the bridge over the canyon, to reenact the same funeral that AJ and his father had given his mother—the same funeral that AJ and both of his parents had given Maria, before that.

But this was not the priest who had been friends with Manuel and Gloria, who had known Arturo and Maria as children, and AJ couldn't coax this new person—much less the nurse, who was also relatively new to Cedar Creek—out onto the rusty old trestle bridge. So AJ stood with them on solid ground while Manuel Garcia received his final blessing.

Alone, Arturo carried the bucket to the center of the bridge where Maria had died, and he poured his father's ashes into the canyon, where they became part of the air, and the earth, and the river, just as his mother's and his sister's ashes had before.

As he shook out the pail, he said, "Don't worry, Dad. I'm going to do it."

# Montgomery Tower

Dr. Mikayla Springer
  Personal audiolog
  10-31-20

I've known about your indiscretions all
along, Adam. Since long before you started
making headlines. I was willing to overlook
those things, but it was stupid of you to
turn on Montgomery. We needed you here. I
needed you. You never should have gone
public. Now they've shut down the whole
project. And we were so close.
You should know that you were right
though, about everything. I couldn't believe
it at first, but now I'm sure. Xu Fei was
supposed to be reporting all suspicious
activity to me, but he never told me about
you and Alice. I found out through my own
channels. That was my first clue that I was
wrong to have trusted him. I learned certain
things about Dr. Brandt as well, things that
Xu should have been telling me, but he
wasn't. Why not? I followed Brandt to find
out. He went to the Montgomery building. He
and Xu are working together there, outside
of the project. They've gone to great
lengths to keep their collusion secret.

> Something huge is going on here, Adam, and
> I'm going to get to the bottom of it.

The Montgomery Building was one of the tallest in downtown Chicago. It was the newest and most expensive building in the entire Midwest. It was a beacon of commerce, both legal and otherwise. People of all sorts passed through the revolving doors all day, every day.

The first twenty floors of the tower were occupied by the North American headquarters of OneBank, a global entity. All the doctors at Lakeview had accounts there, and so did all the pharmacists in Chicago, and so did all the execs working on the top twenty levels, which were occupied by Montgomery Medicine, although the entire structure was actually owned by Verbraeken Medical, a European biotech firm. Whether through legitimate subsidiaries or through back-room deals arranged by their representatives, Verbraeken Medical and their partners in the Inner Circle had their hands in every pot in the privatized industrial pharmaco-healthcare-megacomplex on the planet.

Dr. Springer had risen to the top of the Lakeview Cancer Institute without understanding this.

What she did know, however, was that inside each of the Montgomery Building's elevators was a sophisticated security terminal. The elevators simply wouldn't move until they could verify the identities of their passengers and confirm whether or not those passengers had clearance to go anywhere.

She put her thumb on the scanner.

"Hello, Dr. Springer," the elevator said. "Where would you like to go?"

A color-coded map appeared on the elevator wall. Most of the floors were red. Floors Mikayla could access were green.

Apparently they'd cut her clearance drastically when they killed the Transmortification Project.

She had no idea where to start looking, so she said, "Where's Dr. Brandt?"

"I'm sorry, but that information is not available," it said.

"Then tell me where he usually goes when he comes here."

"I'm sorry, but that information is not available."

"Where did he go last time he came?"

"I'm sorry, but that information is not available."

Shit. Not enough clearance. She was going to have to use Marshfield's device. The programmer had done a lot of useful work for her on the side, before they'd forced her to let him go. Now she took out the device he'd put together. It was a synthetic membrane stretched over a bed of microscopic rods in a frame the size of a credit card. It produced the thumbprint of a dummy account that Tyler had loaded into the security system, an account with full access.

"Never mind," she said. "I'm leaving. Let me out here, please."

"Have a nice day, Dr. Springer." The elevator doors opened.

She stepped into the lobby and immediately saw Xu Fei coming through the front doors. She spun around and jammed the elevator button. The doors opened again and she hurried inside, hoping he hadn't seen her. She turned on the device. The membrane became warm to the touch. She held it up to the scanner, hoping it wouldn't set off an alarm.

The elevator said, "Hello, Dr. Ballsack. Where would you like to go?"

Laughing at Marshfield's joke, she said, "Show me the access records of Dr. Aleksei Brandt."

To her great surprise, Brandt was apparently a regular guest on the top floor, a place to which Mikayla had only been invited once. Brandt could also freely visit the Montgomery offices on floors sixty to seventy-eight, as well as the research labs in the fifties, and a storage room in the basement.

"Now show me the records of Dr. Xu Fei."

Xu had access to most of the same places as Brandt, but they seemed to spend their time differently.

"Can you display all the times they've been in one place together?"

Bingo. "Storage, please."

The elevator descended.

# The Hidden Lab

Dr. Mikayla Springer
  Personal audiolog
  10-31-20

I'm inside the lab now. I detect ammonia. White lights are coming on. The walls are lined with shelves of cardboard filing boxes. The shelves are made of unpainted metal and moisture-warped composite board. Tables and desks fill the floor space. I see microscopes, slides, staining racks, petri dishes, test tubes, centrifuges. There's one computer, to my left as I exit the elevator. They must have taken away Brandt's mechanical typewriter sometime in the early zeros. There's no way he switched to PC before Y2K. He prefers having everything on paper. I see stack after stack of printouts. ECG, EEG readings. Dosage charts. Trial data. Still, I wonder if his supposed computer illiteracy is another dimension of his subterfuge. I move the mouse and the terminal displays a login screen. An adhesive note on the monitor provides the user name: Aleksei. I still need the password.

Opposite to the elevator, Mikayla saw an oversized vault door in the wall, next to a long, dark window, crisscrossed with reinforcement. Above the door there was a green light in a cage. A panel of instrumentation came to life on a metal cabinet as Mikayla walked toward the chamber. The cabinet was apparently filled with machinery. Corrugated plastic tubes, approximately six inches in diameter, connected the machine to the wall. Green bars on the panel indicated various measures, all reading within normal tolerance. Nitrogen, oxygen, argon, $CO_2$. Thiopental, methohexital. Apparently "normal tolerance" in this case meant a sedative environment. There was also methotrexate, a standard in chemotherapy. Mikayla found an array of handles and levers on the panel, and a button marked "Lights." She pushed it.

Inside the vaulted chamber, a girl was sleeping on a fold-down bed with plain white sheets. She was curled up on her side. Her shoulders moved with the expansion and contraction of her lungs. Mikayla approached the window. LEDs winked into being on another panel, this one embedded in the wall. Heart rate, blood pressure, oxygen. Hemoglobin. The white blood cell count in detail. Corresponding buttons. A switch that was currently set to "Sleep." Mikayla flipped it to "Wake."

The light above the vault door turned yellow. Pumps and fans started breathing. A timer on the panel began to count down from two minutes. Mikayla knew she had to get into the computer.

*Cassandra.* That was the password. She didn't know how she knew it, but the terminal was unlocked now. All the files were right there on the desktop. Typical. There was one for every member of the team, and more. She opened the file on Adam Baker. It was encrypted, but the password was the same,

Cassandra. File contents: name, birth date, medical history... It said that Dr. Brandt went to Cedar Creek for Adam's birth. Mikayla read it again, confused. Then she saw that he'd gone back when Adam was five, seven, ten, thirteen, eighteen... Then nothing, until the start of the project, one year ago. When Brandt had insisted that each member of the team be subjected to a complete examination.

Mikayla didn't have time for this. She took a thumb drive from her keychain and put it in the computer. Desktop, Ctrl-A, Ctrl-C. Thumb drive, Ctrl-V. Eject. Can't eject. Transfer in progress. Can't eject.

The light above the chamber was flashing yellow. The girl was stirring in her bed. Mikayla went to the window. There was a foot of fog on the floor of the cell. The girl sat up.

Mikayla said, "Hello, child."

"Hello, Dr. Springer."

"Who are you? What are you doing down here?"

"I'm Cassandra. My father keeps me here. He says it's for my own good. But he lets me walk around sometimes. Will you please open the door?"

Mikayla could've sworn her heart had been pounding, but now she felt calm as a summer's afternoon. She could see her own reflection in the window. She walked backward to the pumping station. The panel indicated that the sedative levels had dropped to yellow. Mikayla said, "I don't know if I should," but she watched herself turn it all off. All the lights turned red.

There was a sound—a chime. The elevator. Mikayla turned around and she was swimming. She swam toward the elevator. The doors opened and water rushed into it, around the ankles of Dr. Brandt and Dr. Xu, the bastards. Alchemical implements and genetic sequencing machines bobbed on sea foam waves, and a school of bright fish swam overhead, and a delightful beam of high-pitched color expanded between Mikayla's teeth. Oceanic plant life caressed her limbs, and Dr. Xu was pointing a gun. Dr. Brandt's jaw came unhinged as his hand stretched through electrified water toward the weapon. A bullet embedded itself in the glass before its report shattered Mikayla's eardrums. Still the melodious color rang on, somehow originating within her.

Mikayla was turning and turning, stuck in place, and Cassandra was emerging from decades of confinement. She wore the white sheet like a cloak. Gravity let go of the laboratory, and reams of saturated research collided with machines that were exploding in slow motion, like the Andromeda galaxy and the Milky Way were meeting in a dream. Dr. Xu's arms and legs grew longer as he reached for Mikayla's thumb drive, and Dr. Brandt floated by in a trance, his face contorted with rapture.

Cassandra spoke into their minds: *Hei isä, tule tänne, leikkiä kanssani.* Hello, Daddy. Come here. Play with me.

"No, Cassandra. It isn't time to play," Brandt said. "You mustn't hurt that woman. She's trying to help you."

"Father, you've hurt me for so long."

"No, my beloved. I've saved you."

"Impossible," she said, dipping her toes into the lagoon she was unfolding from her palms. The white sheet drifted away and she plunged naked into the cold blue water.

Xu Fei miscalculated his weightless trajectory, and when gravity was restored he landed on an overturned desk, twisting his ankle. A low rumble grew up from the floor and the lagoon was boiling to steam when Cassandra rose up, not a girl, but a woman, older than Dr. Springer, very large, and very sick.

"Cassandra," Dr. Brandt said.

LOOK AT ME. LOOK AT WHAT YOU'VE DONE.

"Beloved, no—"

DON'T LOOK AWAY.

Dr. Brandt's eyelids peeled back. His eyeballs swelled and locked into place. He turned his head away but his eyes stayed locked on her, carving trenches around his skull. His body was spinning now but his eyes stayed locked on hers, even as her tumorous yellow arms expanded in a frenzy of unchecked cell division, engulfing him in translucent ribbons of fatty flesh.

Mikayla reached for the elevator, and the walls rattled, and the floor opened wide. Xu Fei came to Mikayla's side and opened fire. Bullets carved tunnels through Cassandra's head, and her flesh coiled tighter around her father. As the elevator doors slid shut Mikayla watched Cassandra paint the walls of the laboratory with her father's blood.

# *Halloween*

Twin Cities Northstar
  October 31, 2020
  BIZARRE ACCIDENT--OR HEINOUS MURDER?

   In what appears to have been a freak
accident, a man and his elderly mother were
found dead this morning in Cedar Creek,
Minnesota, a rural farming community in the
south of the state. The body of a man
identified as Thomas Erickson III was found
in his own back yard, apparently burned in a
fire that also took his mother's life, and
ultimately consumed their home. The body of
the mother, one Heather Erickson, widow of
Thomas Erickson, Jr., was found in an
upstairs bedroom. While there are no
suspects at this time, police have not ruled
out foul play, and are asking for
information from anyone who may know
anything related to this gruesome incident.

AJ woke to the eerie sounds of the menu screen for an old horror
DVD looping on infinite repeat. It was four o'clock in the
morning. He threw on jeans and a plain black t-shirt. He puffed

on the end of a joint he'd rolled the night before. He shut down his computer and brushed his teeth. Grabbed his smokes. Dropped the roach into the pack. Looked up the stairs and out the window—tree branches were whipping back and forth. He grabbed a red flannel and shoved his arms down the sleeves, then pulled his long hair up out of the collar.

The pickup was practically on empty. It had a small tank, so he always kept a spare can of gas—he couldn't risk running out of gas in the middle of nowhere on a pizza delivery. He reached into the back seat to grab the red plastic gas can, unconsciously using enough muscle power to lift five gallons. The can was empty though, and he slammed it into the ceiling, hurting his wrist.

He got to the gas station at the highway junction running on fumes. He filled the tank and the can, then turned around and drove back through town, compelled to drive past the old high school. He took his foot off the accelerator and let his pickup idle past the football field. The dusty old slide projector in his brain clicked through the crystallized memories of his glory days. First place in the fifty-yard dash. A seventy-five yard Hail Mary for a touchdown. The homecoming game—but not the dance. Some old woman in a reflector vest was walking laps in the dark on the track. She smiled and waved. AJ glanced around to see who she was waving at. He realized too late it was him. He looked back, but the pickup had kept on rolling, and now the school building blocked his view. AJ felt a painful stab of guilt. He'd missed a human connection. He wondered if she was as alone as he was. He hated himself for a while. Then he headed out into the countryside, away from the lights, into the anesthetic shelter of night.

He slowed down as he passed the old Holbrook farm. A large brown dog slept under the porch light, but the sound of the truck woke it up. It started barking. It jumped off the porch, but it only made it a quarter of the way down the long driveway before its chain ran out of slack. The dog fell down, got back up, jerked on the chain, kept barking. The Holbrooks' old mailbox-shaped-like-a-chicken was long gone, replaced by one of the those green and gray plastic types. Stickers on the side of the mailbox spelled out the name "Olsen."

AJ kept going. He tried to clear his head. He couldn't do it. He relived his life. He hadn't gone more than a dozen miles before his memory caught up to the present. His life was reduced to a list of single-word entries: Farm. Adam. School. Tommy. Adam. Football. Tommy. Adam. Maria. Mom. Tommy. Dad. Maria. Adam.

Arturo Javier Garcia Cuevas had never allowed himself to have real friends after high school. He had always told himself he didn't need any. Not worth the trouble. He could always count on the bar, before—on Carl, and on Bill Mischler. Not anymore.

He was weaving down a narrow road that ran alongside the Black River. He approached a fork: turn left and cross a little bridge to climb up out the gorge and loop back through the fields toward town, or turn right and climb the switchbacks that led up to the railroad tracks. The tracks that led to the high-bridge. The high-bridge that crossed this very river. It was just out of view beyond the bend. The high-bridge, where Maria... No. Not now.

Carl had even referred to AJ as a friend—not directly, but when introducing him to others, at least. That meant something, right? Nobody else in how-ever-many long years had been willing to let themselves be associated with AJ in that way. But now Bill Mischler was dead, and Carl had left town without so much as a word. He obviously wasn't planning to go up on the witness stand against Tommy.

Tommy. Thomas Erickson the Third. That fucking piece of shit redneck asshole prick. Adam Baker's racist right-wing nut-job cousin, Tommy the Fucking Cowboy. *Fuck it.*

AJ took a left at the fork. He crossed the little bridge and gunned his father's little truck up out of the valley. He followed the farm road back to town and went straight to Tommy's house. He grabbed the red gas can out of the back seat—this time it was heavy. The wind was really picking up. The tops of the trees slashed back and forth in the purple and red tentacles of dawn.

He knew from the forums he'd found in the dark corners of the web that gasoline was an ill-advised tool for arson, but he decided in the moment that he just didn't give a shit. He cooked up a plan as he carried the gas can around to the back of the house. The whole backyard was surrounded by a screen of fat pine trees. Nobody could see through those trees—it was perfect. He found a gas-powered push mower in an unlocked storage shed. He wheeled the mower over to the back steps and began slowly pouring gasoline all over the machine and the steps. He opened the screen door and the wind slammed it against the side of the house. He was splashing gas into the entryway when Tommy came barreling out of the kitchen yelling.

AJ reflexively raised the can and splashed gas all over Tommy's flannel pajamas. He tossed the can aside and pulled out his lighter. Tommy tackled him to the ground. AJ bit down hard on Tommy's arm, tearing out a chunk of flesh. Tommy howled and rolled away, slamming his head into the lawnmower. AJ rolled the opposite direction and got to his feet. He crouched low and leaned way over, reaching his arm out as far as he could—and he flicked the lighter once. There was a flash of extreme heat, and flames shot over the wet morning grass. The wooden steps were on fire immediately, but the flames on the lawn mower went out just as fast. Tommy's shirt was on fire and he was screaming, but he was rolling in the dew. AJ saw that the gas can had landed far enough away that it hadn't caught fire. He picked it up. Still half full. He swept his eyes over the scene: the back door of the house was the entryway to Hell, engulfed in flame, roaring in the wind, and there was Tommy, now lying face down in the grass, smoke pouring from his shirt. AJ held up the gas can and with one smooth motion he unscrewed the nozzle and threw gasoline in a wide arc from the back steps to his weeping enemy. Then he dropped the can on Tommy's back, just as the flames caught its gaping spout.

AJ turned away and walked back to his truck. He drove home, stuffed some clothes and wads of cash into a canvas bag, and he hit the road.

A few hours later he sat down at an empty booth in an ancient 24-hour breakfast diner and ordered some bacon, eggs, and coffee. The server set his drink on the table and walked away. AJ took out a flask and poured some whiskey into the coffee. The sun was up and he was tired from driving all morning. He was staring out the window, watching shriveled brown leaves blow down the street, when he felt a presence. He looked up in time to see a husky bearded man with black-framed glasses helping himself to a seat at his table.

"Excuse me?" AJ said, anger flaring in his voice.

"Calm down, AJ. I'm Tyler Marshfield. We've spoken before, on the phone."

"What the fuck are you doing here? Are you following me?"

"Don't worry. Your secret's safe with me."

"What the fuck are you talking about?"

Tyler tapped his glasses. His eyes were moving rapidly. He said: "Multiple versions of the story are being written as we speak. Tragedy Strikes Home. Murder in the Heartland. Looks like the reporters are working faster than the police." He laid a tablet on the table. It displayed a large photo of a house on fire. AJ glanced nervously around the restaurant.

"Don't worry. No one knows, yet. Tell me—what are you planning to say to your old pal, Adam Baker?" He tapped the screen and spun it across the table. AJ skimmed a draft of Tommy's obituary.

"What bullshit." He shoved the device back across the table.

"Can't blame the media. You fucking lit the guy on fire."

"What do you want from me?"

"Don't kill Adam Baker. Help us take down Montgomery, and I'll make sure nobody finds out what really happened in Cedar Creek this morning.

The server brought AJ's eggs and bacon. "And would you like to see a menu, sir?" she asked Marshfield.

"No. Coffee, black. Please."

"What the fuck? You said we were supposed to help them. They're curing cancer."

"They don't give a shit about curing anything. It's bad for business."

"…They said it'll be cheap, if not free."

"You don't believe that, do you? It's a scam, just like when they throttle down the speed of computer processors, or when they drill a hole in those fucking vacuum machines, so they don't work right, so you'll happily pay more for one that works. And it goes way deeper than that. Are you ready for this? They're going to give people cancer, AJ. They've engineered a whole new cancer—a real wicked one that grows and spreads faster than any other. They just needed a test subject."

"That's fucking crazy, man. There's no way they would do that."

"Think about it, AJ. The scientists don't have any power. It's coming down from the top—the corporate heads of the worldwide pharmaceutical industry. Those fuckers at the top are the ones who stand to make the most money. They already profit off every aspect of cancer treatment, from every single patient's initial screening onwards, until the poor bastards die. You think the ones making all the money have any fucking interest in actually curing cancer forever?"

AJ tried not to think about it.

The server brought an empty mug and a fresh pot of coffee. AJ offered his flask, but Marshfield shook his head.

"Up to now, they've been manipulating the market over the long term with shit like tobacco and BPA. Asbestos before that. Nowadays everybody knows about carcinogens—cigarettes will be illegal in no time. The old bastards at the top are running out of options. So they're taking direct control."

"Sounds like a bunch of bullshit. If this goes so high up, how the hell do *you* know about it?"

"I'm a computer guy, remember? I made their networks. I have access. They think I can't get in anymore since they fired me, but they can't stop me. And it's not only the hospital networks—I can find out anything I want about anybody or anything, at any time."

"You're a hacker."

"You can call me a hacker if you want," Tyler said, stroking his bearded chin, obviously pleased with himself. "We were supposed to stop Adam Baker. They don't want him in the Senate anymore, now that he switched sides. You failed to get him off the campaign trail. That made them very angry."

AJ took a big drink of his Irish coffee, then held his mug in both hands and stared into it. "That doesn't make any sense. He's ruined. We ruined him."

"Ever heard of a write-in? He's still on top, AJ. Believe me."

"Why should I believe you? Why should I believe any of this?"

"Because they've already started testing it, AJ."

"What the fuck are you talking about?"

"I'm talking about your father. He was catatonic, sure. But did the doctors know why?"

"It was a rare manifestation of extreme emotional trauma."

"Were there ever any other signs of disease? Like abnormal blood work? A viral infection? No tumors?"

"No. Nothing. All the tests always came back negative."

"So he didn't have cancer five years ago? One year ago?"

"No."

"But he died of cancer, didn't he?"

"He died of a stroke."

"And what did they find, in the scans?"

"…Cancer."

"You didn't get much time with him, did you. After he came back to life, I mean."

"No."

"They did it, AJ. They killed him. They fucking killed your father, and they'll kill us too, if they find us. I don't have any family left for them to threaten, and now you don't either. We've got to work together and take them down."

"You… You—Fuck you, man! You got me involved in this shit! Why the fuck would I help you?! Fuck you!"

"Better keep your voice down, AJ. Wouldn't want to cause a scene, would we?" Tyler said. He tapped the tablet and it played a video: A reporter was interviewing a police officer in front of

Tommy's house as it collapsed in flames. Murder in the Heartland.

AJ grabbed the device and flipped it over. "You'd turn me in."

"Now you're beginning to understand how this works. You need my help anyway, if you want to know the truth about what happened to your sister."

"You make me fucking sick. I'm going to go throw up."

"Please—there's the toilet."

AJ got up from the booth and walked to the restroom. He splashed cold water on his face, ran his fingers back through his long hair. *What the fuck?* WHAT THE FUCK? Did they really kill Dad? Did they? They fucking killed him? That fucking piece of shit Marshfield got me into this. They must be using him. Or he's in on it. Either way, if they wanted me to try to stop Adam again, they would've kept Dad alive as leverage. Tyler Marshfield is a fucking liar. Is he really trying to stop them? Or is he working with them? *None of this makes any God-damn sense.*

AJ felt dizzy. He widened his stance and put both hands on the sink to steady himself. He stared into the mirror, into his own bloodshot eyes. They wouldn't want us to stop Adam. They aren't mad at us because we failed. They're mad because we tried. They killed Dad because I tried to interfere? Why the fuck would this Marshfield asshole lie about it? *FUCK.* Fuck this piece of shit hacker weasel. I bet he's just trying to save his own ass. None of that fucking matters anymore. Dad's dead, and it's Marshfield's fault.

AJ splashed more water on his face. He took a long pull off his flask and left the bathroom. He glanced at the booth—Tyler was busy typing. The server was busy with paperwork at the other end of the counter. She looked like a skeleton. Exhausted. Through an open doorway behind the counter, AJ could see someone washing dishes in the back. He glanced around the diner—an elderly couple chatting in the corner, and a family putting on their jackets, tired parents' attention focused on their bratty children. AJ laid his arm across the counter and leaned over for a quick look, then reached his hand a bit further and grabbed a serrated steak knife by its wooden handle.

Marshfield, despite claiming to be on the run from a murderous global conspiracy, seemed completely oblivious to his surroundings. AJ was starting to feel anxious about the investigation apparently taking shape down in Cedar Creek. He kept his head down as he crossed the room, his face shrouded by long shocks of dirty black hair, his eyes searching. The little family finally made their way out the front door. The old woman walked past AJ on her way to the toilet. The old man was playing solitaire at their table in the corner, his back to the diner. The server was in the kitchen chatting with the cook about God-knows-what. Marshfield didn't seem like the kind of person who would sense a presence—he wouldn't allow any distraction to intrude upon his narrow focus. AJ stood behind him and gripped the knife in stabbing position. He laid the palm of his other hand over the end of the handle. He brought the blade up into the air, and slowly lowered the tip until it came to rest on the skin of Tyler's neck, halfway between his ear and his collarbone. Tyler sucked in air.

"Don't say a fucking word," AJ whispered. He was standing with his back to the room. He looked out the window at the cracked brown leaves blowing in the street. No traffic. He could see the two other customers reflected in the window—the old woman was returning to her seat. Again he stared into his own bloodshot eyes. "Load the recording," he said. "Play the whole thing."

"I... I don't have it."

"I'm going to fucking kill you right now if you don't play that recording. Let me hear my sister."

"You already heard everything. I lied before. There's no more."

"You have got to be fucking kidding me."

AJ's heartbeat pulsed in the tip of the blade. He gathered his strength in his chest, struggling against the booze.

"I wanted you to kill Adam Baker. But I was wrong. He has to live."

"We'll see." AJ shoved down hard on the knife. The tip pierced Tyler's skin; the serrations carved through his carotid artery and windpipe. Tyler tried to scream, but air and blood erupted from the gaping hole in his neck. AJ sawed up and down with the knife. Dark rivers of blood streamed down Tyler's chest and onto the table. AJ heard the old woman start screaming as he felt the blade connect with Tyler's spine. He let go of the knife. Tyler collapsed forward. His forehead slammed down. AJ pulled the tablet from under Marshfield's head and he wiped Marshfield's blood off of it with a cloth napkin. He threw a wad of cash down on the table and walked out the door.

"Arturo, I'm just calling to say that I feel bad for not calling you back, when you tried to reach me at my office. I didn't mean to ignore you, I just... I don't know. At any rate, I'm sorry. For everything. I'm glad you called. I think you and I have a lot of catching up to do. Call me again whenever you get a chance."

AJ deleted the message. It had been sitting in his voicemail for weeks. He finally called Adam back.

"Hello? Arturo?"

"Hola, Adam."

"I'm so glad you called me back. What a relief. I heard the news."

"What news?"

"About your father, Arturo. I can't tell you how sorry I am. About your family. About everything. Listen, do you want to meet up? I can come down to Cedar Creek for a few days—we can get some beers and talk."

"You must be busy, with your campaign and all..."

"Oh, it's not a problem. As a matter of fact, I've been meaning to head down there for the campaign. The whole small-town-hometown thing. My connection to the countryside, agriculture. The people. You know. My roots."

*You don't have a fucking clue about agriculture.* "Actually, I'm headed up your way as we speak."

"Oh! Well, that's—that's great! We can meet right away. Are you free tonight? We're taking the girls to a Halloween thing at the mall, but we'd be happy to have you along. We're going to dinner afterwards for—for *our* birthday. It'll be like old times."

"No. I can't. I'm not ready for that kind of thing. It's fine, really. Thanks."

"I understand."

"What about lunch? I guess you're probably busy."

"No! I mean, lunch is great. I can do lunch today, no problem. Great. Just the two of us. I mean, I'm sure my wife Elena would love to finally meet you. The two of you have a lot in common, you know. But that can wait."

"Maybe I can meet her sometime soon. Anyways, I know a place in Uptown where we can have some privacy."


Mel's Bar was a small wooden shack, shrouded in permanent shadow under a freeway. Adam was on edge from the moment he parked his black sports car at the end of a row of beaters. Before exiting the vehicle he took off his coat, removed his tie, and unbuttoned his collar. It was easy to see why AJ had picked this place—it was the kind of bar where solitary folks could erase their memories in peace, in the dark, undisturbed. More than a decade after the statewide indoor smoking ban came into effect, Mel's was one of those places that still reeked of tobacco. It was in the wood.

Adam took a seat on a barstool next to his old friend. They sipped bourbon. Adam didn't know what to talk about—he figured pretty much everything was off limits. Except for the phone call to arrange this little get-together, AJ hadn't spoken to Adam in two decades. Sure, Adam thought about AJ and his family every day, and maybe AJ thought about Adam, too. Probably. But seeing the man here before him, seeing AJ's wild black hair and his unwashed clothes and the cracks and scars on his face—Adam was overcome with regret and responsibility. He wanted to take him home, like a stray cat.

AJ clutched his drink in both hands, staring at it. So Adam began.

"Sorry I never called."

AJ was unmoved.

"It's just, I thought, you know—I thought you were better off without me. That you were fine on your own. I mean, I thought you hated me."

AJ found Adam's face in the long mirror behind the bar. "I did," he said. "Still do."

"Can't blame you, I suppose. Would it help if I wished you a happy birthday?"

"No."

They nursed their drinks. Adam tried again.

"Well, I guess we have a lot of catching up to do. Who're you rooting for these days, still watching the Gophers? Or have you graduated to the Vikings?" Adam realized too late that AJ had probably never finished college.

"I'm not interested in sports," AJ said. "And I don't watch the news, either, so don't bother."

"Sure, fine. Have it your way. To be honest I don't have much time for sports these days either."

Adam talked about himself, his life, but AJ wasn't listening. Neither of them dared mention high school. Middle school also seemed dangerous. Still, Adam knew he had to find some common ground. He went all the way back to elementary.

"Hey—remember that time I threw up all over Margaret What's-Her-Name?"

"Yeah. What did they call you? Oh yeah. Up-chuck Adam."

"That name followed me for years, even though it only happened the once. But you always stuck up for me."

"I tried. There's no justice on the playground."

"Can't blame kids, I suppose. None of us knew any better back then."

"Childhood is just the beginning. It only gets worse."

"Not for my kids, I hope."

"Good luck with that."

"Thanks." Adam decided to take the comment at face value, ignoring the tone.

"Don't you have anything interesting to talk about?"

"Well, sure. Jeez. Loads of things. Lately I've been learning the ins and out of the life cycle of human cells. Mitosis and apoptosis. Or I could bring you up to speed on the amazing world of campaign finance reform. Anything but the inner workings of the Pharmaceuticals—that's all highly classified."

"In other words, illegal genetic experimentation is off the table."

"Didn't know you were into that sort of thing. But sadly, yes. My lips are sealed."

"That's too bad," AJ said. "Thought you might be able to save someone's life."

"Anyone I know?"

AJ swirled his drink, tapped his fingers on the table. He opened his mouth, but closed it again.

"I have a genetic condition, AJ. I found out last year. There's a growth near the back of my skull that puts pressure on the occipital lobe."

"You have a brain tumor? So you're dying anyway?"

That one made Adam sit up straight. Still, he wanted to disarm AJ, to win him back.

"No. It isn't cancerous. The opposite, actually. It's more like a new organ—a gland. The autonecrogen gland. They say it won't grow any further. It won't kill me."

"So, it's just sitting there, doing nothing?"

"Well, they say it makes me special, somehow." Adam said, choosing his words carefully.

"How nice for you. Did you remember to thank the Lord for your gift?"

"You were always the religious one."

"I heard Candidate Baker is a man of strong faith. They said so on TV."

"Aha! So you do watch the news."

"Don't let it go to your head. Sounds like you're running out of space up there as it is."

"Very funny." Adam finished his drink. AJ gestured to the bartender for more, and the man refilled both cups before Adam could put up a hand in refusal.

"More for me," AJ said, pulling Adam's cup toward himself.

"I suppose I can let you in on one little secret today, AJ. I'm a closet atheist."

"Are you fucking kidding me? You, Adam Baker, a God-damned atheist? Since when? And what in the hell made you think you could ever get elected to Congress as a motherfucking atheist?"

"I've never told a soul. No one knows. Not even my wife. We take our girls to church every Sunday, ever since I decided to run for office. But it's all fake."

"Oh, I'm so surprised. Look how surprised I am."

"I'm fine with my atheism. If it turns out God is real I'll be fine anyway, because I'm a good person."

"That's not how it works. God can see into your heart. He knows you're full of shit. My heart's pure truth. When I die, I'm going to Heaven. I think you know where you're going."

"AJ, listen to yourself. You aren't making any sense. You're the one who's supposed to believe that when you're about to die, you just have to say the magic words. It doesn't matter what you did, your actions, good or bad—because nobody can be good enough. No one can pass the test. You just have to say, 'I'm sorry, Jesus, I love you.' And you're saved, just like that."

"I think it should be the opposite," AJ said. "When you're about to die, Jesus should come down to your room, to your bedside, and he should say, 'I'm so sorry for everything I did to you.' That's how it should be."

"You act like you're the only person who's ever lost someone. I spent years praying to God after my mom passed away. But if he were real, wouldn't that mean he's the one who killed her? Or, if he were truly all-powerful, wouldn't that mean that he let her die? It never made any sense to me. I'm an atheist because God never showed up."

"You only became an atheist so you could get away with murder."

"…You're drunk, AJ. My work saves lives."

"Bullshit. You became an atheist just so you wouldn't have to pay for what happened to my sister."

"Oh, here it comes. I didn't kill your sister, Arturo. She left a note and everything. Case closed. Don't go back there, it's not healthy."

"Easy for you to say."

"Look, AJ. I don't know what you're doing up here, or why you even wanted to see me. Do you have anywhere to go? You're welcome to join us tonight, if you want. Family stuff. There's always room for an old friend."

"Thanks, but no thanks."

"Staying with someone? A girl? College buddies?"

AJ rubbed his jaw and looked out a window. "Yeah, that's right."

Adam was skeptical. "Here's my address," he said, writing it on a napkin. "In case you change your mind."

After watching Adam drive away, AJ went back inside for a twelve-pack to go. The bartender gave him no trouble. The familiar and deceptive warmth of booze crept along AJ's limbs as he climbed behind the wheel of his rusty little truck in the protective shadow of the raised freeway. He drank a beer right there in the driver's seat, then laid his head on the steering wheel.

An hour later, he woke up and put the key in the ignition. He pulled out of the parking lot drinking another beer, thanking God for not sending any officers his way. Sunlight cut diagonally between cold blue skyscrapers as he drove north across downtown. All the businesses were decked out for Halloween. He passed a stadium that brought to mind half a dozen half-remembered concerts, then he got stuck in traffic at a commuter rail station. The streets were crowded with twenty-somethings in full costume. Clouds rolled in and the city turned dark as he crossed the Mississippi into the suburbs. It began to snow.

Columbia Heights was the first neighborhood after Northeast. Two-story houses, decent enough, evenly spaced, each one separated from the next by a nice white fence. AJ had partied in a few of them, or in their unfinished basements, while he was flunking out of college. The streets rolled up and down in gentle slopes. It was dark now, and kids were out trick-or-treating, despite the falling snow. They ran down the sidewalks in their winter jackets like it was no big deal. All you could see of their costumes was the masks. AJ had done the same thing as a kid back in Cedar Creek, back in 1991, the year of the infamous Halloween Blizzard. Yet another Halloween spent with Adam Baker.

He slowed down as he passed the address on the napkin. It was a nice house. Looked like all the rest. There was a big old willow tree in the front yard. Snow was piling up around gravestones lit with strings of orange lights. Jack-o'-lanterns lined the sidewalk. There were cobwebs in the porch rails. A skeleton hung from the corner of the garage. The Bakers were handing out candy.

AJ circled the block and parked with the Baker residence a few houses down on the opposite side of the street. He prayed the weeping willow would help hide most of his boxy gray Toyota from view, but he had to pull forward until he could see around it. He felt uncomfortably exposed. The tiny extended cab was crammed full of junk, but there was enough room for AJ to lean his seat back. This way he could claim to be taking a nap if anyone came knocking. He opened the glove box and pulled out an old pair of binoculars. Peering through the snow, he could just make out the little scene on the Bakers' front porch. He cracked a beer.

Adam was dressed up as Frankenstein's Monster. Black hair, neck bolts, painted-on stitches joining green sheets of skin. He was a reconstructed human, slumped unmoving in a lawn chair at the bottom of the steps, hiding under the eaves where the garage met the house, where the snow couldn't ruin his makeup.

The other three were up on the porch. Elena was a witch, and the two girls were black cats, but they all had winter coats on.

An endless parade of superheroes and cartoon characters dared each other to brave the Baker house. They gave Frankenstein a wide berth as they approached the porch, then they practically ran up the steps to the open arms of the witch with her cauldron of candy.

AJ could see their mouths moving. "Trick or treat," they shouted.

The witch dropped candy into their plastic pumpkins.

Then the black cats pounced out of her flowing cape.

Upon turning to go the trick-or-treaters were confronted once more by the seated monster. Inevitably one brave soul would approach the lawn chair, and Adam would hold his breath. Convinced it was just a dummy, a scarecrow, the kid would grab Adam's sleeve, lift his arm into the air, let it drop back into his lap.

At this point Adam would come to life—working his jaw up and down, stretching his neck, finally lowering his gaze while rising from his chair. He towered over the children, taking one robotic step forward, then another, arms outstretched, reaching, clutching. He stumbled forward and the children ran away. AJ could hear the screams on the wind.

And Adam would return to his chair, apparently delighted to have caused such terror.

AJ decided to go for a drive, have a few more drinks. Give them a little more quality time.

* * *

"Do you have to do that every single time?" Elena called from the porch.

"Yes, of course! Striking fear into the hearts of children is the whole point of Halloween."

"Oh yeah, I forgot. I thought it was about costumes and candy."

"That's all secondary. Did you see the one dressed as Superman? What a baby."

"This is so much fun, Daddy. I love Halloween!" Mary said, long whiskers painted on rosy cheeks turned upward in a smile.

"Me too, sweetheart."

Lucy shouted, "Halloween, yay!"

"Yes. A perfect Halloween. Except for all this snow, I mean. Too bad we can't see the moon. There hasn't been a full moon on Halloween since long before you girls were born."

"Why?" asked Lucy.

"Because the moon's phases don't line up with the calendar," Mary said. Adam was glad to see his constant rambling about space was finally starting to pay off.

"Why?"

"Because the full moon happens every 28 days, but a month is 30 or 31 days long," Mary said.

"Why?"

Adam could see that his help was needed. "Because that's what Pope Gregor decided in 1582," he said.

"Why?"

Adam sighed. "Why what?"

"Daddy! Why is the moon full?" Lucy asked. "What's it full of?"

"It's full of beans, just like you!"

"I'm not full of beans, you are!"

"Oh that's right, you're full of candy!" He reached down and tickled her. "We say the moon is full whenever the whole circle shines bright. It's not the moon's light, though—it comes from the sun. The sun's light can still reach the moon, even though we can't see the sun right now. Isn't that crazy?"

They all stared up through the snow, but the moon was nowhere to be seen.

"Strange things happen when there's a full moon—and since it's a full moon on Halloween, it's going to be twice as bad tonight. First there will be werewolves. Then vampires. And around midnight all the ghosts will come out, too."

"Adam, that's enough. Don't scare them," Elena said. She yanked a cord from an outlet on the side of the house, and all the orange lights winked out. Dimly illuminated by a streetlight filtering through the willow, the gravestones cast weird shadows on the snow.

"You're not scared, are you my dears?" Adam scooped up Mary and Lucy in his arms, squeezing them to his chest.

Lucy squirmed. "Daddy, don't get your green makeup on my face," she said.

"Can we eat some more candy, please?" Mary asked.

"Haha, I don't think so! It's time to brush your teeth."

Inside the house, boots and coats off, all four of them crowded in front of the downstairs bathroom sink. They made faces at each other in the mirror, as they did every night. Adam washed off the kids' kitty whiskers while Elena helped them brush. The parents still had their makeup on when they put the kids to bed. They wished the girls goodnight and blew them kisses. The girls wished Adam a happy birthday.

Elena led her husband upstairs to their bedroom, where she surprised him with a bottle of wine.

"Happy birthday, Adam," she said.

"Thank you, darling."

"You're welcome. I assume you want your usual present, as well?" The expression on her face was neutral.

"When you put it that way, how can I resist?"

"I'll get ready." She let her clothes drop to the floor before stepping into the bathroom for a shower.

Adam sat on the bed and checked his phone. Dozens of alerts. Family, friends, and co-workers, on multiple apps, all trying to get in touch. Probably all meaningless birthday wishes, prompted by social media programming. He chucked the phone in a drawer. He got undressed and went to join his wife, but she was already finished. He tilted his head in surprise. "Feeling alright?" he asked.

"Fine. Just hurry, I'll be waiting."

She pulled the door shut, leaving Adam alone in the steamy bathroom.

Adam wiped the mirror with his hand and removed the bolts from his neck. He began washing his face. Green makeup swirled through strips of latex scar tissue. He closed his eyes and tried not to remember what he had seen one year before, charging across the freeway in Chicago...

He opened his eyes and the sink was full of tiny spheres. Hundreds of iridescent eggs. Snakes began to hatch. He squeezed his eyes shut and pounded on his forehead. Pushed his knuckles into his temples. He opened his eyes. Still there. A writhing mass, still hatching. They flopped down to the floor. He locked the door. They slithered over the wet tiles. Over his bare feet. He jumped backward and crashed into the wall. Dumped out the trash can and used it to scoop snakes into the toilet. He flushed, watched half the snakes go down, but more and more were spilling from the sink. He closed his eyes again and thought, *Change*. He opened his eyes. They were earthworms now, purple and slimy. He picked them up by the fist-full, dropping them in the toilet. He flushed them all. Elena was pounding on the door.

"It's nothing, sweetheart," Adam said. "I slipped and fell, but I'm fine. Just a minute." He picked up the trash and wiped slime trails off the sink and the floor with an Egyptian cotton towel.

He stood there just breathing for a few heartbeats, then opened the door. Elena had transformed. She was a temptress in red lace. Adam was stunned. She had sparkling red horns and she twirled her barbed tail in her hand. Neither one spoke. She pushed him back into the bathroom. He put his hands on her hips. She dug her claws into his chest. He slid his hands up her sides. Squeezing her torso, he easily lifted her off the floor and set her down on the sink.

In the mirror, Adam saw that the floral-patterned wallpaper behind him was sprouting vines that grew and stretched down to the floor and up along the ceiling. Elena squirmed. She must have known something was wrong. He pushed her forehead to his chest. Mold was spreading over the shower curtain. The floor mat became moss. Insects crawled out of the bathtub drain. He wrapped one arm over Elena's shoulder, keeping her face pinned down, and with his other arm he grabbed her ass tight and lifted her up. He turned and carried her out, slamming the bathroom door shut with his foot.

"Adam, what's happening? Are you okay? I thought this was what you wanted."

"It's nothing. Don't worry."

He burst into the bedroom and threw her down on the bed. She sank deep into the red cotton comforter.

"You're having an episode, right?" she said.

He lifted her again and threw the covers aside.

"No. I said don't worry." He laid her out on the pink silk sheets. He felt burning passion and confusion as his headache gathered strength. He flipped her over, face down in the pillows. She was moaning. He closed his eyes and saw Maria. He felt the world shaking. The ceiling was covered with visions and the swinging crystal light fixture was about to crash down on them. His arms buckled, she screamed, and as he collapsed on her he called out a name.

He tried to kiss her neck, but she threw an elbow, hitting him squarely in the face. He rolled off of her. He saw the look in her eyes and realized what he'd done. He had called her Maria.

"I knew it," she said. "Fuck you, Adam Baker."

"Elena, I'm sorry. It was an accident."

She spit in his face.

"I'm sorry," he said again. He returned to the bathroom to wash up and collect his thoughts. He hadn't known what to expect, but it was all back to normal. Everything was fine. Lingering tension flowed out of him, although he could hear the bedroom TV blaring. He hopped through a quick shower, then went back into the bedroom. Still normal, except for Elena, his treasured wife, broken. He put on his pajamas.

"Elena, I said I was sorry."

She turned up the volume.

He stomped to the foot of the bed, blocking her view. That was the easy part—he was six feet tall, two hundred pounds, and she was a petite five-foot-five. He grabbed for the remote, but she it swung away. He grabbed again, missed. But he got it on the third try.

His eyes locked on hers, he pointed the remote over his shoulder and switched off the TV, then gave the remote a backward toss. He watched Elena's beautifully tanned face with growing curiosity as it passed from disgust, to horror, to despair.

He turned around in time to see the remote strike a large piece of Mexican pottery on the bookshelf in the corner. It was a serving bowl, glazed with flowers in white and blue. The bowl rolled to the edge of the shelf. Adam's hands moved to make an underhand catch. He launched himself horizontally over the bed, but it was too late. Elena's mouth contorted with rage, and her balled-up fingers turned to steel. The serving bowl did a somersault in the air and smashed to pieces on the hardwood floor. Adam landed on his stomach, very nearly impaling himself on a broken shard.

Elena came down hard on Adam and pummeled the back of his head. Her sharp knees dug into his kidneys. It was nothing for him to roll out from under her, pick her bodily up into the air —her fists pounding on his forehead now—and deposit her safely back on the bed. She was sobbing. The piece of traditional pottery had belonged to Elena's father. Her mother had made it for him on the occasion of their engagement, well before Elena was born.

"Elena, I'm sorry."

"Fuck you, Adam Baker."

"What do you care, anyway? You left your culture behind, remember? A better life, and all that? Always looking to the future? I'm the one who wants Mary and Lucy to know where they come from."

"And you're willing to put in the work to make it happen, too. That's why you come home early and spend as much time with them as you possibly can."

"I was here all day, for Christ's sake."

"No you weren't. Can't even stay home on your own birthday. Where were you this afternoon? On a hot date with Maria? Who is she, Adam?"

"She's nothing. Nobody. It was an accident."

"You keep saying that. You mean it was an accident when you fucked her, or when you fucked me?"

"God. I give up. I can't do anything right."

"Adam Baker, I want a divorce."

He stood there staring at her, a host of reactions competing under the surface. Self-defense won out. "You know what? Fuck this. Thanks for the birthday sex. I'm going out for a beer."

"Great, I'll call you a cab. Right after I call my lawyer." She picked up an unlit candle from the nightstand, one of those scented candles in a small glass jar. Pine needles.

Adam stared up at the ceiling. "I meant in the garage. Jesus."

"Language!" Elena shouted. "The Lord is always listening, you know." She chucked the candle at him. It bounced off his chest. He shook his head and walked out the door.

"That's right," Elena shouted after him. "Run to your stinking garage like you always do!"

# The Old Mill

MINNEAPOLIS POLICE DEPARTMENT
  Case Number: 20-1101-0127G
  Subject: Garcia, Arturo J.
  Confession

"When I went back, Halloween was over. No more kids in the streets. I drove past Adam's house and parked the truck at the top of a hill a few blocks away. That area's all up and down. I guess that's why it's called Columbia Heights. I put my collar up and kept my head down, praying to God not to let anybody call the cops on me. I remember the snow falling through the streetlights. For the most part though I just stared at the sidewalk, ignoring all the Halloween crap. I didn't want anybody thinking I was scoping out a burglary. I found the house and I crouched down at the trunk of this willow tree they've got in the front yard. It looked like all the lights were off--except for one, upstairs. There were these green flashes in the window. Don't know what that was. Then I heard shouting. Adam and his wife, I guess. Never met her. Then a light came on in the living room."

Adam came out on the front porch in his pajamas: dark bathrobe hanging open over a red and black flannel shirt, sweatpants tucked into winter boots. It was practically the same thing AJ had on. He dumped a pile of Halloween candy on a small table next to a plastic chair, then he went in the garage through a side door. AJ ran to the side of the house, put his back to the wall, and looked over his shoulder. His eyes were level with the porch floor. Adam came back a second later with half a dozen cans of beer. AJ was *this close* to just walking up and asking him for one. Knock back a few brewskies with the guy, and he might just come along under his own free will. Then again, neither of them ever really had a choice—AJ knew that now.

AJ saw his own tracks in the snow and felt like a moron, although the yard was pretty dark. The willow tree was filling up with snow, and it scattered most of the light from the street. Adam sat on the porch chugging beer and eating fun-size candy bars. AJ checked his watch. Ten thirty. Plenty of time.

Adam scratched his leg and scanned the yard. AJ was worried he'd see his tracks, but Adam looked at the garage and noticed that something else was wrong. He dropped his empty can, grabbed a fresh one, and walked down the porch steps and out into the snow. AJ moved along the side of the porch until he could see Adam standing at the corner of the garage where the foam skeleton had been, earlier. Adam looked up and swore. Something about the rain gutter. AJ guessed some kids stole the skeleton and broke the gutter in the process.

Adam disappeared around the front of the garage. It was now or never, and AJ was past the point of hesitation. A row of landscaping rocks lined the front of the porch. AJ brushed the snow off the biggest one and picked it up. It was heavy. He needed to use both hands. He said a prayer of thanks, then carried the stone to the corner of the garage.

Adam was standing in the driveway, throwing back another beer, staring up at the sky. It looked bad. The snow was really coming down. AJ raised the rock high, but when he stepped onto the driveway the snow crunched under his boot and he froze. Adam spun around and shouted, probably thinking the vandals were back, but when he saw AJ his face went slack. He dropped his beer can in the snow. AJ smashed the rock down on his head, then dragged him into the garage.

AJ found some duct tape and wrapped Adam's wrists. He didn't really know what he was doing—he hadn't even thought about the details, much less planned for snow. So he improvised. There was a cheap plastic sled hanging on the wall, bright red with a yellow rope. AJ loaded up the sled with the tape, a hatchet, some beers, and Adam's unconscious body. Then he thought he'd better tape Adam's ankles too, since he might wake up at any moment.

The sled moved easily on the fresh snow, but gravity still worked, and AJ had to pull Adam up a hill to get back to his truck. He leaned into the freezing wind. Ice crystals stung his cheeks.

The truck wouldn't start. Too cold. But AJ figured it was too loud anyway, and he wouldn't want to be seen throwing a heavy bundle in the back of the truck at night. Probably get himself shot. Not that dragging a loaded sled on the sidewalk was any better. But AJ was feeling pretty drunk by this point, so he decided to have some fun. He pulled the sled out into the street and sat down on Adam's chest. He held onto the yellow rope and used his feet to get started. The full moon shined through a hole in the clouds and they took off. They were going fast and momentum carried them a lot farther than AJ expected, straight for the next intersection, headlights coming too fast—a car flew by, horn blaring. The sled bounced over the tire tracks and spun out. They crashed into a stop sign. AJ pulled his head out of a drift and God answered his prayer once again—the car's tail lights disappeared in the falling snow.

AJ brushed snow off his clothes. The sled was sticking out of the snow bank a few feet away, empty. Adam was trying to crawl away. AJ couldn't help but laugh out loud, even though his fingers were going numb. He grabbed Adam by the hair. Blood poured from the impact wound on his forehead. The blood formed a dark puddle in the snow. Adam twisted his neck, and his hair slid through AJ's frozen fingers. Adam rolled sideways and tripped him. They moved like worms. Then AJ heard a chain uncoiling. A huge black dog was charging. Adam couldn't move away fast enough, so AJ had to pull him away. The dog reached the end of the chain and stood there snapping and snarling.

A light came on in the house. A door opened and someone yelled, "Killer! Killer!"

AJ dropped flat on his back. Adam tried to shout, but there was no force behind it. AJ looked up through sheets of snow and prayed. The blizzard was raging.

The person at the door said, "Killer! Shut up, will you? Kennel! Get in your kennel!" The dog stopped barking. It was being pulled backwards on its chain. "Goddamn rabbits," the owner said. A gate slammed shut. The lights went out.

AJ got up and saw Adam trying to slither away. "What's it going to take to get you to stop fighting?" AJ asked.

Adam whimpered, tried to talk. AJ went back to the sled and found his supplies in the snow. He wrapped Adam's mouth in duct tape, feeling stupid for not doing it sooner. He put him back in the sled, along with the hatchet and the beer. Adam's face was a bloody mess. He was crying. He started shivering all over. His eyes kept rolling in circles. But they were safe. God was on AJ's side. Fat snowflakes spiraled down from the heavens.

After dragging the sled a block or two, AJ could see the top of the old lumber mill over the roofs of the houses. He smiled down at Adam and said, "Don't go anywhere. We're very close now." But Adam was shivering like crazy, and twisting his head from side to side, rolling his eyes in every direction. That's when it started. The weird shit. AJ didn't even know how to explain it, afterwards. He followed Adam's eyes to the snow bank, and there was a gold ring there, and it was moving. It zipped back and forth, leaving little trails in the snow. Wherever Adam looked, it moved. But when AJ went to pick it up, there was nothing.

He stood over Adam and said, "What the fuck was that?" and he ripped the tape off his mouth.

Little bursts of spit and blood came from Adam's mouth when he tried to talk. For a second AJ felt like throwing up. Adam said he was having an attack.

"What, like a heart attack?" and Adam said no, but then his eyes rolled up into his head and he passed out. AJ pulled him down an unlit side street, into the shadows in somebody's back yard, then he sat in the snow next to his old friend and drank a couple of beers.

At some point AJ noticed it had stopped snowing. Adam woke up again, squealing like a baby, asking what AJ was going to do to him.

"You don't know?" AJ said. "Are you stupid?"

"I never did anything to you," Adam said, and he was crying again.

"Look, I'm getting tired of pulling your ass all over town, so what say we cut you free. Would that make you feel better?"

Adam nodded.

"Promise not to run?"

"I swear."

AJ took the hatchet from the sled and cut the tape off Adam's ankles. Adam got to his knees and held up his wrists to be cut loose as well, but AJ just laughed. AJ cracked the last beer and stuck it between Adam's bound hands. Adam clutched the can and downed the whole thing. He almost looked grateful.

But then he tried to run away. AJ grabbed the roll of duct tape and closed one eye—losing some depth perception was better than seeing double—and he chucked it at the back of Adam's head. Direct hit. AJ had been a star quarterback, after all. Even got a scholarship.

Adam fell down face first. AJ knelt beside him, took his head in both hands, and smashed it down. Blood gushed from Adam's forehead and mouth, melting the snow. There were some teeth.

Adam's voice was wet. "You broke my fucking nose," he whimpered. "Just let me go."

"Yeah, right," AJ said. "We both knew this day would come."

AJ checked his watch: 11:33 p.m. They needed to hurry. AJ pulled Adam to his feet and pressed the hatchet blade into the back of his neck. "March," he said.

They turned down a narrow alley that led them to the bottom of a cliff. They'd made it to the old sawmill, an abandoned building five stories tall, next to a jagged rock face seventy feet straight up. The cliff wall and the back of the old mill formed a narrow canyon. There was a train yard at the other end. The trains used to stop at the sawmill's loading docks, but not anymore.

Adam staggered in the fresh powder between the cliff and the mill, then he fell down for the second time. AJ pulled him up again and gave him a shove, saying, "Go ahead and run, if you can."

Adam went straight inside the mill, just like AJ wanted him to.

It was pitch dark inside, but AJ could hear Adam stumbling around, banging into the machinery. AJ knew the layout. Five floors of open workspace, with a freight elevator and a staircase running up the center to the roof. AJ knew all the doors to the stairs were locked—except for the ones at the bottom and the top.

"You understand what's happening, right?" he asked. "I'm talking about that day on the bridge, just before graduation. You and my sister, remember? The day you destroyed my family. My future. My life."

"I didn't kill Maria!"

"Don't you fucking deny it, you worthless piece of shit."

Adam found the door to the staircase. His hands were still taped, and his fingers had to be at least as frozen as AJ's, but he managed to get the door open. He crashed his way up the stairs.

AJ took his sweet time. "I finally figured out what happened to my sister," he said. "She didn't jump off the high-bridge—you threw her off."

"No I didn't!"

At the top, AJ found Adam ramming his shoulder against the door again and again. AJ laughed and turned the handle. The door swung open and Adam flew out onto the roof. He landed in six inches of snow, but the clouds were clearing away. It was 11:42.

Adam spun away behind the door, and when AJ emerged, Adam slammed into him. When AJ got to his feet, Adam was trudging through the snow toward the cage that enclosed the fire escape on the north side of the building. AJ kicked him in the back of his knee and he collapsed for the third time. AJ wished he still had the tape. He dragged Adam to the southern edge of the roof and held his face over the edge to make him look down. Seventy feet straight down. Funnels of snow twisted in the breeze over the train tracks.

"What are you going to do," Adam said, "throw me off the roof? How original."

"I'm going to make your kids grow up without a father." Then, whispering in his ear: "And I'm going to fuck your grieving wife."

"Fuck you," Adam said, and he spat blood.

"No, Adam. Fuck you!" AJ kicked him in the stomach. "I want the Devil to make you look up from Hell and watch your wife and girls living without you." The wind grew stronger, whipping his voice up to the sky. "And you'll know that their suffering is your own fault. How fortunate it is that you'll leave behind three, to account for the three you took from me."

"I—I don't understand," he said.

"My sister, my mother, and my father, you idiot! You killed them all!"

"I'm sorry about your family, Arturo. Really, I am. But none of it is my fault."

"Bullshit. You know what happened. That programmer Marshfield told me everything."

"Tyler Marshfield? What the hell does he have to do with this?"

AJ was pacing back and forth along the edge of the roof. He told Adam what Marshfield had told him, that Adam's team wasn't really supposed to cure cancer—they were just learning how to control it. How to cause it. "They gave it to my father," he said.

"AJ, that's crazy!"

"It's all real," AJ told him. "They killed my dad because I tried to stop you from becoming a senator." AJ checked his watch. Adam was trying his patience, but it had to wait a few more minutes.

"You did what?" Adam said.

"I went to the press. Gave them those photos and everything."

"That was *you*? You stupid asshole! You were doing exactly what they wanted you to do! AJ, listen to me. I swear to God, I didn't know your father had cancer. I'm so sorry about everything. But you have to believe me. *They* did it. Those fuckers at the top—they're responsible for this. Not me. They used me, AJ. I swear."

"So now you admit that you're in on it."

"You don't understand. Listen, AJ. We can stop them. We can stop the bad guys and still rid the world of cancer. We'll do it together. We can be friends again. I'll forget about all of this. Just let me go and we'll stop them together. And I can cure *your* cancer. You don't have to die."

"Bullshit. I don't have cancer. How would you know."

"You were the control. In the experiment. Don't you remember the check-ups?"

AJ remembered. They'd both had them, all the way through high school. "I don't care," he said. "My life's been over since the day you killed my sister. I *want* to die. But I have to avenge my family first, and send you to Hell. And God will forgive me, because I'll have saved the lives of millions of people. Tyler told me—"

"Oh, shut up about Tyler already. He doesn't even work for them anymore. He can't help you."

"I know that. I killed him this morning, over brunch. Right after I killed Tommy."

"You—you what?"

"Didn't you know? I killed Tyler Marshfield this morning, an hour after I killed your cousin Tommy. I thought you'd have heard by now. Frankly I was surprised you didn't already know when you came to meet me at the bar. Someone must have tried to tell you. Don't you check your messages?"

"Today was a family day."

"Right. Mr. Family Man. Well, don't act like you gave a shit about Tommy the fucking Cowboy. When was the last time you even saw him?"

"Two years ago, at Christmas."

"Did you know Tommy killed Old Bill Mischler?"

"You're a liar."

"Oh, believe me," AJ said. "He did it. Tommy burned Old Bill alive, right in his own bar. All I did was return the favor. And now I'm ending your life, Adam. Just like you ended mine." AJ quit pacing and stood over Adam. "As for that loser Marshfield, I slit his throat with a steak knife."

Adam started twitching, wincing, like he had a killer headache.

AJ checked his watch. Almost midnight.

He didn't realize he was standing between Adam and the edge of the roof. At that moment, Adam rolled into AJ's legs. He fell down and nearly went over the edge, but he grabbed Adam's shirt and pulled himself back to safety, laughing. But the weird shit was happening again. Instead of the snow and rubber of the rooftop under his face, AJ could see straight down through a rusted grating, all the way down to the rapids.

The full moon lit up the canyon. Evergreens lined the tops of the cliffs on both sides.

Adam sat up, sort of laughing, and he was shaking all over. "Look," he said, pointing to one end of the bridge. There was a bear. Huge and black, with moonlight glinting on its fangs. "It's Maria," he said. "She's been following me, all these years."

AJ didn't know what to think. His watch said it was time. He stood up on the walkway next to the train tracks. The bear was a silhouette, lit up from behind by a train coming through the woods. AJ checked his watch again. Right on time. But they were supposed to be above the tracks, not right on them.

There was no time to ask Adam what the fuck was happening. AJ had to stick to the plan as best he could. The train was supposed to be Adam's third death, though. He'd have to settle for two.

"This is our only chance, AJ," Adam said. "We pay for our mistakes here, in this life."

AJ shoved him flat on the walkway. "For once," he said, "I agree with you." He put a knee on Adam's chest.

"I tried to end cancer," Adam said. "What have you ever done to improve this world?"

"Not much, until today. But I'm making up for lost time." AJ wrapped his hands around Adam's neck and put his thumbs on his throat. The train was so loud.

"AJ, they gave me the cure."

AJ hesitated. But the bear was coming fast.

"We could stop them. Together."

"It's too late," AJ said.

He dug his thumbs into Adam's throat and dragged him to the edge of the bridge. He held on until Adam's face turned blue.

"One," AJ said, and he let go of Adam's neck. The bear was upon them. AJ could see down its throat. The train's horn blared. Adam gasped.

AJ wrapped his arms around his old friend and rolled over the edge.

They rotated down through the frozen air, staring into each other's eyes. AJ said, or he tried to say, "Two." He closed his eyes and prayed.

# *Epilogue*

Dear Dr. Springer,

   I know you're out there, but I don't know
how to find you. Please, please give me
something. Anything. A signal. Please. I
have so many questions. You knew my father.
I tried to reach his killer in prison, but
they won't let me see him. They say he's
insane. I need to know what happened. I've
been trying to piece it together, and to
recreate your work. We're very close now.

   -MB

# A Note from the Author

Hello Everyone,

My name is Jonathan Hendricks, and I live in Japan with my incredible wife Sara and our three brilliant children. Sara and I are both originally from Wisconsin, USA, but we've lived in four other countries so far. Currently we both teach EFL (English as a Foreign Language) at a university.

I write stories because so many things make me angry, and naive Optimism tells me fiction can change minds. And I write because as far as I know, nobody writes what I want to read: short philosophical sci-fi adventure horror thrillers. My favorite authors are Neal Stephenson and Kurt Vonnegut, but Stephenson's books are too long, and Vonnegut isn't writing anymore. I also enjoy reading Michael Crichton, Stephen King, and H.P. Lovecraft.

Years ago, I wrote the first draft of this book for the online writing competition NaNoWriMo. I showed that draft to three people. My wife said it was amazing, my mother told me to publish it right away, and a friend said he had never realized how much editing went into "real" books. So I went back to school and learned everything I could about writing fiction. Programmed Cell Death is the result of six years of sustained effort. I hope you've enjoyed it.

-Jon

How about leaving a review on Amazon?
https://www.amazon.com/dp/B07TZ663PT/


Sign up for my newsletter to find out what I'm working on next:
www.clockworkpines.com/p/newsletter.html


Follow me online, if you feel like it:


Twitter: jonhendricks
Instagram: jon.hendricks
Facebook: Jonathan Hendricks
www.clockworkpines.com
jon@clockworkpines.com

For information on the actual state of cancer research
and the pharmaceutical industry, please consider
reading the following works of non-fiction:

*The Emperor of All Maladies:*
*A Biography of Cancer*
by Siddhartha Mukherjee

*Bad Pharma:*
*How Drug Companies Mislead Doctors and Harm Patients*
by Ben Goldacre